False alibi

'The plan is that we will stage a fake murder investigation . . .'
The top secret directive to Detective Superintendent Mark
Pemberton, quick-tempered high-flier in a northern county's
CID, came from the Chief Constable himself. The idea was to
get local villains on the run, obtain their admissions and
confessions, clear up lots of minor crimes, secure a wealth of
valuable information about the criminal world – and, primarily,
to flush out any threat of violence to a forthcoming top-level
visit by the Prime Minister himself.

So, an anonymous, naked female corpse – her remains
bequeathed for the benefit of the nation – is planted by the
police in Green Lane. But at almost the same time, the body of
a popular, good-time bar maid is discovered in Blue Beck with
a massive shot gun wound.

Mark Pemberton now has more on his plate than he or his
Chief Constable bargained for. And the town's people are
terrified: is this the work of a maniac, a rapist, a sex-killer? And
is there a link between the slayings of the two women?

Besides a handful of murder suspects and a major drugs
dealer behind bars on a different rap, the threat of an IRA
mainland bombing blitz also keeps Pemberton and his Detective
Constable lover, Amanda, at fever pitch. And hours before the
PM's visit, Amanda disappears . . .

False alibi is a police procedural novel of awesome pace and
excitement. It reveals a writing talent to rival the best in our
revered history of detective fiction.

Books by Peter N. Walker

CRIME FICTION
The 'Carnaby' series (1967–84)
Carnaby and the hijackers
Carnaby and the gaolbreakers
Carnaby and the assassins
Carnaby and the conspirators
Carnaby and the saboteurs
Carnaby and the eliminators
Carnaby and the demonstrators
Carnaby and the infiltrators
Carnaby and the kidnappers
Carnaby and the counterfeiters
Carnaby and the campaigners
Fatal accident (1970)
Panda One on duty (1971)
Special duty (1971)
Identification Parade (1972)
Panda One investigates (1973)
Major incident (1974)
The Dovingsby death (1975)
Missing from home (1977)
The MacIntyre plot (1977)
Witchcraft for Panda One (1978)
Target criminal (1978)
The Carlton plot (1980)
Seige for Panda One (1981)
Teenage cop (1982)
Robber in a mole trap (1985)

Written as Christopher Coram
A call to danger (1968)
A call to die (1969)
Death in Ptarmigan Forest (1970)
Death on the motorway (1973)
Murder by the lake (1975)
Murder beneath the trees (1979)
Prisoner on the dam (1982)
Prisoner on the run (1985)

Written as Tom Ferris
Espionage for a lady (1969)

Written as Andrew Arncliffe
Murder after the holiday (1985)

NON-FICTION
The courts of law (1971)
Punishment (1972)
Murders and mysteries from the North York Moors (1988)
Murders and mysteries from the Yorkshire Dales (1991)
Folk tales from the North York Moors (1990)
Folk stories from the Yorkshire Dales (1991)
Portrait of the North York Moors (1985) *As Nicholas Rhea*

THE 'CONSTABLE' SERIES
Written as Nicholas Rhea
Constable on the hill (1979)
Constable on the prowl (1980)
Constable around the village (1981)
Constable across the moors (1982)
Constable in the dale (1983)
Constable by the sea (1985)
Constable along the lane (1986)
Constable through the meadow (1988)
Constable at the double (1988)
Constable in disguise (1989)
Constable through the heather (1990)
Constable beside the stream (in preparation)

EMMERDALE TITLES
Written as James Ferguson
A friend in need (1987)
Divided loyalties (1988)
Wives and lovers (1989)
Book of country lore (1988)
Official companion (1988)
Emmerdale's Yorkshire (1990)

FALSE ALIBI

Peter N. Walker

For Olivia Tolfree

With congratulations for
winning the Hoyas Bank
Crime Story Competition,
1991.

Peter N Walker

Constable · London

First published in Great Britain 1991
by Constable & Company Ltd
3 The Lanchesters, 162 Fulham Palace Road
London W6 9ER
ISBN 0 09 470700 6
Set in Linotron 10pt Palatino by
CentraCet, Cambridge
Printed in Great Britain by
Redwood Press Limited
Melksham, Wiltshire

A CIP catalogue record for this book
is available from the British Library

To Rhoda, for her patience

1

'What I am about to say to you, Detective Superintendent, is top secret.'

It was late and the Chief Constable moved around his office with an aura of stealth as Mark Pemberton watched from the chair before the huge oak desk. The Chief was tall and slim; his immaculate dark grey suit, pale blue shirt and striped tie provided the necessary air of authority and his polished black shoes made no sound on the thick carpet. He prowled like a sleek black panther as it decided how best to tackle its prey.

Charles Moore was always well-dressed, always clean and crisp, and he set a visual example of smartness and style which he expected his subordinates to emulate. With neither a hair out of place nor a piece of fluff on his clothing, Moore made Mark wait and wonder what he had done wrong. Had his report on the rise in house burglaries fallen short of the Chief's high expectations? Had one of his detectives got himself into trouble? A disciplinary tribunal on the way perhaps? But nothing of that kind could be regarded as secret, let alone top secret . . .

While his chief padded around the room, Mark strove to anticipate the content of his speech, but Moore made him wait. It was as if he was struggling to find the right words, yet this man never struggled for words.

He never struggled for anything or with anything – he was an achiever, he was always confident, always polished, always in control, a self-made man who had risen from being a police cadet at sixteen to Chief Constable by forty. That he was ruthless and ambitious was beyond doubt but he was fair – and Mark Pemberton felt he was sitting like the panther's prey, awaiting some action. Then after yet another circuit of his office, Moore was speaking and Mark concentrated on every word.

'This will set a precedent, Superintendent, an important one. A national one, in fact. I like to establish precedents, you know, I see myself as an innovator. Do you realize the police service rarely sets precedents? As a service, it hates to initiate anything, it's incapable of genuine innovation. We prefer someone else to put ideas to the test and then we adopt them for our purposes. But even if the scheme I'm about to unfold is a precedent within police circles, it is not entirely new. A similar one has already been used by the military. So there's nothing new under the sun, as they say, is there?'

He paused, did another circuit of the office, and then continued, 'Now, Superintendent, do you know of the "Man Who Never Was"? Like me, you'll be too young to recall the war years but during the last war, the Allies placed a man's body in the sea along with forged documents and clothing. They gave him a fake identity and even a false nationality.

'He was provided with some documents containing secret data and the plan was that this body would be found by the Germans who would examine it and then be deceived about the timing and venue of a major military invasion. The Army used a genuine corpse. So, Mark, I ask myself – and I ask you too – why shouldn't the police do the same? We're fighting a war; ours is a real war too, except that it's against crime. I believe we must use every device at our disposal if we are to win our war. So why shouldn't we take the initiative? Why wait for a murder to be committed before we carry out a major investigation?'

'I'm not sure I follow your argument, sir,' Mark frowned as he wondered when the Chief was going to explain himself.

'I propose a murder exercise, Superintendent.' As the Chief switched between Mark's Christian name and the more formal address, he anticipated something of importance. 'I propose that we stage a murder investigation in the form of an exercise, with realism added through the medium of a real corpse. Now, some would say it's unethical, that I'm asking for trouble, that things could go wrong . . .'

'A real corpse, sir? Why?'

Moore continued. 'We need to create a murder-style enquiry at this time of abnormally high crime. In that way, we will establish the crime-fighting initiative. You know as well as me, better than me I'd say, that we have a very high crime rate and a very low detection rate.

'There are many factors affecting that, but you are equally aware that when we *do* have a full-scale murder investigation, we turn up all manner of other things. We get villains on the run, we get admissions and confessions from them and we clear up lots of minor crimes – and some serious ones; we secure a wealth of valuable information about what's going on in the criminal world and we gather crime intelligence of a most useful and lasting kind. It happens because the petty villains try to get themselves out of our net by volunteering good information, by informing on other criminals, by admitting crimes even. That's the real value of a murder investigation, Mark – it goes beyond the satisfaction of arresting the killer. But we can't organize murders whenever we want them, can we? We've got to wait for them to happen. So those benefits are at the root of my proposal. The plan is that we will stage a fake murder investigation so that we can produce genuine results.'

'But with a real bloody corpse, sir?' Mark asked as Moore strode backwards and forwards in front of him.

'Yes, Mark, with a real corpse. That's the whole idea. We haven't had a long-running murder enquiry for over a year, yet other crime is on the incease, especially minor stuff like burglaries and thefts, so we will create a murder investigation. Only those who need to know will be told the body is not a genuine victim.

'Even the CID – and by that I mean everyone from the enquiry teams to the photographers – will not be told the body has been planted. They must believe they are dealing with a real murder, Mark. And if you think I'm crazy, I do assure you that I am not and that this scheme is feasible.'

'You've got to be joking, sir! This will never work – we can't mess about with bodies like that and besides, our lads would soon sus it out for what it was. It would turn into a farce.'

Moore halted in the middle of his office floor to smile at Detective Superintendent Pemberton. Mark recognized that smile – it was the smile of one who had made up his mind.

'I've considered all the risks, Mark. The plan can work and it will work. I've seriously considered the details involved and it's now time for positive action. This is why this discussion is top secret. There must be no leaks, no hints even, not to other

9

police officers of whatever rank. No one must ever know it is just an exercise. It wouldn't succeed otherwise.'

As Mark's unease made him shift in the chair, Moore began another circuit of his office, hands clasped behind his back like the Duke of Edinburgh. Was this one of the Chief's curious ways of testing him for future leadership, he began to wonder. If the plan was crazy, Mark must be bold enough to say so; he must make known his reservations and objections. Moore had no time for yes-men.

'Sir,' he began. 'I can understand the need for realism. Like you, I've been involved in umpteen exercises – I've done the lot – war duties, fire hazards, dangerous chemicals, major incidents, NATO, escape and evasion. The lot. They've all been useful even though we knew they were exercises. But this is so bloody different, it's got so many risks – what if the press discovered we'd borrowed a dead body, that we'd faked a murder? They'd accuse us of using underhand methods to gain entry into private houses or question innocent people, they'd say we were becoming secret police, wanting to pry into every aspect of life in this town. Imagine the fuss, especially from our Labour council and its band of merry red men if that allegation broke! They'd have our guts for garters, sir, our jobs would be on the line. And we'd not be able to deny it.'

'They will not find out, Mark. No one will. We will ensure that they don't!'

'But there's always a risk!' Mark pressed. 'If anyone did learn the truth, how could we explain our actions in a way that would satisfy the public? Or the Police Authority and town councillors? You know what they're like! They're addled with lefties just aching for a reason to slag us.'

'All that's been taken into consideration, Mark, but I repeat my belief that the exercise could never work satisfactorily without a real body; a dummy just would not produce the required results. It must be a real corpse.'

Mark was about to repeat his reservations when Moore continued, 'If those involved knew it was just an exercise, we'd lose the vital realism that's necessary. So, if we are challenged, we'll admit the simple truth. We'll say it is an exercise designed to test our CID officers, our resources and our Serious Crimes computer system. We won't make excuses. And because it's an exercise, we needn't worry about having an undetected murder on the books when we don't find the killer. Besides, an exercise is to highlight failures, Mark. We all learn by our mistakes.'

'I'm sorry, sir, I don't share your confidence or enthusiasm, I just cannot see this working.'

'It must be made to work, Superintendent.'

'And supposing it goes ahead, sir. . .'

'There is no supposing about it, Mark. It is going ahead, I can assure you of that.'

'I thought this was just an idea you were floating for an exercise? I thought you were seeking my views.'

'I am seeking your views – and I am also seeking your professional co-operation because the plan is going ahead.'

'Forgive me for appearing stupid, sir, but where would you get a dead body?'

'From the pathology department at the hospital. Where else? There's a cadaver there now, it's available at this very moment, ready and waiting for you to collect, hence my urgent summons. We must move quickly, the timing is perfect.'

'Me? You mean I'd be responsible for seeing this through?'

'In the absence of Detective Chief Superintendent Foulds who's at the Police Staff College, you are deputizing as head of the CID. So this task is your responsibility. It will be your duty to implement this exercise, to make it work. It is an official exercise, and you will treat it as an order, Mark. It will be done, and it will be done properly with professional skill and competence. And it will be under your command.'

Mark Pemberton began to wish he had never thrashed that child-molester . . . was this Moore's way of reminding him of that other occasion he'd stood before this very desk – he'd stood to rigid attention in front of Moore wondering whether he'd be sacked or demoted. The Chief had lectured him about losing control of his temper, warning him that a police officer who could not control his emotions was unfit for higher office or senior command. Mark had explained that the enquiry had made him so damned frustrated because he couldn't secure sufficient evidence to justify an appearance in court, let alone secure a conviction. The result was that he'd exploded and beaten up the nasty piece of work. The molester, sporting a black eye and bruises, had lodged an official complaint of police brutality and Mark had found himself upon a disciplinary charge. Moore had found him guilty, there had been no other possible verdict, and he had been fined one month's pay.

Mark accepted he had done wrong, if only under extreme provocation, and promised he would try to curb his quick temper. But the lapse could seriously retard his career. And now, as he was confronted by Moore's latest scheme, he wondered if this was a chance to redeem himself? Is that why the Chief had picked him for this strange task? If he succeeded, would his career be resumed? Or was Moore merely making use of him to further his own bizarre plans? Whatever the answer, Mark Pemberton knew he had to make the plan succeed.

'Am I right in thinking the body would come from one of those willed for medical research?' he now tried to think of a logical question.

'Roughly right, Mark. But when someone donates their body for medical research, you can't purloin it for a murder enquiry exercise! You just can't muck about with corpses like that! But we're lucky. I have access to one, a female corpse, and I quote from the woman's will, "to be used for the benefit of the nation". It's not restricted to medical research, you see, so there's scope for other purposes. We can use her, which is why I want to press ahead immediately.'

'It all seems pre-arranged, sir.'

'Let's say we have not gone lightly into this project and I will tell you that we do have the approval of higher authority. Such opportunities don't arise very often! And, I might add that Doc. Andrews saw nothing wrong with the idea.'

'He wouldn't!' snapped Mark. 'He goes over the top from time to time. I've heard tales from the hospital, like that fancy dress he wore at the annual dinner/dance. So, if he can fix us up with a corpse, sir, who is she? Is she someone ashamed of a pauper's burial, some poor soul not wanting her funeral to be paid for by the council?'

'Far from it. She was a respectable woman, a widow in her sixties with no criminal record. She is a cancer victim and she is not from this town or anywhere nearby. She was sent to the cancer specialist and died here, she has no relatives or known friends in this part of England. But she has relations by marriage in the Home Counties. They know she has left her body to the hospital and they think it will be used for medical research.

12

They have not complained about that. I've had her antecedents checked. She's ideal. What I've told you is what she specified in her will. She wants her body to be used for the good of society, and surely the detection of serious crime qualifies as that? Through her help, we can trace drug-suppliers, burglars, shop-lifters, subversives, sex offenders . . . we could go through some of our worst ghettos and no-go areas with a big brush, cleaning up the tower blocks and council estates. And all because we can use her mortal remains. Of course, you'd have to make sure she was never identified; in the unlikely event of any relatives turning up, they must never be aware of her starring role with us. This has to be achieved in total secrecy.'

'I can see why!'

'I'm sure you can, Mark.'

'We could always claim we'd used a tailor's dummy if anybody starting asking daft questions?'

'That shouldn't be necessary,' said Moore quietly.

In spite of Moore's polished confidence in the plan, Mark felt vulnerable for in a scheme of this kind there was so much that could go wrong, so many problems that could never be anticipated. He stood up and joined his boss who was now staring out of the bay window of his first-floor office.

'Sir, I must record my distaste at this, it is most unethical.'

'So is crime, Mark, so is raping old ladies and young girls, robbing banks and killing people, so is stealing their belongings or getting them hooked on drugs . . . it is our job to stop that sort of thing, and this is one method of doing so. I view this as a legitimate tactic to detect crime in very difficult times.'

Mark remained silent for a few moments and then said, 'So sir, correct me if I'm wrong. You would have us secretly deposit this body where it would be found, hopefully by a member of the public who would raise the alarm. We would then follow that discovery with all our call-out procedures just as if she was a real murder victim; we'd set up the entire machinery of a full-scale enquiry?

'Incident Room, computer, SOCO, the lot? And we'd run the investigation until you, me or some other senior officer decided to wind it down, even with the so-called "murder" undetected?'

'That's right, Mark, with the reminder that it will remain top secret. No other senior officer will know it's an exercise. Not even my deputy or my two assistant chiefs will be told. I will know, you will know, Doc. Andrews will know and so, of necessity, will the coroner. But absolutely no one else. The exercise will start tomorrow, Monday. I want you to commence in the early hours and it needs to be concluded before the new PM arrives on Thursday – you will have received advance notice of his visit to our derelict industrial sites? He's coming to regenerate our decaying relics of nationalization, they're going to build a supermarket and a small business complex there. At 2p.m., he's going to dig the first sod with an earth-remover and says he intends to show how capitalism can continue to produce new businesses and jobs where socialism has failed.'

'The security arrangements are in hand for the visit, sir. I can confirm that.'

'Good. As you know, the precise itinerary will not be revealed to the public until twenty-four hours beforehand, but there's always concern for his safety.'

'We've done a lot of groundwork already. SB will be making the final security arrangements.'

'I know, so in your absence on the murder enquiry, I will put Detective Inspector Curtis in charge of what you've been doing. That way, you can concentrate entirely upon this exercise. In fact, the exercise should benefit the security plans for the visit. Our scheme will enable us to round up any incoming ne'er-do-wells and would-be assassins before the visit. So, Mark, where are you going to plant the corpse for maximum effect?'

'Me, sir? You want me to plant it as well?'

'There's no one else to do it, is there?'

Mark Pemberton had not yet anticipated just how much responsibility would rest upon him, and knew that his reservations had been rejected by the Chief. He was under orders to carry out this task, and said, 'Well, sir, I'd have to make sure it was placed so that it would be found in a way we'd gain the maximum benefit.'

'And to make it look like murder, Mark, you'll need the expertise of Doc. Andrews.'

'How much does Doc. Andrews know?' asked Pemberton.

'I've talked it through with him,' smiled Moore, his clean white teeth bright against his natural tan. 'He knows the general idea and he'll help to lay out the body so that she looks like a murder victim. He's sworn to secrecy.

14

'The body is in the deep-freeze and will need thawing out before you position her. Her name is Mrs Wanless, by the way, Margaret Wanless, and she's from Nottingham. Obviously, for this exercise, she will always remain anonymous.'

'But if we're seen placing the body, we'll be suspects ourselves . . .'

'Then you'll have to ensure you're not seen! Placing the corpse is a two-man job and I can help by authorizing the use of a Q-van, the one that looks like a struggling plumber's van.'

'I might still be seen by our own patrols, sir. That's always a practical risk.'

'Then set up a diversion. If criminals can do that in an attempt to fox us, why shouldn't we do the same to fox them? Didn't you tell me only a fortnight ago that you wanted to do a drugs-raid in the near future? Pennine Flats, wasn't it? Weren't you aiming to catch a supplier? Roe, wasn't it?'

'We do want him, sir, we've been targetting him from time to time, when we've had enough men. He's a weasel, that one, as slippery as hell. Terrified of his own shadow, and yet we know he's dealing in drugs in a big way . . . I've known him for years, he was once straight but now I'd love to nail him, sir.'

'So why not carry out that raid without waiting for the necessary intelligence? If the beat lads are detailed for that operation at the other side of town while you're in the act of dumping the corpse, you should avoid scrutiny. Now, what about planting the body? Tell me how you'd achieve that.'

Mark walked about the office, striving to think of a useful plan and then he remembered Mayhew. Frank Mayhew, another target criminal. Another villain he wanted to bring in and keep in. With this exercise, he might just nail that bastard. He might be able to salvage something for himself after all . . .

'To get the maximum benefit, sir, I'd plant the body on the known route of one of our target criminals – I'd select Frank Mayhew. It's time we nailed him, he's the suspected Shotgun Raider. I'd make sure he found the body and then we'd have an excuse for quizzing him about his recent movements and we might even get to searching his house – and our net should catch a lot of smaller fish.'

'Perfect,' smiled Moore. 'So Frank Mayhew, for his past sins and because he finds the body, lands himself as a murder suspect for a crime that's never been committed?'

'It would do him good to sweat a bit! He's a strong suspect for several armed robberies on building societies, sir, here and further afield. We're sure he's one of those travelling villains *Crimewatch* is trying to find – other forces want him too.'

'You've targetted him before?'

'Several times, without success. He seems to know when he's being observed; he's clever.'

'You realize that if our local council and the Police Authority get a smell of this, they'll have a field-day,' Moore reminded Mark, halting before him.

'I am aware of that, sir, I just hope our plans are secure enough to avoid that.'

'Then make sure they are. Don't treat this lightly – remember that we're going to terrify the town into thinking there's a killer on the rampage, we're going to quizz half the town's population about their private lives and scare the remainder into staying indoors at night . . . if the truth breaks in the Press, Mark, our esteemed civic leaders will have my guts for garters. And yours. Bang will go our pensions!'

'It will be done properly, sir. Now, what about the more mundane side of things. The costing of man-hours, for example?' Mark was thinking of the administrative problems too. 'With any murder, we incur lots of overtime.'

'And to make this realistic, we'll do the same. Any costs incurred will be written off as being due to a normal crime enquiry; they'd be absorbed in the general accounting system. I will authorize any overtime payments and other costs. Regard this as a genuine enquiry in every detail, right down to toilet-paper, ball-point pens, cups of tea and chocolate biscuits!'

'Thanks, sir.'

'Now, one other thing that is important, Mark. I want you to instigate lots of house-to-house enquiries. Get among the townspeople, the ordinary folk. Stir them up. Get them aware of the crime, get them involved in helping you solve it, get them thinking about their neighbours, get them worrying about what's going on next door, or about friends in the office or events in their street . . . get them to help the police, Mark.'

'That is standard procedure during a murder enquiry, sir.'

'Yes, I know, but for this particular exercise, I need more commitment, I need sheer determination among your teams – the excuse for this heavier-than-usual bout of house-to-house will be your urgent attempts to name the woman. OK? Get the public involved, stir up the town. Use the BBC's *Crimewatch* if you think it will help.'

'Yes, I understand, sir.'

'Good, well, that's it then. It's on. Start immediately, Mark. You'd have no advance warning if it was a real murder. Go and see Doc Andrews, he's expecting you. Removal of the body has been cleared with the coroner. Arrange to plant the body tonight and wait for developments. I'll keep myself in touch, but do feel free to call on me if there is any problem, however small. I must be made aware of all your on-going problems.'

'Yes, sir,' and as Detective Superintendent Mark Pemberton walked out of the Chief Constable's office, he knew the success of this strange plan now rested entirely with him.

Moore had astutely shifted the entire responsibility to his shoulders. So whose career was at risk now?

When Mark Pemberton had left, Charles Moore picked up the secure telephone at his desk, dialled a London number and announced his name.

'We're starting now,' he said.

2

It was 1.15 a.m. and Detective Superintendent Mark Pemberton was in the Control Room. With the Chief Inspector in charge of the night shift and the sergeant in charge of 'A' Division's Drug Squad, he was sipping coffee from a chipped mug while eating chocolate biscuits. They were all in the Chief Inspector's small glass-walled office which overlooked the staff at their consoles; the buzz of the town's continuing dramas kept them busy beyond his door. Even at this time of night, it was non-stop action. The night-duty officers both in the Control Room and out in the town were coping with domestic rows, traffic accidents, drink-and-drive cases, yobs and idiots, fights outside pubs and clubs, break-ins and criminal damage. For them, it was a routine night's work . . .

'You look worried, sir?' Chief Inspector Elsworth smiled at Mark. 'You've no need, everything's going to plan.'

'The best laid plans can go wrong,' Mark Pemberton, youthful looking for his forty years, sipped from the mug. 'Remember that so-called secret raid by the Met? The Broadwater Farm drugs swoop? The Press, television cameras and dozens of bloody councillors and Socialist Nosy Parkers turned up to watch! It was more like a television drama than a raid.'

'Ours will be more discreet, sir. It was arranged too quickly for moles to operate.'

'Let's hope so, but moles can move quickly too, you know. At Broadwater, everybody was waiting for the police to become racist pigs by arresting a black man. Somebody had tipped them off . . . I just hope that hasn't happened here.'

'This isn't London, sir, our staff's honest. We've some good ones, things are secure.'

'I hope you're right. The duty inspector's got his men positioned, has he?' asked Pemberton for the umpteenth time.

'Yes, he's got his foot patrols lined up and all the night-shift mobiles briefed and stationary within a thirty-second response range. Are you going to the scene, sir?'

'No, I'll keep a low profile, this is Division's show, not mine. DI Rhodes is in charge on the ground, I'm just observing. I'm going to disappear soon – I'll be in Queen 36 if there's anything urgent. I'll call in when it's all over, though, just to see how it's gone.'

Detective Sergeant Paul Barnett, the drug-officer, said, 'I'll go now, sir.' He had called in to update the Control Room Chief Inspector verbally instead of relying on the radio channels which might be overheard. He addressed Elsworth. 'My lads are all ready, we're going in at two hundred hours, sir; I want to be there.'

'Well done, Sarge,' smiled Pemberton. 'Thanks for the gen. I hope you turn up some good stuff.'

'We know it arrives at Roe's flat, sir, cocaine chiefly. It's a distribution centre, and we think he uses another room some-where in that block of flats . . . it'll be like searching a giant rabbit-warren for a single black rabbit . . . the pushers haunt the bloody spot and the addicts are always waiting for their next fix, all gaunt-eyed and nervous. I'd like to bring the lot in, but tonight I'll settle for Roe.'

18

As Barnett left Pemberton checked his own watch and said, 'I'm off now, Walter. Best of British!'

Pemberton was pleased the drugs raid appeared to be progressing so well; the test would be the actual forced entry. It would be dramatic with several officers simultaneously gaining access at different points. From that moment, the flat would be a riot of noise and action, with blue lights flashing, pushers, buyers and druggies running for cover, innocent residents wondering what was going on, dogs barking, police photographers lighting the scene, people fleeing from capture, protestors protesting . . .

Outside the Control Room complex, Pemberton climbed into the Q-van, switched on the official radio and drove to the General Hospital's pathology department. Doc Andrews was waiting at the rear entrance, the one through which all bodies entered for post-mortems. He raised a hand in acknowledgement even before Pemberton entered the building, then vanished along the deserted corridor. Pemberton went inside and waited.

Seconds later, Doc. Andrews reappeared with a trolley bearing a body tidily covered with a crisp white sheet. He wheeled it towards the exit.

'No problem,' beamed the pathologist in his Welsh lilt. He was a big man, a former prop forward and a daredevil in his youth. He'd once danced nude on the turf of Cardiff Arms Park moments before a festival of Welsh choirs arrived in procession. The assembled Women's Institutes had loved him. 'Don't look so worried, man, this is a normal sight, me or my staff wheeling corpses about the place.'

Pemberton helped to guide the trolley to the rear of his vehicle. It had all the appearance of a nondescript and rather battered white van of the kind used by self-employed plumbers. He opened the doors and, aided by Andrews, slid the corpse along the floor aboard its wheeled stretcher. It was immediately covered with a dark blanket. Andrews steered the trolley back into the corridor, closed the laboratory doors behind himself and locked them, leaving the lights on.

'Let's go,' he said. 'You know, Mark, I'm enjoying this. It's more exciting than using a cadaver for medical research, eh? It reminds me of my student days. I wonder if Mrs Wanless knew what she was getting involved with? I took her out of the fridge some time ago, by the way, so she's thawed nicely. Her temperature will be about right when she's found. It's a strange way of helping your country.'

Mark agreed. 'I suppose we ought to be grateful to somebody who cares enough about the rest of us to donate their mortal remains for the benefit of the uncaring masses. But I just hope my boss hasn't gone off his rocker with this one! You know, Doc., it's a pity we can't thank her in person.' Mark Pemberton, with the police radio burbling in the van, drove into the estate behind the laboratory, wove through several side-streets and eventually emerged onto the main road. It was precisely two o'clock as he reached the junction with the trunk road and at that moment, a voice on the radio shouted, 'Go, go, go.'

'That's not for us, is it?' chuckled Andrews, who was clearly enjoying this escapade.

'No, I've set up a drugs raid on Pennine Flats,' said Pemberton. 'The lads are going in now. It's a diversion,' he added. 'We don't want any police vehicles checking us!'

'Nice one,' said Andrews.

As the radio filled with the burbled chatter of lots of police officers being co-ordinated within their well-planned raid, so the anonymous little van turned away from the drama. It slunk into the peaceful southern outskirts at the opposite side of the town. Pemberton was heading for a quiet lane on the edge of suburbia, and a few minutes later he turned down the deserted track with its cinder base. It ran adjacent to the railway line and after driving about a hundred yards along the lane, he halted.

He made sure he parked on the solid surface to avoid leaving any identifiable tyre-marks. Then he doused the lights. Each man then changed his footwear, using old wrong-size shoes Pemberton had bought from two different Oxfam shops. Then Pemberton stepped outside to look and listen.

'Not a soul,' he said with pride at his own earlier reconnaissance.

'Great,' murmured Doc. Andrews.

Operating without lights and relying on the overglow from the town around them, the two men allowed the stretcher to remain in the van as they lifted out the corpse. It was still covered with the dark blanket. They laid it on the grass beside the track and Andrews quickly removed the cover. The woman, emaciated and grotesque in her cancerous death, was naked.

'She's no beauty,' commented Pemberton.

'Cancer's a bastard. But somebody loved her. Now, she's got no clothes as agreed,' said Andrews. 'Clothes can be traced or recognized, no jewellery either. I've cut her hair, too, to change her appearance a little and I've painted her toe-nails and fingernails with varnish, red, Max Factor. She never used make-up in life. We don't want any relatives thinking they recognize her . . . her relations think the body's being used for medical research, not this!'

'So Moore explained,' Mark whispered in the hush of the night.

The cold white body was arranged on the grass to look as if she had been dumped from a car. Her light grey hair, thin frame and miserable breasts were ghost-like, and exposure to the cold air of this December night would provide the necessary touch of macabre chill and mystery.

'Is that OK?' said Andrews eventually.

In the dim light, Pemberton, now sweating, said, 'Fine. Now, let's get the hell out of here.'

Having checked they had left no evidence of their presence, they drove quickly away after changing back into their own shoes, throwing the discarded ones into the rear of the van. Pemberton said he would incinerate them later.

'What happens next?' asked Andrews, shouting above the voices from the van's noisy radio. It sounded as if a lot of things were happening at Pennine Flats. This was good; the present activity and the follow-up arrests and paperwork would occupy the night shift for some hours. Pemberton was confident the body would not be found by a police patrol.

'Our target criminal should find the body before the first train passes the scene. That's due at seven-eighteen. Chummy's a dog-lover and walks his dog along that lane every morning about six-thirty; he's always the first person along. We know that from time to time he goes off to raid a building society or something. Catching him has been our problem. But he always sleeps at home. That's one of his character quirks.'

'You've been spying on him?' said Andrews.

'We call it targetting, we use it for known criminals. Now, according to my reckoning, he'll come across our body first thing in the morning and he'll call the police. Like all those who find the body, especially those who've committed murder, he'll

21

want to report it to make us believe he's innocent of any involvement. Anyway, Doc., the usual procedures will be put into action. I repeat, only you, I, Moore and the coroner know this body is a plant.'

'And I'll be called out in the usual way?'

'You will. You'll be called to examine the body at the scene – and after the post-mortem, you'll state she has died from asphyxia as discussed . . . and you'll compile your usual report as if you've done a PM for a murder investigation. I'll establish an Incident Room and away we go, just as if it's a real crime. We'll wind it up within the week.'

'Great! Now the fun's over, you can take me home!'

Doc. Andrews, a bachelor, lived in rooms at the hospital and so Pemberton returned him to his laboratory where he let himself in. After disposing of the stretcher, Andrews switched off the lights and vanished into the depths of the building. Pemberton then drove across the town towards Pennine Flats. He found a scene reminiscent of a riot, with people arguing with the police, blue lights flashing from several vehicles and excited dogs straining at their leashes as the volatile residents hurled abuse at the assembled officers.

Pemberton located the duty inspector.

'Now, Inspector,' he said. 'How's it going?'

'A good raid, sir, we've got Roe, would you believe? He was caught with the stuff in his bedroom, a new delivery. Talk about a stroke of luck. Cocaine I think. We'll get it analysed. We're sure some pushers were waiting for him, but we got there before he'd had time to hand over the stuff. We got him in possession, but not them. We caught him within minutes of coming home . . . a bloody good night's work, remarkable in fact. We need this sort of luck once in a while.'

'Well done,' said Pemberton, pleased that he had established his presence at this raid. It was almost as if he were creating his own alibi, and the chance discovery of a cache of drugs and the surprise arrest of this known dealer was a good omen, a bonus in fact. Sometimes you deserved luck of this kind. He'd hoped to catch minnows, but had netted a big fish, as someone said. It was 2.50 a.m.

He must now return the Q-van to base and then go home. Amanda would be waiting.

*

22

At 6.15 that same morning, a 999 call was received in the Control Room. It was accepted by Julie Thorpe, one of the civilian staff.

'Police Control Room,' she said pleasantly. 'How can I help you?'

A breathless male voice with a strong local accent gasped, 'There's a body, a woman, in Green Lane, dead . . .'

'And your name, sir?' she was accustomed to remaining calm when her callers were excited. Julie was known for her unflappability; she'd worked here for over ten years.

'Downes, Harry.'

'And your address, Mr Downes?'

'Look, there's a bloody corpse . . .'

'Yes, but we will need to talk to you later, sir. So your address please?'

He gave an address in town, adding that he was the driver of a milk-tanker who had just started his daily run.

After establishing the precise location, she asked him to remain at the scene until a mobile arrived. It would take about three minutes – the day shift had just begun. Having gained his agreement, she radioed Delta 15, as the body lay in D Division.

'Delta One-Fifer, are you receiving? Over.'

'Delta One-Fifer, go ahead.'

'Delta One-Fifer, report of woman's body in Green Lane. Finder is a Mr Harry Downes who is remaining at the scene pending your arrival. Please investigate and report. Over.'

'Ten-four,' acknowledged the officer.

The early-turn inspector came across to her.

'Emergency call, Julie? So what have we this time?'

'Report of a body, sir, in Green Lane. A dead woman. Delta One-Fifer is attending.'

'It might be a druggie left over from this morning's raid,' he laughed, heading to his office for his first cup of coffee.

Six minutes later, Delta 15 provided his sit. rep.

'Delta One-Fifer,' he radioed. 'Am at the scene of the body, Green Lane, western end. There is the body of a mature woman; she is naked, she appears to be dead and the circumstances look suspicious.'

'Received One-Fifer,' acknowledged Julie. 'Remain at the scene, preserve any evidence, detain any witnesses. I will call a doctor and the CID – wait there pending instructions.'

'Received and understood,' said Delta 15.

Julie checked the list of senior officers' home numbers, then lifted the telephone to call Detective Superintendent Mark Pemberton. Having alerted him, she would await his orders to set in motion the procedures for calling out the cavalry, as the first flush of members of murder team was often called. But now she must summon a doctor to examine the body and formally to state the woman was dead.

It looked like being a busy and interesting day.

3

Mark Pemberton, aroused from a fitful sleep by the jangling of his telephone, struggled from Amanda's bare arms and legs, and crept downstairs to make himself a coffee and some toast. Even though he'd been anticipating this call, it was still coated with the ingredients of drama. There was a hint of the unknown and the thrill of a man-hunt even if it was a staged exercise. But even on the most dramatic of early morning call-outs, he tried to calm himself by first having a light meal because, when on such duties, he never knew when he'd be eating again. Even if this had been a genuine murder call-out, he would have eaten something before leaving home.

He recalled the custom of one of his bosses – a past Chief Constable – who'd said "Always let the staff get there first, give them time to get the mail read". Well, he'd allow his preliminary teams to establish themselves at the scene before he arrived. They knew their jobs. No discovery of a dead body demanded a Batman and Robin type of response unless there were aggravating circumstances. It would be different if the killer were standing over the corpse or threatening to kill others or had kidnapped someone. But this very routine murder call meant the body had been found and, having called out his men, he could arrive cheerfully at his own pace. The discovery had been right on schedule. Another good omen.

As the kettle sang in the peace of his kitchen, Amanda came to join him at the kitchen table. She had wrapped a pink dressing-gown around her small, slender but delightful naked body, yet still shivered in the cool of the morning. The heating hadn't come on yet, it was dark outside, but the sky was brightening as the morning moved towards a new day.

'Call-out?' she was rubbing the sleep from her eyes.

'A woman's body in Green Lane,' he said. 'You'll probably get a call yourself if it's suspicious.'

'I'd better get home then. It'll be nice working with you on a big case. I hope we catch whoever did it, if it's murder,' she said. The kettle boiled and she made two mugs of coffee. After eating, Mark made sure his thick blond hair was neat and tidy, that his moustache was trimmed to perfection and that his tie was knotted correctly. His shoes were shining and black, and his dark suit was immaculate. Behind his back, he was known as the best-dressed man in the Force – even pipping the Chief to that honour, according to some. Pride in his appearance was a vital ingredient of Mark's busy life. He reckoned that if you cared how you looked, you gained respect and that's why Moore had achieved so much. People respected him because he dressed well. Satisfied with his own appearance, Mark gathered his brief-case and opened it to throw in an apple, two bread buns, a slab of cheese and a tomato. Then he kissed Amanda.

'Might see you in the Incident Room?' she returned his kiss.

'I hope so,' he said. As he left, she settled down to sip her coffee before driving to her own modest flat.

On the approach to Green Lane, Mark could see the familiar indications of concentrated police activity amid multi-coloured illuminations. A police car with its blue light flashing sealed one end of the lane and he knew that a similar ploy would be used at the other, about a mile away. There were white lights galore, some amber ones and a green rotating one on the doctor's car. The light and colour almost matched the Christmas decorations that adorned the town-centre shops and streets each evening. Now, though, at this time of day, this was the only patch of brilliant colour in the greyness of morning.

Clearly, the exercise was rapidly gathering momentum. The scene had been preserved and a uniformed constable wearing a reflective poncho stood in the main road, waving past the beginnings of the Monday morning rush-hour traffic. Drivers would slow down in their curiosity, thus becoming accident hazards and so the constable had to keep them moving. Scenes of Crime had arrived along with the police photographer and video crew; one of them was encircling the area with yards of yellow plastic tape, pinning it to the railway fence, the hedgerows and the trees.

The duty sergeant, in uniform, was in attendance and so were several detectives, conspicuous in their civilian clothes.

In the dim light of this early December morning, Mark noted a milk tanker parked in the lane with sidelights showing. It was trapped within a web of yellow tape, and a large and anxious-looking driver stood on the verge of the main road, his overalls declaring his role. Mark saw no sign of Frank Mayhew, his target criminal, or Frank's Labrador.

He parked two hundred yards away and walked towards the action, those at the scene recognizing the slim, fair-haired Detective Superintendent. He was acknowledged with cheery calls of "Good morning, sir" as he passed, for uniformed officers did not salute high-ranking detectives, a relic of the days when the CID was almost secretive. Mark scrambled down a grassy bank towards the milk-tanker, ducked under the tape and hailed Detective Sergeant Derek Thornton, the man in charge of the Scenes of Crime team.

'Morning, Derek. So what have we here?'

'A woman's body, sir. Unclothed with no sign of clothes lying nearby, and therefore suspicious. Middle-aged to elderly, she is. Thin as a bloody rail. No visible marks of violence. Dumped from a vehicle by the look of it.'

'Any ID?'

'No, she's not known to any of us. No jewellery, no handbag lying about so far as we can see from a cursory visual scan by arc lamp, although a fingertip search in full daylight might turn up something. It'll soon be light enough for a real search.'

'Has a doctor seen her?'

'Yes, Control called our Dr Cowen; he certified death but could not give the cause. He's in the van now, giving his statement. No one else has touched the body and the scene has not been searched.'

'Right, well, full steam ahead them. It looks like murder, eh? I'll confirm that the Incident Room needs to be set up and the teams called out. Control will put things in motion. We'll need Doc. Andrews to examine her *in situ* before you cart her off for the PM. You'll video the scene? Stills are needed too, in colour. We can fingerprint her later, in the morgue . . . bloody funny thing, stripping her like that.'

'It'll be somebody thinking it'll stop us identifying her, sir. There's no identifying material left at all, she's been well and truly stripped of everything, even her jewellery.'

Pemberton smiled. 'Concentrate on her ID, get cracking on that straight away,' he said. 'Has the Press been onto us yet? It's a wonder their early shifts haven't picked up our radio calls.'

'I've had none here yet, sir.'

'Good, well, I'll arrange a news conference for ten-thirty this morning, at the nick. Now, who found the body?'

'That tanker driver, sir,' and Thornton pointed to the solid man in overalls who stood on the fringes of the activity. It wasn't Mayhew! Mark felt a twinge of surprise and some dismay, even regret, but he could not let it show.

This was the first problem . . . a minor one, but a problem none the less. He had wanted Mayhew to find the body, he'd wanted that villain to get himself in the frame. So where had Mayhew got to?

'What was he doing down here with his tanker? I thought this was a bridleway?'

Mark covered his disappointment by asking that question.

'He was late for his rounds, sir, so he took a short cut; he reckoned it would save him a few minutes. Well it didn't, he found the woman, so it's cost him at least half a day, I reckon. We've sealed his vehicle for SOCO's once-over.'

'Is he in the frame then?' asked Pemberton. Those who reported finding murdered bodies often became Suspect Number One but the sergeant shook his head.

'I doubt it, sir, he left home just over half an hour later than usual, about five-past six. He says his wife can corroborate it, so she'll have to be interviewed. He says he came along here hoping to catch up on some time and gain the main road at this point. It chops more than a mile off his usual route. He was late and could have missed seeing the body, but he did see it and to his credit, he did stop and report it. He rang from that kiosk just over the railway bridge. I suppose he could have bumped her off and dumped her, then claimed he'd found her.'

'It's the sort of trick some killers do,' said Pemberton.

'We'd better check his wife is still alive then!' said Thornton. 'And give his tanker a careful check to see if it ever contained the corpse.'

'We'll do those as a matter of priority, I'll see a team is allocated the wife action,' agreed Pemberton. 'Now, has anybody else used the lane this morning?'

'No, sir, not that we know of. It's busy at night with courting couples, we'll need to trace some of those to determine when she was dumped.'

'How long has she been here, any idea?'

'No, not the foggiest, sir. She was cold, though, so she's been dead some time. Poor old biddy, she must have looked ill in life, eh?'

'She certainly wasn't the most robust of ladies, was she? Right, well, as soon as Doc. Andrews has done his stuff, you do yours. I'll have words with the tanker-driver now but I won't press him about our suspicions of him, not just yet.'

The driver, worried what his bosses would think, could tell Mark very little. He was more worried how the farmers along his route would react to the non-collection of their milk and then there was the milk factory. It would be expecting his delivery . . .

He confirmed he had left home a few minutes after six o'clock, some thirty-five minutes later than usual, and, knowing the area well, had used Green Lane as a short cut to make up some lost time.

In the headlights of his tanker, he'd seen the thin white figure lying in the grass and had stopped to see if he could help. He'd tried to rouse her and when he couldn't, he'd touched her and found her stone-cold. So he'd rung the police.

'Did you get a good look at her?' asked Mark.

'Not at first, I just cleared off to call you fellers when I found how cold she was. Then that constable took me back, showed me her face. Never seen her before, though. No idea who she is. Sorry.'

'Was anybody else in the lane when you came along? Walking? Out with dogs maybe? Jogging? Cycling? Keep-fit fanatics, that sort of thing? Or did anybody come along after you'd stopped?'

'No, nobody. Never saw a soul. It was dark, mind.'

'Have you used the lane before, like this? As a short cut?'

'No, I bloody well haven't. Trust this to happen the very morning I was late . . . the only bloody morning I've been late on this run, the only time I've come along here . . .'

'Well thanks for your public-spiritedness,' said Mark. 'Now, have you given a statement to my men?'

'Yes, a young detective did get me to sign what I'd seen, I told him what I told you just now. So can I go?'

'We'll have to give your tanker the once-over first. Our Scenes of Crime lads will do that. To eliminate it from suspicion, you see, tyre-marks and things.'

'So how long will that take?'

'They'll be done within a couple of hours. Now, what about your firm, have they been told?'

'The lad who interviewed me first said he'd tall them.'

'Well, I'm sorry, but you'll just have to hang about for a while. The Press might want to talk to you, by the way. If they do get hold of you, just tell them what you've told me. There's no harm in that.'

'I can't say that appeals to me, getting my face plastered all over the bloody newspapers . . .'

'It's the penalty for doing the right thing, Mr Downes. Thanks for being so public-spirited. We'll get you mobile just as soon as we can. Now, I must have words with my Detective Chief Inspector. I see he's arrived.'

Detective Chief Inspector Rodney Abbott, known as Bud to friends and colleagues alike, had been given an up-to-date situation report and now turned away from the knot of officials with Pemberton at his side. Abbott, in charge of the Divisional CID, and in whose area the body now lay, was a detective of the old school, a no-nonsense man who hated criminals and who regarded it as his life's mission to arrest every one of them. In his late forties, he was stockily built with a balding head of short, dark hair. He always wore brown suits and white shirts. His colleagues wondered if had just one suit, but he hadn't; he had several, all the same colour.

But he was a popular fellow, a man's man who liked his pint, his fish and chips and his Saturday football match. With five children in their teens and twenties, he had a happy family life, too.

The two senior detectives wanted a few moments of discussion without interruption. As they promenaded away from the action, Pemberton formally placed Abbott in charge of the investigation, which was really a matter of routine because the body did lie within his jurisdiction. Pemberton would maintain a supervisory role and said he would take the first news conference at ten-thirty, but he'd like Bud to be present and perhaps conduct any future ones. Having established those priorities, they discussed minor aspects of the enquiry, such as agreeing to the usual overtime commitments for the men. They'd all work a daily 9 a.m. to 9 p.m. shift – detectives liked murder enquiries because of the large overtime payments.

Both Abbott and Pemberton knew they need not elaborate the proposed details of the enquiry, each knowing and trusting the other's capabilities.

'Just one more thing, Bud,' he added to this preliminary chat. 'Mayhew. Frank. Our one-time target criminal. I know, and you know, that he always takes a morning walk along this lane with his dog. From what I've learned so far, nobody's seen him this morning. You might regard that as significant.'

'That puts him firmly in the frame for starters,' smiled Bud. 'Right, sir, we'll give him priority. It's nice to have a good suspect from the start. But after what Thornton's told me, I'm not happy about that lorry-driver. It's too much of a coincidence that he came along here today of all days. He admits he never comes this way as a rule.'

'You don't like coincidences, do you?'

'I don't believe in them, sir, not in a crime enquiry. I reckon they're all part of the event. I don't reckon coincidences ever occur in crime . . . too many snippets of genuine evidence have been written off as mere coincidences . . . and I wonder if it's more than a coincidence that the lorry-driver came this way today.'

'He sounds honest enough to me,' admitted Pemberton.

'I'll check his story with a fine tooth-comb,' affirmed Bud Abbott.

'That's what we need and I know you'll sort it all out. Now, here comes Doc. Andrews right on cue, let's see what he can tell us.'

Climbing out of his little Renault 5 a couple of hundred yards away, the pathologist looked even bigger than usual. Then, armed with a medical bag, he hurried to the scene, nodding to acquaintances as he sped along. He greeted Mark and Bud with a cheery 'Good morning', and then ducked beneath the yellow tape to speak with Detective Sergeant Thornton whom he knew well, the two often having worked together.

The video camera started to record this examination. Pemberton and Bud Abbott stood aside during these moments, knowing that Andrews liked to work undisturbed. They saw him examine the body visually, then take temperatures from various parts of the corpse and the earth, measure the body and finally make a rough sketch depicting its position. Having conducted a careful examination without moving the remains, he shouted, 'Has she been moved at all?'

'No,' said Thornton, speaking for everyone.

'I'm going to turn her over, I want to examine her back, maybe she's been shot there or stabbed or something.'

With tender care, he knelt before the corpse and hauled her towards him, the stiff body resting against his legs as he looked at the back of the head, neck, chest and other parts.

'Nothing,' he said, allowing her to fall back into her original position. Then he stood up and addressed Thornton, by which time Pemberton and Bud Abbott had edged forwards. 'Well, gentlemen,' he smiled, his Welsh accent sounding stronger than normal in this situation. 'She is a mature adult woman, undernourished I would say; aged between fifty-five and sixty at a guess. She's 5 feet 6 inches tall, brown hair turned mainly grey and cut short, grey eyes, she has all her own teeth in good condition. There are no visible scars or signs of injury, no visible wounds and no ligatures around her throat. No tattoos or other identifying features. The head and skull do not appear to have been damaged.

'No external evidence of a sexual assault. In other words, I cannot hazard a guess as to the cause of death but would think it is probably asphyxiation. I will determine that from my postmortem – maybe I shall find some internal bruised neck muscles or some other indication like a blockage in the trachea or of course some semen in her vagina. I cannot definitely state how long she has been here, but would estimate between four and eight hours. I reckon she was dumped sometime between eleven last night and three this morning.'

'When it was pitch dark!' said someone.

'Precisely. Now, if you want an opinion, the death is suspicious simply because she is wearing no clothes and no jewellery. Someone wants to hide her identity. I'll make a full written report when I've done the post-mortem.'

It was enough to be going on with, enough to provide the investigating officers with several starting points, so when the pathologist had left, the Scenes of Crime officers began their own examination of the body and of the scene. Task Force officers were assembling to begin their fingertip search of the grass and surrounding ground, and a detective was now making plaster casts of the milk-tanker's tyres. Everything was being recorded by a stills camera and a video tape-recorder, now able to work in full daylight. The sun was rising on a bright morning with a chill in the air. As Doc. Andrews hurried back to his Renault, Mark Pemberton caught him. Alone and out of earshot, they could talk.

'Thanks, Doc, for going along with this,' said Pemberton.

'I'm enjoying it, you know,' the pathologist beamed. 'It's bloody good fun. A smashing idea for an exercise – your lads are responding well, it's all very realistic. Now, when your lads have done with her, they'll fetch her to the lab and I'll do a PM, a real one, just to maintain the illusion. I'll make a report too, I can fake that to say she died of asphyxia. I'll stick her in the fridge again, she'd better be available just like a real murder victim, especially if someone comes forward thinking they know her.'

'OK, do that. Keep her as long as possible.'

'So your man found her on time, eh?'

'She was found as I expected, but not by my villain!' and Mark explained what had happened.

'Lovely,' said Doc. Andrews. 'So now you've two suspects instead of one, haven't you?'

4

By ten-thirty, the parade room had been converted into an Incident Room, The HOLMES computer had been installed, teams of detectives were arriving for their first briefing and the clerical staff were organizing cups of coffee, sorting out stationery and allocating newly installed telephone numbers and extensions. The correct and swift establishment of an Incident Room for a murder investigation was vital, but these officers and civilian staff were well trained and rehearsed. They had established this room on many previous occasions in many different locations.

As they worked, Bud Abbott followed Mark Pemberton down to the staff lounge where the news conference was being held. As he entered, he found a knot of about eight journalists chatting informally with the Force press officer, Inspector Dodd.

'Morning, Les,' he addressed Dodd. 'Any more to come?'

'Not at this stage, sir, it's still low key and only of local interest, isn't it?'

'So far as we know, yes. OK, introduce us and I'll get this show moving.'

Dodd introduced the two senior detectives who were in fact well known to most of the assembled journalists, and then Pemberton explained the current situation, adding a brief description of the corpse with a rider that his first priority was to identify her.

He followed with the basic facts, adding that at the moment, the cause of death was not known but a post-mortem was being conducted this morning and that the incident was being treated as murder. When the pathologist's report was complete, the media would be informed. He added that the scene had been sealed off and a fingertip search was being conducted by the Task Force; news photographs could be taken if required. No one was in custody or helping with enquiries and an Incident Room had been established. Teams of about forty detectives were being drafted in to begin house-to-house enquiries, their priorities being to identify the deceased and to interview anyone

33

known to have used Green Lane since tea-time yesterday. In response to their questions, he did say none of the woman's clothing was lying nearby, her handbag had not been found and it was possible she had been killed elsewhere, then dumped there from a vehicle. The journalists all said they would issue appeals for witnesses through their columns or broadcasts, and they would ask the public to reflect on any ladies of this age or description who might be absent from their homes or usual haunts. The police also asked for any found handbags or women's discarded clothing to be notified to the Incident Room. Those items had clearly been dumped somewhere; all waste-disposal tips would be searched. This preliminary news conference was quickly completed and there would be another at four o'clock that afternoon.

As the journalists drifted away to file their stories, Pemberton's next step was to address the detectives who had assembled in the Incident Room. Members of the advance group were still at the scene but they were aware of the facts; the officers now gathering around him had been drafted in from outlying divisions and had to be provided with all the available information. They had to be fed and watered, space had to be found for them to work on their reports and he was aware that it was a major upheaval in their daily routine.

As they seated themselves around the Incident Room, Paul Larkin, the Inspector in charge of admin., chalked some brief details on a blackboard. This gave the location of the woman's body, the time and date of discovery, and the name of the tanker-driver who found her. It also described the body.

'So,' Pemberton stood on a chair to address his teams and saw Amanda's pretty, alert face among the crowd. 'We need to know who she was. That is our first priority. Inspector Larkin will allocate actions for that task. We might need several teams working on that action because we have so little to go on, no clothing, no jewellery or tattoo marks. No handbag even. Nothing except her red toe-nails and fingernails. So it's down to house-to-house enquiries, lots of them, persistent enquiries. Don't give up. And get around the pubs and clubs, find out who's likely to have had women of her age-group visiting them, maybe a bus tour who's lost a passenger or some locals who've lost a granny.

'Check hospitals for missing patients, especially mental ones, old-folk's homes, that sort of place. We've taken a video of the scene and of the body, that'll be ready for your next conference, so you can see what she looks like, and there'll be photos too.

'Suspects? Well, our tanker-driver is Number One. He found her. Name Harry Downes, his address is in his statement and copies are on the desk. Paul, put a team on him. He never drives that way as a rule; he says he was late this morning and used Green Lane as a short cut. Could he have done her in and dumped her, covering up by claiming to find her? Is it his wife? Make sure she's alive by talking to her. Check him thoroughly. See if he has a record of any kind. Suspect Number Two is Frank Mayhew. Some of you know him – he's been a target several times, but always avoids detection. He's clever and dangerous. He could be armed, bear that in mind if you have to confront him. He's known to the police as an armed raider, building societies mainly, which he robs well away from here with a shotgun. He's the Shotgun Raider some of you might have seen featured on *Crimewatch*. But we've never had enough evidence to nail him. Lots of forces want him but we can't prove a thing against the bastard. Paul, put a good team or two onto him, dig up everything. He always sleeps at home and usually walks his dog along Green Lane at half-past six. This morning, for some reason, he wasn't seen out with his dog. So where was he? Why didn't he make this trip today?

'With him and Downes, we've got two good 'uns in the frame . . .'

After the briefing, one of the detective sergeants asked whether there was any possibility that the body was an outcome of this morning's drugs raid at Pennine Flats and Pemberton said the idea could not be ignored. A check must be made on known drug-dealers, -pushers and -users and their movements and all known contacts should be investigated. The dead woman might have been involved, he suggested; was she a friend, user, mother? He did say that so far as he could recall, her body showed no signs of drug abuse, no needle-marks, bruises and sores. The PM, and tests on body tissues, would show whether or not she had taken drugs. The idea created a buzz of interest among the detectives, after which Pemberton said that all addresses in flats and pensioners' homes must be checked to see if anyone of her description was missing. The

DSS might help, although their trade union could be obstructive to the police.

Pemberton said that all the social and welfare agencies must be approached to see if they were willing to co-operate and any problems of overt union or official hostility should be referred to him. And as Mark Pemberton addressed his men, he realized he was being carried away with enthusiasm . . . he was treating this like a real crime, a genuine murder, so surely his men would produce something worthwhile?

By eleven-fifteen, the teams were leaving the Incident Room to go about their actions, with Amanda Wallbridge being detailed for house-to-house enquiries. An action was the name given to each specific enquiry. Every action was given a consecutive number and logged in an Action Book and it was the duty of the Incident Room Inspector to ensure that each was completed and the result logged into the system. Each team comprised a Detective Sergeant and a Detective Constable, and each would take written statements from everyone they interviewed, even if they could say nothing. Statement readers would abstract every fact and log every one into HOLMES, the computer known as the Home Office Large Major Enquiry System, with cross-references so that the origin could be traced. Every statement would then be filed after being photocopied for distribution so that every detective had access to all the amassed information. As the office hummed with activity around him, Pemberton rang Andrews.

'Hi, Doc, it's Pemberton, calling from the Incident Room. Any joy with the PM?'

'Ah, yes, thanks for calling, Superintendent,' he used a very formal approach in case he was overheard. 'Asphyxia, I'm sure. You'll get a copy of my report by runner, but I believe she was suffocated with something like a pillow or cushion.

'There was no damage to her neck muscles, so indicating she was not strangled, nor did I find any evidence of manual pressure on her bone structure; sometimes, with manual strangulation, we get minor fractures to the neck bones, as you know. These were non-existent. She was undernourished but that is sometimes a feature of growing older and it in no way contributed to her death. I'd say she was well into her sixties, Inspector. So there we are, asphyxia by direct application of a blockage over the mouth and nose, I reckon. Cushion or pillow, something soft like that. Murder, in other words, but no evidence of sexual assault or such activity immediately before death was found. So she wasn't raped. I'll be sending selected internal organs and samples of brain to our scientists to test for drugs, but I've not located any indication of drug-dependence.'

'Can we put a time on her death?' asked Pemberton.

'Very loosely. I'd say she died between 6 p.m. last night and 2 a.m. this morning, but that is not a very scientific assessment. I think she was dead before she was placed in Green Lane. I don't think we can gauge the time any closer than that.'

'Thanks, doctor. I'll inform my teams.'

Later that morning, Detective Sergeant Roger Daniels and DPC John Watson presented Mark with his first real problem.

After their initial enquiries into the background of Harry Downes, they came to see Pemberton.

'Sir,' said Daniels. 'Downes, the tanker-driver, he's our action. We've discovered he's lying. In his first statement, he said his wife could confirm his late departure this morning, well, she's not there.'

'Bloody hell! You've searched the house?'

'Yes. There's no sign of her. He's at home now, the firm gave him the day off, so we went to talk to her. He admits he was lying about her being there to confirm the time he departed. He says he has no idea where she is.'

Mark's heart sank; he did not want an innocent man to be pilloried. 'So what's his story, Sarge?'

'They had a row, he said, they were fighting and arguing. She's been having it off with another man, she works in a pub, sir, behind the bar of the Black Lion. We've had words with the licensee, he confirms that. She was there last night, working till closing time at eleven, and was sent home by taxi after washing the glasses and clearing the bar. She left the pub just before midnight and got home at midnight as near as dammit. Nobody's seen her since, except Downes. He claims she did come home, they had a row and she walked out on him half an hour later. He says he spent all night looking for her, driving round the town in his car.'

'And?'

'He never found her, so that's what made him late this morning. He left home after no sleep and then came across our corpse . . . It's not his day, is it?'

'And his wife? What's she look like?'

'Nothing like that corpse, fortunately. She's thirty-eight, busty and blonde. I've got a photo, from him. She's called Sheila Downes, 5 feet 6 inches, blonde hair, plump build, wears heavy make-up, works part-time as a barmaid at the Black Lion and has been seeing a chap called Stan Miller, a regular at the pub. He's at work today, he's a salesman for animal foodstuffs and is out on the road, so we can't see him yet.'

'So why did Downes make up the tale about his wife seeing him off late?'

'He didn't want his domestic life to become public, sir, so he says. He never thought we'd check.'

'I believe him. OK, so it puts him higher in the frame, but that's all; mind, we'd better find his bloody wife, hadn't we? Do you need another team helping you?'

'Not yet, sir, we can handle this.'

'Have you searched his house for things his wife might have taken?'

'Yes, we first went through every room looking for her, outhouses, attic, wardrobes, the lot. She's not there. So we checked the bathroom and bedroom. Her make-up is there, her toothbrush is there, all her clothes are there, suitcases, and so on. If she's left home, she's taken sod all with her.'

'Right, then we'd better set about finding Mrs Downes. And when you do, see if she knows our dead woman – and see if her fancy man knows our corpse, too. The corpse might be his wife, eh? Might the fancy man have killed his missus and run off with Mrs Downes – what age is this Romeo?'

'Late fifties, so the licensee says.'

'Now, there's a thing. Miller marries an older woman, gets tired of her and finds a fresh piece of skirt, so he knocks off his missus and clears off with the new crumpet . . . and the corpse is found by the husband of the new crumpet . . . no, that's hardly likely, is it? Too much of a coincidence!'

'It's not impossible, sir,' said Daniels. 'And we know what Mr Abbott thinks about coincidences!'

'True, anyway, lads, it's up to you to sort out this scenario. Well done.'

'The reason we're here, sir, is to ask should we bring him in? Downes, I mean, to help with enquiries?'

'Good God, no!' snapped Pemberton, before immediately bringing his temper under control. He mellowed and said, 'Sorry. I mean not just yet. I think that's a bit premature, don't you? We know this stiff is not his wife, don't we? And there's no evidence he's bumped our corpse off, or his wife. Mrs Downes is just missing from home, and we don't pay much heed to mature people who clear off with new lovers.'

'But it's all a bit odd, sir, a bit of a coincidence . . .'

'So you think it's suspicious? I think we need more to go on, don't you? I know you want the arrest, and I agree your tanker-driver is a suspect, a bloody good one, but we lack the hard evidence we need to fetch him in – remember we're into the realms of the Police and Criminal Evidence Act now, so we must be sure of our ground before making any arrests.'

'Yes, sir.'

'Good, well, keep digging. If we don't find Mrs Downes, then your man will be a good suspect and if he has done her in, then you'll get the arrest.'

This cheered them up; it was every detective's ambition to arrest a murderer and Pemberton knew he must honour their ambition if at all possible.

But he couldn't allow Harry Downes to be arrested . . . unless the fellow *had* killed his own wife? It was a possibility he could not ignore.

5

Detective Chief Inspector Wilfred Draper, the officer in charge of the Special Branch, had commissioned some covert photographs of two men thought to be involved with the IRA. The request for the pictures had come from the Eighth Floor of New Scotland Yard following discussions between the Special Branch at the Yard and the Security Services. Draper was pleased that a local police photographer, aided by his long-distance lenses, had succeeded in obtaining some good black-and-white shots. They included a full facial of the major target and the prints were now ready for collection. Draper said he would pop into the studio around 4 p.m. As good as his word, he thrust his burly frame through the swing-doors promptly at four and sought Detective Sergeant Thornton. He found him poring over some freshly produced sets of fingerprints which were spread across the preparation table on A4 sheets of paper.

'Hello, sir. Your prints are over there, in the CID tray. Blue envelope. They've come out well, nice and crisp.'

'Thanks, Derek, your lads did well to get those shots, it wasn't the easiest of jobs. So what have we here, then?' and his attention was drawn to the array of reproduced fingerprint forms which were spread haphazardly across the table.

'The Green Lane woman, sir, these are her prints. We took them directly from the corpse before the PM.'

'Prostitute, is she?'

'We don't think so, she seems to have led a decent life. Late middle age, thin as a rail, clean, nails tarted up a bit perhaps, but nothing to say she's been on the game.'

'But you'll be doing a previous cons. check?'

'Naturally, we're sending sets to the CRO and to our own bureau for comparison; if she is in our records, they could throw up a name.'

'Funny job, that,' said Draper.

'They're all funny jobs, sir,' agreed Thornton. 'I've never known a murder that was straightforward . . .'

'I mean the body – no clothes, no signs of injury, nothing personal lying nearby . . . it was just as if somebody had wanted rid of a corpse rather than pay to have it buried. It *was* murder, wasn't it?'

'Asphyxiation according to Doc. Andrews, cushion or pillow or something soft over the air passages. Smothered, according to him. No sex motive, it seems. She wasn't assaulted.'

Draper, arguably the Force's most experienced and skilled detective, picked up the prints and examined them. Then after what was at first a mere casual glance, he scrutinized them more closely, his thick dark eyebrows showing his concentration.

'What do we know so far?' he asked, the interest now strong in his voice.

He had a warm face with a square chin and heavy features beneath a good head of dark hair; touches of grey were showing at the temples now, but his eyes were sparkling and his brain was constantly alert to every kind of villainy. Although the detection of murder was not within his normal duty, he had lost none of his interest in this most serious of crimes. 'Has anything positive turned up yet?'

'Not yet, sir,' and Thornton told him the story so far.

'So Mark Pemberton's got a puzzle on his hands, eh?' smiled Draper. 'It'll test him while the boss is away. Now, have you a couple of spare sets of these prints?'

'Sure,' said Thornton. 'Help yourself. We always run off more than we need.'

Draper took two full sets of each hand and begged a file cover to contain them.

'Thanks,' he said, leaving the studio with this file and his requested IRA photos.

Detective Sergeant Thornton puzzled momentarily over the Special Branch chief's interest in this body, but when the telephone rang with a query about some colour negatives of a recent road-traffic accident, he put those thoughts to the back of his mind. Besides, the more officers who saw these prints, the more likelihood there was of an identification.

Back in the seclusion of his office, Draper spread the prints across his desk and used an old-fashioned magnifying glass to study them.

It was the right thumb that attracted him – even when glancing at the prints in the studio, the mark had been prominent. Now he could examine it more clearly; set among the ridges, loops and whorls was what was probably the result of a knife cut, a scar perhaps, but there was a definite irregularity. It was in the rough shape of a letter D with the flat face nearest the joint. It was the sort of scar that might result from a small but deep cut with a sharp kitchen knife – the skin would be sliced, but the flap would be replaced to heal and so leave permanent evidence of the cut. A mark like this could endure for the person's lifetime, albeit fading a little with the passage of the years. But on those black-and-white inked reproductions, the outline of the rough D was very clear. It was about the size of the nail on an average woman's forefinger.

And he had seen that outline before. He recognized it.

But where? He knew he had once perused this very same set of fingerprints, but where had that been? And when? And

41

under what circumstances? At this moment, he could not remember.

His own telephone rang so he pushed the prints into his top drawer, closed it and locked it so that no one else would have access to them. He wanted as few as possible to know of his interest. Identifying those prints was a job he would do with some discretion, for it would please him greatly to provide a name for the murder victim.

He would like to succeed if Pemberton failed, for wasn't Pemberton now occupying the post of CID Superintendent that he himself should have been awarded?

The call took his mind off the prints because his immediate attention was redirected towards the IRA suspects. He opened the blue envelope which contained their photographs, then rang for his sergeant. There was work to be done on these terrorists. The Green Lane lady would have to wait.

As Draper worried about the IRA on that first afternoon of the investigation, the scene was being cleared. The body had gone. It was now bearing the enormous butcher-like cuts of the pathologist's saws and knives and was stored in a fridge at the mortuary. The milk-tanker, having been closely examined by Forensic scientists, had been restored to its owners and the Task Force had completed their search of the grass and hedgerows without finding anything significant.

Plaster casts had been made of several footprints and tyre-marks which had been discovered in the softer parts of the lane. These would serve for elimination purposes. No female cloth-ing, hangbag contents or jewellery had yet been found in spite of a meticulous search of the undergrowth and surrounding countryside, and so far there was nothing to suggest the woman's identity or origins. The entire scene had been photo-graphed in stills and video, with and without the body in position, and these pictures would be shown to all officers.

The investigating officers and British Rail police had been asked to interview all known passengers of trains which had passed the scene since six o'clock last night. The Incident Room was now operating at full capacity for twenty-four hours per day and the initial excitement of a new murder enquiry had created a strong team spirit among the assembled detectives.

In the town, news of the murder was carried on the front page of the *Evening News* and Pemberton was pleased to see that a description of the woman, with his appeal to the public for suggestions of her identity, was prominently presented. There would surely be some response. The request for readers to report finding any clothing or handbags was also printed.

There was the inevitable photograph of the scene, minus the body, but with the assemblage of detectives and vehicles portrayed so they suggested an aura of efficiency and activity coupled with more than an element of drama. The 4 p.m. news conference had been a minor one, Pemberton's only amendment to the first being that it was now established that the woman had died from asphyxia. He declined to specify the precise nature of that asphyxia, knowing some of the Press would say she'd been strangled and others would say she'd been smothered.

The Incident Room was enjoying a period of temporary peace and quiet because the detectives had all left and were all in the town, asking their questions during house-to-house visits and taking their statements.

The office staff had started the laborious task of reading and processing the statements already filed and as Pemberton strolled around, pleased with the progress to date, Bud Abbott hailed him.

'Sir,' he said. 'A word in your ear if I may.'

Pemberton followed the Detective Chief Inspector into his tiny office and Abbott closed the door.

'This lorry-driver,' he began. 'Downes. Daniels and Watson have given him a thorough grilling and asked me to follow with my own questioning. I've just come back from his house.'

'And?'

'I think we should have him in. I've never been happy about him.'

'Bring him in? On what grounds, Bud? What evidence? As I said to Daniels, we're not investigating him for killing his wife, are we? She's just cleared off, and that's no crime.'

'That's according to him; he could be covering up a crime of his own. I mean, the circumstances of finding the woman's body . . . the coincidences involved . . . I'm wondering if he's done both jobs, I never believe in coincidences where murder is

43

concerned. Well, any serious crime for that matter, but murder especially. It all stinks to me, sir, I think he's hiding something.'

'Bud, old son, let's not get carried away with this. If that corpse had not been found, Mrs Downes' absence wouldn't have caused a ripple, would it? Married women are always running off with fancy men and our official policy is "good luck to 'em".'

Abbott refused to back down. 'But the woman's body *has* been found, sir. It's not a hypothetical question I'm posing, it's actually happened, it's real. That changes everything, it means the events could be linked . . .'

'OK, Bud, point taken, so what are you proposing?'

'That we bring in the tanker-driver, that we give him a taste of the cells and some close questioning to see if he cracks . . . he might just tell us what's happened to his wife.'

Pemberton thought hard. 'OK, invite him in then, don't bring him in under arrest. Let's get this cleared up in a civilized way. Tape his interview, having Daniels and Watson present, but do it by the book, crossing all the t's and dotting all the i's.'

'Aren't we being a little cautious, sir?'

'No, we're not. Do it, but do it right. Now, how's the search for Mrs Downes progressing?'

Abbott explained that his teams had visited the Black Lion where Sheila Downes worked. They had interviewed the taxi-driver who confirmed he'd dropped her outside her home at 12 midnight and he'd watched her go in. He always did this.

He always waited until his lone lady-passengers had entered their homes, a piece of old-world courtesy from him.

The landlord, Dennis Lewis, confirmed she had been seeing Stan Miller while her husband was away on long-distance runs, and sometimes they met in the pub. Sometimes, she'd say she was working just to get out of the house and have a night out with Miller. Lewis had gained the impression it was not a serious romance, certainly not the kind that would compel her to leave home; he regarded it more as a long-standing flirtation than anything serious. So far as Sheila's work was concerned, she was a good barmaid who was popular with all the regulars, young and old alike. Buxom and at times bawdy when the moment required it, she could charm the older men and tame the younger ones. She had a warm personality which made her ideal for her work and she had gained a lot of friends and acquaintances of all types, all over the town. She was honest too – he'd never once had cause to worry about the contents of the till or his cellar stock while Sheila was in charge.

'Has she done this before?' asked Pemberton.

'Not that we know of,' replied Abbott. 'According to her husband, she's always enjoyed a flirtation, but there's never been anything serious, so he says. He admits, mind, that at times he did get annoyed with her, especially if she chatted up her beaus while he was around. There had been rows, fights even about her men friends, but never in public and the heat always blew over very quickly.

'Downes reckons she was a good, loving wife. He did admit that sometimes when he was on an overnight trip, he did worry about her, wonder whether she'd brought a man in . . . but he'd never found any evidence of that. There's no children, by the way.'

'And Downes? Anything on him?'

'We've run a check, he has got form, sir. Three recorded convictions for causing ABH and one for GBH, all when he was in his twenties.'

'That's about twenty years ago, then?'

'About that, sir.'

'Nothing since?'

'One minor conviction for driving an overloaded timber-wagon and another for careless driving in Scarborough. That's all.'

'These wounding convictions? What were the circumstances?'

'His record card is a bit vague, sir, but when I put this to him, he said he'd had a habit of getting into fights about girls; if he saw a lad with the girl he thought should be with him, he'd clobber the other fellow . . . Dangerous Downes, they called him, he reckons . . . he laughs about it now, says all that behaviour is in the past. He's grown up now, he says.'

'And you don't believe him? You reckon that if he caught his wife at it, or knew she was having it off with another chap, he'd blow his top and hammer the suitor? Just like he did in the old days?'

'Or hammer his wife . . . or anyone else who happened to be in the way . . . Dammit all, sir, he's done it before, he admits that. Leopards don't change their spots, as they say, even if

45

they do grow older. I knew a bloke of eighty-six who would lash out at anybody he thought was eyeing his wife!'

'So how does all this square with Downes being a top suspect for our Green Lane victim?'

'At this stage, I don't know, I need to learn more about Downes and his private life. We've found nothing to link him with our victim, except that he found her. Or claims he found her. If Mrs Downes had been naughty, there might be links between her and our victim. It's these coincidences that worry me, sir, they're too convenient . . .'

'So we need to find Mrs Downes, Bud?'

'Yes, sir, and urgently.'

'OK, do as you say, but have him volunteer to come in. He might know more than he's told us so far. Have we made sure there's no link between him and the Green Lane woman?'

'No, but if there is, I'll find it.'

And Bud Abbott smiled and went on his way. When it came to interviewing suspects, a police station was infinitely superior to the comforts of one's own home. It was surprising how the truth emerged after a few hours in the calm of a police cell, and so Bud was now a happy man.

Mark Pemberton, on the other hand, was now striving to remember that this was merely an exercise.

He could not admit it to Abbott at this stage and so Abbott's plan, with all the ramifications that it threatened, had to be allowed to proceed, even if it was something of a worry. In the circumstances, it was feasible to bring in Downes due to the worries about his absent wife. Poor old Harry . . . he was already being treated as a genuine suspect.

Mark wiped his brow. Harry Downes was going to go through hell simply because he'd done what any member of the public would have done and should have done. If the people who found dead bodies knew what faced them and how they were immediately under suspicion from the moment of their discovery, then none would volunteer their help. It was little wonder the Great British Public did not want to get involved with crime and its detection.

Pemberton considered the dead woman's ideals in donating her body for the good of society, but what about Harry Downes' forthcoming anguish? Did that matter? Was Harry's torment the price to be paid for increasing the local rate of detected crime?

Pemberton went over to the statement file and began to read those already logged in HOLMES.

At five-thirty that same evening, a twitcher called Cedric Halliday was returning from a hike in the hills behind the town.

He had been to the reservoir to observe the wintering wild geese, including some pink-foots and beans, although earlier reports had indicated that a very rare bird, a migrant black woodpecker, was living in the woods on the lower slopes. This outing had not produced a sighting of the woodpecker, but the water had attracted its usual winter complement of migrating flocks of geese. He would return tomorrow, armed with his binoculars, camera and notebook and he could continue his vigil until he saw the woodpecker. His return journey took him down the route of the Blue Beck, a fast-flowing stream which rises in the hills. Its route and watershed have been dammed to create the inland water known as Blue Beck Reservoir which now forms a massive lake midway down the stream's fast-flowing run from the moors. The reservoir's gushing outlet forms the lower half of Blue Beck.

This pretty stream rushes down the slopes in front of the dam before meandering towards the town across an expansive plain. Today, much of its route near the town is underground, for roads and buildings have been constructed above it. It emerges into the river to the north of the town centre. But between the hills and the town, before reaching the more heavily built-up areas, the stream widens and deepens as it absorbs other tributaries from the surrounding moors. On the flat plains and in the fields, there are places where it is as wide as a river and as deep as a house.

There are bogs and marshes, too, the result of many centuries of erosion upon this plain of soft and marshy land. The area has become a haven of wildlife as the Cedrics of this world are aware.

A footpath runs beside the river for most of the way, sometimes crossing it by small foot-bridges or diverting wide where the river has entered the marshy areas. But Cedric knew the route. He used it frequently to walk from his home in Victoria Terrace up to the distant moors and he was familiar with every curve in the stream as well as its more dangerous stretches. But as he hurried home in case his mother started to worry, he was aware of a red object in one of the pools. At first glance, it looked like an old coat, but then he realized the coat contained a person. . . .

'Oh God!' he breathed. 'Oh, my God . . .'

Taking a deep breath, he clambered down the steep, sandy bank until he was able to gain a closer look. It *was* a person, a woman; she looked very still and her blonde hair was drifting on the surface like strands of feathery weed. And all the time, the gentle flow made one of her hands move like the fin of a basking fish . . .

'Oh my God,' cried Cedric again. Bravely, he ventured closer and tried to touch her, but she was out of reach so he jumped feet first into the water and waded to her. The water was waist-deep and she was floating face down, apparently anchored by clinging weeds which secured her legs.

He tried to lift her head from the water but it was grotesque and swollen and he knew she was dead.

He ran towards the town.

6

After two hours of intense questioning, Harry Downes admitted that Sheila was not his legal wife. He was a widower. His first wife had died of cancer when she was twenty-nine and Harry was thirty-one. Then he'd met Sheila. Her real name was Sheila Wynn; she was from Birmingham where they'd met ten years ago when he was driving furniture vans. After several meetings, they had set up home as man and wife. She was a divorcee; her maiden name was Hatfield, he volunteered. They had decided to live together in the days when convention demanded that common-law wives adopted the names of their men, and so Sheila had lived and worked as Mrs Downes.

But in volunteering that information, Harry could shed no further light upon her disappearance. In that, he was unshakable. He repeated that he had not harmed her and that he had no idea where she was now.

During Abbott's intense interview, Harry's face had become bathed in sweat and he looked exhausted. But Abbott was relentless. A fervent advocate of repeated and demanding interviews, he believed in hammering home the questions until he detected a chink in the defendant's story. Knowing he'd find a chink in Harry's armour, he kept the lorry-driver in the interview room, alternately becoming a harsh and bullying questioner, then a mild and persuasive one.

For Abbott, it was tiring work and it was during this long and tough interrogation, that a detective constable knocked on the door of the interview room. He opened it somewhat gingerly to ask if DCI Abbott could spare him a moment; the matter was urgent and would he please come outside?

'Look,' said an angry Abbott once outside, 'this had better be bloody urgent, I'm in the middle of a major interview and I don't want interruptions . . .'

'It's from Mr Pemberton, sir, he's at Blue Beck Marshes. A woman's body has been found in Blue Beck, he thinks it might be Mrs Downes. He said it looked like murder.'

'Bloody hell! Right, tell him you've contacted me; tell him that I am allowing Mr Downes to go home. I will come to the scene very shortly, I'll liaise with him there.'

Abbott knew that by releasing Harry and then almost immediately confronting him with the devastating news, if indeed it was her, Harry might admit his part in her death.

Abbott returned to Harry.

'OK, Harry, I believe you,' he said amiably with no hint of the shock that was to follow. 'Sorry to have put you through all this. You can go home now. We'll be in touch if anything else happens or if we hear anything of Sheila.'

'Look, you lot might think I've done her in, but I haven't. God knows I haven't and I didn't do that other one. You've gotta believe me.'

'OK, Harry, I believe you, so let's wait until we find her, shall we?'

Harry went home exhausted as Abbott hurried to the riverside. Abbott now knew he was right. Two murders in one day. Two women. One town. And the only known link was Harry Downes, a man with a record of violence, a man who had already lied. If he'd been genuinely worried about Sheila's disappearance last night, why hadn't he reported her missing?

Why pretend she had been there to see him off to work? In Abbott's opinion, that suggested guilt and thus Abbott convinced himself that Harry was a killer. And, given time, he would prove it – and he would do so to the satisfaction of any court.

After viewing the corpse, Abbott knew he would have to break the news to Harry Downes. The dead woman matched Sheila's description and when he learned of her death, it would be interesting to see the expression on the tanker-driver's face.

For the second time within twenty-four hours, Detective Superintendent Mark Pemberton found himself briefly examining a dead woman. This time, however, it was no exercise, it was the real thing. It was late in the evening, the Scenes of Crime officers having completed their work at the riverside. The corpse was in the morgue where it bore a massive wound in the chest, apparently the work of a shotgun fired at close range.

The face looked bruised too, but that could be the result of coming into contact with underwater rocks or obstructions. The body was fully dressed in its bright red coat, white blouse and black skirt, although one of her black shoes was missing. She had black tights too, but no hat or scarf.

The body was awaiting careful undressing before its postmortem. A forensic pathologist, aided by Doc. Andrews, would meticulously examine the corpse and its clothing, then strip it for the medical examination and awful operation before pronouncing the official cause of death. Pemberton had little doubt the death had been caused by a blast from a shotgun but confirmation by formal medical examination had to be sought. After all, she could have drowned.

A search for the weapon in the river and surrounding marshes had been abandoned due to the darkness, but would be resumed at first light.

And now Mark Pemberton was awaiting the unfortunate Harry Downes. Bud Abbott was bringing him here, to the mortuary. When the pre-arranged signal confirmed their arrival, Pemberton covered the body with the shroud, making sure the woman's face was hidden by the top. He also made sure that the length and breadth of the shroud concealed the bloody and gaping wound from Harry's view.

Pemberton went into the ante-room to meet the unfortunate Harry as a uniformed constable remained beside the body, his role being to ensure the continuity of evidence.

Upon entering the ante-room, Mark saw a depressing sight. The tall and powerful driver was pale and drawn; his thick grey hair was unkempt and he was still dressed in this morning's overalls while his face was unshaven and his hands dirty. He looked on the point of exhaustion. It had been an awful day for him . . .

'Mr Downes,' began Mark. 'I'm dreadfully sorry to have to bring you here like this, it's been an awful day for you . . . I'm sure Detective Chief Inspector Abbott has explained things . . .'

'Aye, he says there's another woman been found, that she could be my Sheila . . .'

'Yes. And it means we must ask you to look at her, to tell us if it is her.'

'I had nowt to do with this you know, I mean, if it is her. This chap, this Detective Abbott here, seems sure I had summat to do with that other woman but I hadn't . . . God knows I hadn't . . .'

'He is only doing his job, Mr Downes. We must explore every possibility, unpleasant though it might be. I'm sorry, but we cannot make exceptions . . . Now, can you face this?'

'Aye, let's get it over with.'

'When we're inside the theatre, I will simply turn back the shroud so that her face is revealed; will you look carefully at her and tell me if it's Sheila. OK?'

'Aye.'

'Then when you've done that, the constable will take you into a room to obtain a written statement of identification, a few lines just for the file. If it's not her, then you must say so too – and I hope it's not . . . I really do . . .'

'It's a nightmare, all of this . . . I'm just an ordinary chap . . . trying to earn a living . . .'

Abbott's bright eyes were on his suspect as Mark took the burly fellow's elbow and steered him towards the operating-theatre. Inside, there was the clinging scent of disinfectant and the cloying aroma of death. Mark guided Harry towards the slab. It stood on a solid white plinth like a massive oblong mushroom and Mark said, 'Ready, Mr Downes?'

'As ready as I'll ever be,' he replied.

Mark peeled back the white sheet, halting at the neck until Harry gazed upon the dead face of his common-law wife. Her long blonde hair had been tidied a fraction, but it was still dirty and wet from the river and her features were swollen. Pemberton wondered if they would be out of proportion to the extent that Harry would not recognize her.

'Is that the woman you know as Sheila Wynn, alias Downes?' asked Mark Pemberton in his formal tones.

Harry nodded and a tear came to his eyes. 'Aye,' he said softly, touching her wet hair with his big hand. 'Aye, she is swollen up, but that's her . . .' and he turned away, weeping softly.

Mark guided him out and they returned to the small anteroom, followed by the constable who was clutching a statement form.

'Drowned, was she?' asked Harry, wiping his eyes. 'Did she jump in, do you think? After what I'd done . . . chucking her out . . .'

'No, Harry, I'm sorry to say,' said Pemberton. 'It's not suicide. We believe she was shot and then placed in the river. She was found this evening, by a bird-watcher.'

'Shot? Bloody hell! But why? Who'd want to shoot our Sheila? And why's all this happening to me? It's like a nightmare, honest it is. Why my woman, why did I find that bloody corpse this morning, eh? I know what you fellers must be thinking now but God's honest truth, I had nowt to do with this, with any of 'em . . .'

'OK, Mr Downes, but you appreciate my Chief Inspector will have to ask you lots more questions now, about Sheila, her past, her friends, her haunts, that sort of thing, anything at all might help us track down her killer . . . It's not going to be an easy time, for you or for us. . . .'

'Aye,' said Harry with resignation. 'But what about her funeral, then? I mean, I want to give her a decent burial . . .'

'First, we must conduct a post-mortem and then we will open the inquest, just for identification purposes, but I'm afraid the funeral must be delayed, Harry, for a long time. Several weeks, even months.

'In a murder case, we don't allow burial of the deceased until the court case has been completed or any appeal has been finalized. That's just in case the defence wants another post-mortem examination of the body, you see . . . it must always be available. They could challenge the first findings . . .'

'Oh, bloody hell . . .' and Harry burst into tears, sobbing until the sorrow rocked his huge frame. 'She didn't deserve this, not this . . .'

'I'll leave you with this constable,' said Mark gently. 'When he's taken your statement, Chief Inspector Abbott will take you home.'

Abbott's mouth smiled a fraction as he nodded his understanding. If that gesture appeared to be an act of kindness towards Harry, then it was not. It was often found prudent to allow a murder suspect to go home, to be permitted the feeling that he or she was no longer under suspicion, to be left alone with his or her own thoughts while the intense pressure of the investigation surrounded them or eventually swamped them as they wrestled with their consciences. And then, some time later, there would be the dreaded knock on the door . . .

'See you, Bud,' said Mark Pemberton. 'Look after Mr Downes. I'm going now, I'll be in the Incident Room if I'm needed.'

Ten minutes after he entered the Room, Charles Moore arrived. It wasn't often a Chief Constable came to the centre of operations of a murder hunt, and his arrival had convinced the detectives they were engaged upon a most important enquiry. The appearance of the second body meant that the papers would be headlining a crime wave, referring to the sadistic work of a mass killer and sex maniac and stressing that all women would be advised to stay indoors unless accompanied. And it meant the Press, and therefore the public, would be demanding to know what the police were doing about it. Why weren't the police catching the killer or killers?

'We'll talk outside,' Moore said to Mark. 'We're going for a drive.'

'Sir?' questioned Mark.

'To be alone, without ears flapping,' he said.

In the darkness of that December night, they drove to a car-park where Moore switched off his engine and lights. They were positioned in the middle of an almost deserted car-park and there was just a hint of frost on the cars already there.

'Now,' Moore demanded. 'In view of this second body, what

the hell are we going to do about our exercise? It's become superfluous, Mark, we can achieve our aims without it.'

'We must keep it running, sir,' said Mark. 'It's all we can do; there's no alternative. The two cases are intermingled,' and he explained about Harry Downes, involved in both.

'But our fake murder, was it the cause of the real one? Have our actions precipitated a killing, Mark?' the concern was clear in Moore's voice.

'No,' Pemberton was able to reassure his boss. 'Sheila Wynn left home before our body was positioned. It's highly likely that she met her death before we planted our corpse, her killing is just a freak, a strange coincidence . . .'

'Abbott doesn't believe in coincidences, Mark, he regards them as clues.'

'Well, he's wrong in this case. You and I both know that.'

'But there is a link between the two women, isn't there? It's Downes, Harry Downes. He's the link, Mark, you said so.'

'We know, sir, you and I, that he could not have killed woman Number One. But he could have done Number Two. Now, Abbott thinks he's done both. If all the teams think that, they'll work even harder to prove it.'

'Exactly, so you don't think we should call off the exercise to concentrate on the real murder?'

'How can we call it off, sir? How can we admit we set it up? We can't, we're in too deep now. If we find the real killer and prosecute him, we could even keep the exercise from the public – they would assume that Sheila Wynn's killer also bumped off the other woman; they'd make up their own minds about that, even without the formality of a court case so we could leave the exercise corpse as an open-ended enquiry.

'In other words, we could leave it on file. In view of what's happened, it would be dangerous to declare that the first body was the means of providing an exercise to test our resources. The Press, then the public and our bloody Police Authority, would accuse us of bringing about the second death . . . and I do think the information gained from the first investigation, even if it's only a few hours old, will help us in our enquiries into the real death. There must be benefits in running them simultaneously, sir.'

'Downes, you mean?'

'He could be guilty of killing his wife. So far, he seems to be the last person to have seen her alive. We can't ignore that. Without our Green Lane lady, he wouldn't have entered the frame, well, perhaps not so quickly.'

'So we run both simultaneously. So be it. But you will ensure that the real killing gets priority? You can do that by clever supervision of the Incident Room and allocation of actions, eh? And keep up those house-to-houses, I want those rigourously undertaken.'

'I think I can carry that one off, sir.'

'Good, well, let's hope we get a quick arrest, eh? I want it all wrapped up before the PM comes. I don't want him quizzing us about unsolved murders with the Press listening in.'

'We'll do our best sir.'

'And, Mark, keep the pressure on. Get the public involved, use the Press to persuade them to co-operate. That shouldn't be difficult now. We want to know of any suspicious people in town, newcomers, secretive behaviour, that sort of thing.'

'I'll ensure my teams bear that in mind, sir.'

'Good, well, so far so good, eh? You've done a good job so far, Mark. It seems to be going well. I'm pleased the way you've approached this, you've fulfilled my expectations.'

And with that, Mr Moore drove away, leaving Mark Pemberton to walk back to the police station. He enjoyed the fresh air, but wondered why Moore was so anxious about this investigation; he'd never shown such an active interest on previous occasions and he seemed particularly keen on saturating the town with house-to-house enquiries.

It was now approaching eleven o'clock and when he entered the Incident Room, Inspector Dodd, the PRO, was waiting and hailed him.

'Sir, I'm getting lots of Press calls. I've confirmed that a second body has been found and that we're treating the death as suspicious. Some of the journalists, especially PA and the nationals, want a quote from a senior detective.'

'What sort of quote?'

'Well, is it the work of a maniac? Is a sex killer at large in the town? Is it a maniac rapist? Is there any link between the two deaths? That sort of thing.'

'Right, I'd better be the spokesman. Say this, Les – "*Detective Superintendent Mark Pemberton, in charge of the investigation said,*

'At this stage, there is no evidence to link the two deaths, and sex assaults do not appear to be a motive in either case. We are investigating both deaths as separate crimes, we suspect murder in both. A further thirty detectives have been drafted in and I feel sure we will shortly be arresting the killers."' How's that?'

'Thanks, that'll be fine for now. Shall I fix a news conference for ten in the morning?'

'Yes, that's important. I'll take the conference, Mr Moore has put me in charge of both investigations.'

For the next hour, Mark Pemberton examined the incoming information relating to the Green Lane killing. As a direct result of news coverage, four couples had come forward to admit being in the lane at times varying between 6.30 p.m. and 11 p.m. last night, but none had seen or heard anything suspicious.

The suggestion that she might be Miller's wife had been ruled out and preliminary interviews of regular passengers on trains which passed the scene had also drawn a blank, but there were eight other possible names for the deceased. In all cases, they were women of around sixty who had been missing from their usual haunts or homes in the last year; in one case, the mother of four girls had been missing for fifteen years and every time an unidentified female body was found, her family contacted the police, always in the hope of finding her. They would be happy to find her dead or alive, just so long as they knew.

In all these cases, which were spread from as far north as Durham and as far south as Milton Keynes, the claims would be examined very closely. But the Incident Room was now alive again. A second blackboard had been erected and bore a description of Sheila Wynn, alias Downes, and in spite of the late hour, none of the detectives had gone home. None would claim overtime either – they just wanted to catch the killer or killers.

And at the top of the improvised bookie's frame was the name of Harry Downes, the odds being shown as 5:2 on.

In second place, at evens, was Frank Mayhew, the Shotgun Raider. He seemed to have vanished from the town, so where had he been during these last few hours?

7

During the night the detectives went home for a well-earned rest but the work of the Incident Room continued. A small staff of night-duty officers coped with the more mundane but essential work of filing and record-keeping.

One of their tasks involved Sheila Wynn, née Hatfield. Once her name had been confirmed by Harry Downes, along with her date and place of birth, Inspector Larkin, in his capacity as Inspector i/c the Incident Room, caused the name to be entered into the Police National Computer. Her maiden name and her assumed name of Downes were included. The names would be compared with its records of Hatfields, Hadfields, Winns, Whinns, Wynns, Downes and Downs or any other likely combination of letters. Larkin instructed his night staff to make an additional check by telephone to the Criminal Record Office at New Scotland Yard. In the former case, Sheila's name was not thrown up by the PNC, for she was not a suspected or wanted person, nor was she a vehicle-owner or -driver with dangerous tendencies nor was she sporting a current disqualification. But the CRO did produce results.

A night-duty sergeant at Scotland Yard had found a criminal record in the name of Sheila Hatfield, born in Birmingham on 13 July 1953, described as a machinist. That made her thirty-seven years of age.

He read a brief synopsis over the telephone and confirmed he would post a copy of all the relevant information, plus a photograph of the woman, to the Incident Room. If it was urgent, copies could be faxed through. Pemberton's staff would reciprocate by sending copies of the victim's fingerprints, just to make sure the CRO records referred to this Sheila Wynn. The date of birth almost clinched it anyway. Larkin, who was still working, felt sure this was their victim. He hailed Pemberton who was likewise still on duty. Even though it was almost midnight, he was in his office, chatting to one of the young women detectives, Amanda Wallbridge. They appeared to be deep in discussion, but Larkin opened the door and interrupted them.

The policewoman blushed and said, 'I'll be off now, sir,' to Pemberton and quickly departed.

'Sir,' began Larkin as the girl left the room. 'The Yard has a record of Sheila Wynn. She has form.'

'Has she?' Mark Pemberton was interested now. 'What for?'

'Drug-dealing mainly, three convictions in Birmingham and two in the Met area, about fifteen years ago. It's still on file, fortunately; she got a suspended sentence on her last conviction. Three years suspended for a year. She's also got form for prostitution, a whole list of convictions, dozens, according to the Yard, with fines. Mainly in Brum, some in the Met.'

'So our pretty but ageing barmaid had a murky past, eh? I wonder if Harry knows? So what about her life here?'

'We've nothing on her, sir, her last conviction was in 1978, in London. It seems she's been keeping her slate clean while she's been living here. I've done a check with the collator and local crime intelligence, they've nothing.'

'Well, then, we'd better look into her local life a bit more closely, eh? Maybe her past, or one of her past contacts, has caught up with her? Give Birmingham a call, will you, and set up preliminary enquiries. We'll send a team down there if necessary. Ask them to dig out the usual stuff, background, contacts, family and so on. Now, Paul, anything else before I call it a day?'

'We've got Harry Downes' private car in, sir, for a forensic test. That'll tell us if it carried the Green Lane body or his wife's; I've asked them to check for bloodstains, too, in view of his wife's violent death. It looked clean from a visual check, but you never know. The results will take a day or two. And there's still no sign of Mayhew. He seems to have vanished into thin air.'

'Good, keep checking and if necessary, we can circulate him nation-wide as wanted for interview. Some Force might know where he is, but I'd rather we exhausted every local hiding place before we go nation-wide. We'd look a bit sick if he was kipping down in our patch all the time. So what about poor old Harry Downes? How's he coping?'

'He's at home now, sir.'

'It'll be a sleepless night for him. Now, you lads will be knocking off now, eh?'

'Yes, we've a skeleton staff from midnight until eight in the morning.'

'OK, see you then,' and Mark Pemberton left the room and went out. Amanda would be waiting.

Patrick Roe was in the cells. He had been well and truly caught in possession of the cocaine and accepted that the evidence against him was conclusive. He would plead guilty this time, there was no point in making a contest of it. Under normal circumstances, he would never plead guilty to anything, and tonight, if things had worked out as planned, he would not have been caught. But it had been a series of catastrophes. Normally, he'd have been at the flats much earlier and the stuff would have been distributed. Luckily, the others had got away in time, and he'd got snide remarks from the police when he'd told them his watch had stopped and then he'd got that puncture on the M1. To compound things, they'd laughed when he'd said he'd discovered his spare tyre was nearly flat and too soft for a long trip home and then he had missed his pick-up with the stuff and so he'd come home, with the cocaine . . . and he'd got nicked. Normally, he never brought it home but he'd had little alternative tonight . . . and within minutes of his arrival, the Drug Squad had raided him.

Talk about a night of disasters.

Now aged thirty-eight, Roe regarded himself as a man of considerable wealth with many thousands of pounds tucked away in various bank accounts. But he realized he could lose the lot if his finances could be traced and examined. He'd taken steps to be very discreet about that. Ever since the inception of the Drugs Trafficking Offences Act in 1986, he knew his assets could be confiscated upon a drugs conviction. He thanked his lucky stars he was living in a council flat, otherwise he could lose his house . . . in his profession, house purchase could be a risky business, but the house in Spain should be safe from the sequestrators, as well as his foreign bank accounts . . .

In the discomfort of the cell, he rolled over and tried to sleep, but the bed was unyielding. For one thing, it was too short, being made for a short, lightweight character rather than a heavy man nearly six feet tall. The mattress was hard and the single rough blanket no substitute for a soft warm bed and a soft warm woman.

For the police, the night had been a success, a surprising and unexpected success in fact. Normally, secret raids of this kind were planned weeks in advance, always with the risk of leaks but this one, organized at very short notice, had netted Roe probably because of its secrecy and swift execution. But why had there been no pushers waiting? If Roe had been expected and then delayed, they'd have been hanging around for their supplies, anxiously waiting for him.

But they weren't, and neither were any addicts waiting in the wings; that was odd. Had they been warned off? That was an aspect that Abbott had considered, again rejecting the theory that it was all a series of coincidences. But the raid had been an unqualified success and the men who had conducted it thought that Superintendent Pemberton must have had inside information about Roe's movements. Abbott wondered too . . .

But now, with Roe out of the way, other dealers would try to move in and take over this patch. The police were very aware of that possibility.

Doctor Dai Andrews considered that his part in the day's events had been fascinating and in due course it would make a very interesting paper for delivery at one of his lectures. Students would find it far more interesting than the usual medical uses for a cadaver, although Andrews was curious about the interest shown in the Green Lane corpse by Detective Chief Inspector Draper.

Wilf Draper had called late, about eleven-thirty, and had asked for a look at the corpse's fingers. He had not concerned himself with Sheila Wynn's remains, being content only to look at Mrs Wanless's thin fingers. And he had requested Andrews not to tell Pemberton or any other police officer of his visit. No one must know, he'd stressed. Having examined the fingers, Draper had left without explaining his interest.

When he'd gone, Andrews had then taken a close look at the fingers but had found nothing abnormal except for an indistinct scar on her right thumb. It was like a letter D albeit faded with the years, but he saw nothing odd in that. It was probably the result of a domestic accident in the kitchen, the sort of scar you'd find on many housewives' fingers. So were the police up to something else? And why was Draper apparently acting independently of the murder investigation?

Something odd was afoot and so Andrews decided to watch events with a deepening interest.

So far as the second body was concerned, his post-mortem had been fairly routine. After the body had been carefully divested of its clothing, he had conducted a visual examination. Apart from the massive wound in the chest, there had been bruises upon her face, upper torso and upper arms. These could be the result of being in violent contact with underwater rocks or other obstructions, or they could be the result of physical activity before death. They were the sort of marks that could result from a struggle, so had she been assaulted before death? Had she fought for her life, perhaps?

His further, more detailed medical examination showed that Sheila Wynn had been a heavy woman whose liver was beginning to show signs of deterioration through over-indulgence in alcohol.

She had not been sexually assaulted, thus ruling out rape or sex as a motive, although her vagina showed the familiar evidence of regular sexual intercourse.

This was the hallmark of a busy prostitute, an enthusiastic amateur or a nymphomaniac. She had one or two tattoo marks in curious places, including one on each large breast, and all had been logged for his report. Apart from her liver, which would have caused problems in later life, she had been fairly healthy, if a trifle overweight.

There was no doubt about the cause of death. She had not drowned – she'd been dead when cast into the river, for she had not inhaled any water. There was none in her lungs. Death was a direct result of the shotgun wound in her chest. He expressed an opinion that the weapon had been fired at close quarters, probably from a range of less than six feet having regard to the pattern of the shot and the size of the wound. He did not believe the wound had been self-inflicted; to kill oneself with a full-length shotgun was a difficult task. You had to be something of a gymnast to achieve that and besides, the gun had not been found.

Only one barrel had been discharged into the body just below the heart, and death had resulted from a combination of shock, haemorrhage and severe internal injuries. Mrs Downes, alias Ms Wynn, had been murdered, he believed, although an accident involving a third party could not be ruled out.

In other words, her sudden death was suspicious and required investigation, a fact already formally approved by the coroner. It was odd, he mused, that Charles Moore had finally got his murder enquiry, this time a genuine one, and his team of detectives would cause mayhem as they investigated the underlife of the town. With that in mind, he fell into a contented sleep. Tonight, he had done his duty for his country.

For Harry Downes, the night was everlasting and harrowing. He wished he hadn't stopped to report that body but he'd had no choice. Thank God it hadn't been Sheila . . . Now, he wished he hadn't told the lie about Sheila but who'd have thought they'd check up on simple things like that? And would they talk to the neighbours? Those Curtis women next door but one would surely mention the rows between him and Sheila, like the time he'd thrown her into the garden in her bra and pants because she'd admitted she'd been with another man . . . and now that they'd found her, the pressure would really be on . . . He hated that Abbott detective, he never stopped asking questions, never gave up, always pushed and pushed for answers and every answer Harry gave seemed to prompt another series of questions . . .

Harry sat with his head in his hands, drinking cup after cup of black coffee, not touching the whisky bottle, a quality he'd learned from years of having to drive for a living. Even in this turmoil, he'd drink only if he wasn't driving next day.

You daren't go on a blinder with a lorry to drive next morning. He was scheduled for an early run tomorrow, with the milk tanker . . . he'd make sure he wasn't late for that and even if he was, he wouldn't risk any more short cuts.

But as he sat alone in his scruffy terrace-house with its unkempt garden and flaking paintwork, he knew they would dig up all the dirt about Sheila; he knew most of it. She'd told him about her past, about wanting to make a new life, a clean life with new friends and contacts. She'd explained about her struggle to make something of her life after being dragged up in the back streets of Birmingham, after having to go on the game to earn money just to survive; she'd explained her early brush with drugs . . . But for him, she'd been a good and loving wife. He'd enjoyed with her a life of happiness marred only by her occasional flirting . . . she couldn't help it. When things weren't going as smooth as she liked, she had to have an admiring man around her but that Miller chap seemed not her type, he was too much of a smoothie, he was just using her . . . the bastard . . .

But would Abbott return with more questions? After today's terrible discoveries, Abbott seemed sure Harry had killed his own wife, that he'd shot Sheila, but he'd told the detective that he hadn't a gun. He'd explained how he'd spent hours touring the town looking for her . . . Abbott had asked for proof of his route and timings and he hadn't been able to think of any.

Abbott had said there was only Harry's word that he'd been driving around town and he couldn't remember exactly where he'd been, nor at what time . . . he'd have to work on that, he could remember if he really tried, if he really was given time. When you were just driving about like that, looking at people, cars, crowds outside clubs and things, you never really knew what time it was or where you'd been . . .

Abbott had said he would return because there were more questions he wanted to ask Harry.

But what else could he ask, for God's sake?

In a very self-congratulatory mood, Frank Mayhew had an early night.

He had a very early start planned for the morning because he intended driving over to Keswick in the Lake District, there to carry out a raid on a building society office. His pre-raid scrutiny of the premises showed that its crime-prevention facilities were like something out of Noah's ark. You could walk in, stick the twelve-bore into the face of the lady behind the counter, ask her to fill the plastic bag with cash, and then vanish into the crowds before anyone could raise the alarm. A woolly hat or a trilby or some other headgear was all that was needed as a disguise – the snag with a too-clever disguise was that you had to get rid of it pretty smartish and with just a hat or cap, you could throw it over a wall or stick it in a dustbin.

When the police were called, they'd be looking for a man with a hat and a Tesco plastic bag. He'd be wearing no hat and would be carrying some other plastic bag, with the Tesco one safely hidden . . . and because it was near Christmas, the town would be crowded with shoppers. He liked crowds because they helped him to disappear after his crime.

But his smug attitude was not because of that advance planning – it was because of the success of his midnight flit. Without anyone knowing, he'd moved house; in the middle of the night, he'd flitted to this cottage in Charlton, five miles from his other house, and the transfer had been achieved without the police snooping on him.

He'd paid cash for the house and knew that, for a time, they would not know where he lived – they would find out in due course, that was a racing certainty, but he would have a few days or even weeks of respite from their annoying supervision. In keeping his removal secret, the drugs raid had helped; word had soon spread about that. They'd nailed Roe this time, but no one else. The night-time busies and their CID pals had all been involved in that job and so they'd not seen his furtive removal with a self-drive hire-van. He hadn't much furniture – when you're always on the move, you don't need a lot – just a bed, a table and a comfortable chair or two . . . it had worked like a dream . . . and in a few weeks from now, he would put his old house on the market.

He'd sell the few sticks of furniture he'd left behind, hoping they'd make the house look occupied. The little house should sell well to a first-time buyer; small, clean and modest terrace-houses were always in demand.

Mayhew fell asleep thanking his lucky stars that he had moved when he did; if he'd still been living in Gladstone Street at the end of Green Lane, he'd have exercised Ben yesterday morning as usual. That meant he might have found that dead woman. And that would have caused a few headaches – as he drifted into a restful sleep, he wondered whether or not he would have reported discovery of the body . . . he knew the risks in so doing . . . maybe he would have, maybe he wouldn't. Anyway, it was a hypothetical question and so it need not worry him. He didn't say his prayers, but he did thank Providence, or whoever was looking after him.

For Detective Sergeant Bernard Goddard of the Special Branch, there was a late-night puzzle. He had been given authority to use one of the Q-vans to keep observations for two men, extreme left-wingers, who were suspected of plotting to sabotage the recently privatized water supplies. It was a low-key observation, for the men were not known as saboteurs, merely being suspected by another Force. One was using the name Ian Harris and the other was Martin Fife. Each was in his middle twenties, but apart from that they were not recorded in criminal-intelligence files.

In addition to his own observations, Goddard had been instructed to keep an eye on the name index now increasing by the hour in the Murder Incident Room. That enquiry was throwing up many names, lots of which were worthy of checks via the computer. Harris and Fife might be located in that way.

His low-key observations were simply an attempt to establish their whereabouts, since intelligence had indicated their absence from the West Midlands combined with a suggestion they had moved here. In recent months, the West Midlands SB had become worried about them, even though they had not produced any concrete evidence or intelligence to justify their concern. And so Goddard was doing his lonely duty in an effort to trace them, checking suspect addresses by parking outside all night and watching arrivals and departures. He was to keep observations and report anything of interest.

As Bernard Goddard entered the white van, he examined the rear compartment and found two pairs of old shoes. He picked them up, looked at the heavily patterned soles, decided they'd been used by some other operator and placed them in the rear space. Whoever they belonged to would want to come and collect them in due course – Bernard looked in the mileage log-book which was kept in the cubby-hole and saw that the previous user was Detective Superintendent Pemberton. Goddard smiled – he couldn't imagine such a well-dressed man as Pemberton wearing such scruffy, down-at-heel shoes, but in this profession, you never knew.

He must have used them for a covert operation of some kind. He'd remind Pemberton next time he saw him.

And having completed all his pre-observation procedures, he started the van and moved into the quiet streets to observe yet another address of police interest.

8

At six o'clock the next morning, having exercised Ben around the village green in front of his new house, Frank Mayhew left Charlton to go about his business. He was in the same van he'd hired for his removal; it was a 30cwt. vehicle in pale grey livery with the words 'Jacob's Self-Drive Hire' on the doors and sides, and it was only a few months old. Ben was sitting on the front seat and peering through the windscreen with all the intensity of a human passenger. The van was due to be returned to the hire-company no later than six this evening and so he had a clear twelve hours to accomplish today's objective. He had checked with the company's literature, and he could return this vehicle to their Keswick depot. He would do that.

Frank was dressed like a van-driver. He wore a green overall, black boots and a baseball type of cap with a long peak bearing the words *Coca-Cola*. He had a false driving-licence to show to the police if he was stopped; he carried his real one too, just in case he was known by the officer in question. The fake one was one he'd stolen some time ago. If he was bodily searched, he would claim he'd just found the false one in the van and was going to hand it in to the police. His own local police would not believe him, of course, but how could they prove otherwise?

Mayhew was in his mid-thirties. Tall enough and wide enough to be described as 'well-built', he was a powerful man who could box, play rugger and even make sense of American football. A one-time employee of British Gas, he was single with no family and his dark, but not exceptional good looks boasted no distinguishing features. He wore no spectacles, had no moustache or scars, was not tattooed or balding and sported nothing that would make him stand out in a crowd. It was this anonymity that had aided his past successes – he was far too ordinary to attract anyone's attention but he had the sense to dress differently each time he ventured on a job. For that reason, witnesses could never be totally sure he was *the* Shotgun Raider. Other villains might be emulating the Shotgun Raider, as he had often suggested to the police.

Today, he looked like a washing-machine delivery-man with his bag of assorted tools, and lying in the rear of the van was a shotgun in its gun-case. He made no effort to conceal it; he did possess a shotgun certificate, having never been convicted of a crime that would disqualify him, and thus he was entitled to carry it with him. He'd always used the excuse that he was carrying it for potential sale or valuation. And who could prove he wasn't? But his sawn-off shotgun, the one he used for his raids, was hidden in the panelling. If it was found, he'd deny ownership. There was no ammunition for either – he never carried any, and so he could never kill anyone during his raids. He merely frightened them into handing over the cash and that technique had always succeeded.

Like any other early-morning worker, he drove carefully through the dark town, to all intents and purposes an anonymous van going about its anonymous business as the busy streets came gradually to life. Window-cleaners were at work, bakers were at their ovens and the fish-market stalls were already crowded with customers. As a chill dawn began to brighten the horizon, Frank moved through the traffic on dipped headlights, heading for the motorway which would carry him across the Pennines and into the Lake District. Fortunately, there had been no overnight frost and no hazardous road conditions, although the forecast said light snow was expected on the higher ground tonight.

He switched on his radio and found it tuned to the local radio station's *Good Morning* programme. He allowed it to remain on that wavelength, the mixture of light music and inconsequential chat being undemanding. He negotiated the town but as he passed out of suburbia and into the country lanes before gaining the motorway, the 6.30 a.m. news caused him to slow down as he strained to catch every word. Even so, he had not caught the precise wording of the first sentence, but it announced that a woman's body had been found in Blue Beck. The report went on to say that the police had confirmed her death was from gunshot wounds and that she had been formally identified as

Sheila Wynn, also known as Mrs Sheila Downes, and that the police were anxious to trace her recent movements.

As he eased his van to a gentle halt at a conveniently deserted bus stop, the news-reader was saying,

'Police have drawn in an extra thirty detectives to investigate this latest killing, although Detective Superintendent Mark Pemberton has declined to link the two deaths. He stated there is no evidence of sexual assault in either case. Speaking last night, he did say that the body of the middle-aged woman found in Green Lane had not yet been identified and he is appealing for any information which might name her. We will bring you more news as the enquiries progress. And now to the industrial news. The chairman of Scran Feeds has confirmed that thirty-six new jobs will be created as a result of further expansion in health-food production . . .'

'Bloody hell, Ben,' he said as his dog's ears pricked up. 'That's Stan's woman . . . I need a phone!'

He drove on and soon found a kiosk from where he dialled Stan Miller's number. He was prepared for it to ring a long time, for Stan would still be in bed, but was pleasantly surprised when he answered almost immediately. Stan must have been out of bed; it was rather early for him.

'Hello,' said a rough voice.

'Stan?'

'Aye. Who's that?' Stan sounded awful.

'It's Frank, ringing from a kiosk. Look, I've not much time, but have you heard the news? On the radio this morning?'

'What news?' Stan's voice made him sound exhausted.

'God, this is awful, look, Stan. It's bad news, there's been a woman's body found . . .'

'Aye, that Green Lane job . . .'

'No, another one. In Blue Beck. Last night. Shot by the sound of it. They say it's that lass of yours, Sheila . . .'

There was no response. Frank waited.

'You still there, Stan?' he asked. 'Look, my money's running out . . .'

'Aye,' said the voice, quietly and gently. 'Aye, I heard you, Frank . . .'

'Just thought you'd better know . . .'

'Sure, right . . .' and the line went dead, his money having expired. Stupidly, Frank looked at the handset, wondering whether he should call again, but decided against it. He'd done his bit; he'd let Stan know, but surely Stan would now be quizzed. It wasn't as if his affair with that ex-pro was secret – the whole bloody town knew about it. Mayhew returned to his van, patted Ben on the head and drove off. He wondered if the police would want to talk to him about that one; they seemed to suspect him of every crime that was committed within a hundred miles and they knew he had shotguns. He might need a good alibi but the report hadn't quoted the time she'd been killed, though it must have been some time yesterday.

That meant they'd not be too interested in where he was today. But the night before last, Sheila had come running to talk to him, sobbing that her husband had thrown her out. It would have been just after half-past twelve, he recalled, twenty-five to one mebbe. He'd been busy moving furniture, so she'd gone away, into town . . . to what? Who'd seen her after that, he wondered? He'd never admit to the police that he'd seen her – it would make him a suspect.

'Women are nowt but a load of trouble, Ben,' he said as the van gathered speed. And Ben's tail thumped on the seat.

As the detectives assembled for their morning conference, Detective Superintendent Mark Pemberton was surprised to see Wilf Draper entering the Incident Room. It was a few minutes before nine o'clock. From his office, he noticed the Special Branch man stroll in to examine the notice-board with its photographs of the Green Lane woman at the scene and in the morgue, then watched as he went over to the statement file and began to flick through the index. All the time, he was chatting to various officers. Full details of Sheila Wynn's death had not yet been processed and so photographs of her at the scene were not available. They would be ready later today, although a snapshot was displayed on the board.

'What's he after?' he asked Inspector Larkin. 'Has he been chasing something, Paul?'

'No, sir,' Larkin was as puzzled as his boss. 'He's not been in touch before, so far as I know. There's nothing in this for SB, is there? In either of the deaths, I mean?'

'They're checking our name file, but that's all. That's routine anyway – all the specialist squads do that. I'm sure some of the names we turn up will be given a security check.'

'He's certainly asking a lot of questions . . . hello, sir, he's sitting down, so he intends staying for the conference.'

'I'd better find out what he's up to,' Pemberton went out with his own file under his arm and crossed to Draper who sat with his legs crossed as he began to light his pipe.

'Morning, Wilf.'

'Hello, Mark. Hope you don't mind me dropping in like this?'

'Something bothering SB, is there?' asked Pemberton.

'Nope, nothing like that. I just thought it was a while since I was involved in a murder, so I'd come to the conference to regain a bit of the atmosphere, that's all. I'm not muscling in, Mark, murder's not my problem, unless it's a so-called political job.'

'You sure?' Pemberton was not convinced.

Draper smiled. 'I'm absolutely sure,' he looked steadily at Pemberton, knowing his rival was more than a little curious about his presence. But he was not going to enlighten him, or anyone else; not at this stage.

Puzzled, Pemberton returned to his office to check that Larkin was ready.

Larkin's job included the administrative matters, like paying out daily subsistence allowances, logging the hours of overtime, allocating vehicles and seeing to that host of mundane chores that were essential for the smooth progress of every major investigation. Pemberton allowed him to address the assembly with his admin. matters before he chaired the conference.

Pemberton then addressed his officers, noting Amanda's cheery face in the second row. Every morning during a murder enquiry, this morning conference of detectives was held. It enabled those in command to inform all the detectives of the up-to-date developments, the result of earlier enquiries and of any outstanding matters. It also allowed them to name and target any new suspects who had entered the frame, to check the movements of local criminals and to air everything that the detectives had to know. In this way, everyone had a full grasp of all the ingredients of the investigation – all could assist one another.

But today's conference was special because it was the first since Sheila Wynn's death. New detectives had arrived and so

Pemberton must begin all over again. He did so, once again outlining the circumstances of the Green Lane body's discovery and the progress on that case, and then referring to Sheila Wynn from the time of Cedric Halliday's discovery.

He declined to link the two deaths officially, save to remind his officers that there was one known link – and that link was Harry Downes. He stressed that the movements of Sheila before being found in Blue Beck must be traced – her red coat and blonde hair should make her readily identifiable to any witnesses. Having given his briefing, he then asked for contributions from the floor.

'Roger Daniels and John Watson, you've got the Downes action. What's new there?' he began.

Daniels acted as spokesman. 'Sir, we've asked at neighbours' houses. Downes and his wife, or the woman they thought was his wife, did have blazing rows sometimes, about other men. He's chucked her out on occasions before; Harry Downes is a bit of a ruffian, it seems, he's got form for it. But the really interesting gen has come from the pub where she worked, the Black Lion. We had words with the landlord last night, after closing-time.'

The conference chuckled *en masse* as someone said, 'But you'd not break the law by drinking after hours, would you, Roger?'

Daniels, a teetotaller, ignored the snide comments and said, 'She had a fancy man; Downes knew about him, and there were rows about him between her and her husband, so I'm told. Chap by the name of Miller, Stan Miller, a salesman.'

'His name has been logged already. Have we got anything further on him?' asked Pemberton.

In a murder enquiry, every time a new name appeared it was logged and the person thus named was investigated, if only for elimination purposes. Every named person was checked and interviewed. In this way, the tentacles spread wider and wider . . .

'Yes, this is the interesting bit,' said Daniels. 'Miller's a close pal of our recent target, Frank Mayhew.'

'Is he? How close?'

'Close enough to go drinking with him, visiting each other at home . . . I've checked with Division. They're going to let me have the log of Miller's visits to Mayhew's home when he was under surveillance. The collator's got a file.'

71

Pemberton turned to the team whose action was Mayhew. They were Detective Sergeant George Lloyd and DPC Don Kent.

'George? Got anything good on Mayhew yet?'

'Bugger all, sir, to be honest. He's not at home, his house is deserted and has been for a day or so, but he's still there because the furniture's not been removed. The neighbours haven't seen him for the last couple of days and his dog isn't there. They say it's unusual for him to be away like that, and there was no shotgun raid yesterday. I agree with Roger – Miller's name has come into the frame, he has been knocking off the Downes woman, but we think he's into drugs in some way. We're checking on that, going into his antecedants. He was seen hanging around Pennine Flats when they were raided the other night and there was a woman with him, a blonde.

'But we've got nothing on him, no form. And he wasn't in possession of drugs at that raid, he was searched.'

'Great, keep digging. Now, so this means we need a team for Stan Miller. Who hasn't got an action?'

Several hands were raised, men whose actions had been completed during yesterday's initial surge. Pemberton selected Detective Sergeant Sally Merston and DPC Alex Groves.

'Miller's on the fringes of everything,' he reminded them. 'The Green Lane body – because he's knocking off the common-law wife of the bloke who found the body – and the Blue Beck body because he was knocking off the woman who's our new corpse. We know the Green Lane body isn't his missus, but he's still very worthy of our interest. On top of that, he's pally with our top villain and he was hanging about with a blonde when the drugs raid occurred. Sort something out of all that, will you, Sally?'

'Yes, sir,' smiled Sally Merston, a vivacious thirty-year-old policewoman with blonde hair and a figure that lots of the lads had tried to measure with their hands.

'Pin him down with dates and times, check every alibi with the utmost precision. Now,' continued Pemberton, 'the weapon for the Blue Beck job. The pathologist is sure it's a shotgun, a twelve-bore probably. Our own computer's doing a print-out of all shotgun-certificate holders in the county, and teams will be visiting each one to do a physical check on the weapons they hold.

'And don't forget that Mayhew's a legal holder of shotguns. Another team's getting around firearms dealers, antique shops and so forth to check whether there've been any sales recently. All buyers will be visited and their guns examined. All known villains will be visited and if necessary, we'll get warrants to search their premises if they've no shotgun certificates and if they deny possession. And thefts – check on any recent thefts of shotguns and ammunition. And if anybody does locate Mayhew, ask him to show you his guns, all of them. Was one of them used to kill Sheila Wynn? He uses a sawn-off shotgun for his raids, but we've never found that one . . . see if any has been fired recently. And if you do find him, tell me straight away, I want words. Now, Task Force? Brian, what progress is there on finding the murder weapon?'

'We did a preliminary search last night without success, sir, due to the light fading. We're doing a second sweep along the course of the river this morning, doing both banks and the bed. And we'll be doing a fingertip search of the fields and woods along the riverside.'

'You won't forget the approach routes, or departure routes whichever way you look at them?'

'No, sir, that's in hand. The weapon could have been thrown out of a moving vehicle. We did find tyre-marks nearby, sir, we've taken plaster casts. And we think she was dumped from a vehicle, not shot at the scene. We haven't found any used cartridge cases or blood on the ground.'

'It's not the same vehicle as the Green Lane one, is it? Because that might be another similarity between the two deaths,' said the dour voice of Wilf Draper from the front row.

'Point taken,' acknowledged Pemberton who had almost forgotten the SB chief was there. 'We'll compare plaster casts of tyre-marks. Well, Brian, I know your lads will turn up the weapon if it's there. Where's Downes now, by the way?'

Daniels answered. 'On his rounds, sir. We left him at home, but we stationed a police car a few yards up the street. He's not been out all night, not made any phone calls, but his lights were on all night. He's on an early run this morning, he was reported leaving home just after half-past five in his tanker and we logged him doing his normal rounds. He did see the police car as he left, we made sure of that, and it followed him for the first five miles. We'll replace it outside the house in time for him finishing work.'

'Good, keep the pressure on him.'

And so the conference continued, with every team making some contribution, and with all names, vehicle numbers, locations and other salient factors being recorded and logged into HOLMES. It would soon be time to meet the Press for today's first news conference, but the moment the CID meeting was over, Detective Chief Inspector Draper left without a word.

Mark Pemberton watched him go and could not help worrying about his presence. And Amanda Wallbridge noted the worry on Mark's face, but said nothing.

9

Stimulated by the facts imparted at the news conferences and enhanced by the journalists' individual brands of investigative reportage, the Press, radio and television had already made sure that the townspeople were vividly aware of the crimes. That awareness was amplified by rumours which were circulating in pubs and shops, cafés, and meeting places. There was fear even among upper-class homes in suburbia while the less fortunate felt even more vulnerable, living as they did with crime all about them. There was talk of another Ripper, of a local sex-mad, knife-wielding, gun-toting maniac who preyed on older women. No woman felt safe. The stories, many exaggerated and gory in the extreme, had succeeded in making everyone, especially women and girls, afraid of the unknown killer that stalked among them. They were asking – who would be the next victim?

The Council, at its meeting that morning, had added its corporate voice to the rising concern and chose to do so through its chairman, forty-two-year-old bachelor, Councillor Raymond Hogbin. In addition to being Council Chairman, he was also a member of the Police Authority, albeit not *its* chairman. He was therefore considered the right person to undertake this important role. Indeed, he was personally concerned about the endless questions being asked by the detectives.

Many of those who had been interviewed were residents within his ward. As always, the police seemed to pick on the defenceless, the weak, the out-of-work, homosexuals, lesbians, drug-addicts and others from that mass of under-privileged. Councillor Hogbin, a dedicated left-winger, did not like this overt police oppression, and especially he resented questions being asked in the areas in which he spent so much of his leisure. He had considered voicing his personal concern, but felt that that would not have been appropriate. In his official capacity, therefore, he was able to express his views.

Officially, therefore, and wishing to appear the good socialist that he was, he said he was concerned about the overwhelming and heavy-handed police attention to such places as the Pennine Flats. The police claimed it was a seething mass of lawless humanity; he claimed it was the home of deprived citizens, victims of capitalist oppression and gross neglect. Councillor Hogbin did admit he spent a lot of time there, helping those less fortunate than himself, although he'd not been there at the time of the drugs raid. But he did not want the police upsetting those he regarded as 'his' people. The Labour-controlled Council's official concern was therefore a way of letting the police know they must not overstep the mark. And in his dual role as a member of the Police Authority, he would take steps to regulate the behaviour of the police, ensuring there was no oppression and no infringement of civil liberties.

While Detective Superintendent Pemberton had been chairing his own new conference, therefore, Councillor Hogbin, in the chair at the Council Chamber, and with the approval and assistance of his members, had drafted a statement for the Press. A reporter had been present and had taken down his words for the *Evening News*.

Hogbin's statement said: 'This Council has noted with some concern the serious crimes which have occurred this week and which remain undetected. We trust that the police will prove their efficiency and loyalty to the public by speedily detecting and arresting those responsible, and that they will take steps to reassure the public, especially the women of this town, that there will be no repetition of these awful crimes. The citizens must be confident they can walk the streets without danger or molestation. It is the duty of the police force to ensure that the public is safe from attack at all times but this Council wishes to ask the force not to harass innocent citizens during their enquiries.'

A copy was sent by courier to Pemberton, but it was cleverly timed to arrive in his hands too late for him to make an official response in the Press. Thus the Press would print Hogbin's views without any official comment from the police and some readers would interpret that as a reluctance at the least or a disrespect of the townspeople at the worst. Consequently, when he read those words, Mark Pemberton could sense the political undercurents and the venom in the final sentence.

Instead of supporting the police service, the Council was using this traumatic time to throw veiled criticisms at the police. Pemberton was both saddened and annoyed, for these words would swell a good deal of anti-police feeling which, in turn, would make the public resentful about helping the enquiry teams. If Councillor Hogbin was truly desirous of helping the public, he should have taken this opportunity to ask the people to provide information, to be responsive and co-operative, especially about sightings of Sheila Wynn, or providing suggestions for a name of the Green Lane woman. He should have stressed that the police could not operate without the active assistance of ordinary people. He could have also asked them to keep their eyes open for the discarded shotgun or to search for the clothing and handbag of the Green Lane victim.

But Pemberton knew that Hogbin had once been discovered by a patrolling woman constable when he was in an embarrassing homosexual situation. There had been no court case because the evidence was insufficient, but this lapse in his private life was known to every detective. From that moment, Hogbin had made a practice of criticizing the police service for what he regarded as its failures, and he was astute enough to be overtly critical in a manner which did not permit a public response from the Force. In this case, he had mischievously compounded the pressures being imposed upon them by making them seem inefficient in not having secured an arrest.

'The Chairman of the Police Authority is here, sir, he wants a word with you.'

'Bloody hell!' snapped Mark. 'First Hogbin sounding off, then this idiot. What's he want, Paul?'

'He wouldn't say. He demands to speak to the officer in charge of the investigation.'

'Right, I'll see him in reception, don't let him in here, this is not the place for a man like that to enter.'

'He's at the door now, sir.'

'Then escort him away, Inspector, and if he objects, say those are my orders. Only police officers and those authorized by me, such as forensic scientists, are allowed in this Incident Room. He is not a police officer, he has no jurisdiction over the operational functions of the service and there is a lot of confidential information here, information he'd like to get his eyes on. He's trying it on, Inspector, so take him away. Put him in reception and don't give him a cup of coffee – he might think it's a waste of poll-tax payers' money. I'll be with him just as soon as I can.'

As Paul Larkin went about his mission, Mark settled down.

The confounded Chairman had come without an appointment, so he could wait without his coffee. Mark asked one of the girls to make a coffee for him and settled down to scan the latest incoming statements. He continued for half an hour, then went to speak to the Chairman.

'Good morning, Mr Ruddock,' he spoke coldly but respectfully. 'It's a busy time for us just now. How can I be of assistance?'

Councillor Jonathan Ruddock was Chairman of the Police Authority, a body comprising two-thirds councillors and one-third magistrates. The Authority's role was to maintain an adequate and efficient police force within its areas of responsibility, which meant it approved the finance, regulated building plans and the purchase or renewal of new equipment. The Authority had no jurisdiction over the operational functions of the service. That was the duty of the Chief Constable. The relationship between a Chief Constable and the Police Authority was most certainly not one of servant and master. This fact annoyed many Labour politicians and councillors who repeatedly attempted to breach that protective barrier as they struggled endlessly to gain control over the police.

'I'm here to see what's going on with these murders, Chief Inspector,' he began without a smile. 'You will be aware the Council has already expressed some concern . . .'

'Detective Superintendent, actually,' Mark was quick to correct the error. 'We are investigating them, we are treating them just like any murder enquiry, with every available resource . . .'

'But the town's in turmoil, er, Superintendent, and the Council . . .'

'Ah, the Council! It seems with all due respect, Mr Ruddock, the Council is taking too much heed of the newspapers. There are two deaths which we are investigating and I would remind the Council that it does not run the Force. If you see Councillor Hogbin, perhaps you'd remind him of that?'

'I am here in my capacity as Chairman of the Police Authority, and as such I need to be satisfied that you are doing all in your power to calm the public . . .'

'Perhaps you have seen Councillor Hogbin's statement to the Press? It is disgustingly political in its tone as well as being counter-productive, Mr Ruddock. The Council should be helping us, not making our job more difficult; they could calm the public and reassure them instead of sniping at us. We don't allow murders to happen, we just sort it all out afterwards, we clean up the mess society leaves behind. We are doing our best with the resources that are available. Perhaps you would convey that to the Council and the Police Authority?'

'Then do you mind if I come into the Incident Room to check for myself . . .?'

'That's out of the question. That is only for authorized personnel and police officers, there's a mass of confidential material. As you know, your Authority will receive a full report of the enquiry in due course, as is normal practice.'

'If the Chief Constable were here, he would allow me . . .'

'I doubt that, but he's not here, Mr Ruddock, and I am in charge. I cannot allow any councillor or Police-Authority member even to begin to think he has any jurisdiction over the operational functions of the police. That is totally alien to our method of working and you know it, Mr Ruddock.'

'Aye, well, I was just ensuring you were doing all possible . . .'

'That responsibility is the Chief Constable's, not yours with all due respect. Look, Mr Ruddock, we want to catch these killers, we are the professionals and we will work until we drop in order to do so, but we do need co-operation from the public and positive backing from official bodies, not continued sniping and backbiting from amateur politicians hoping to gain some political advantage . . .'

78

Mark thought he might have overstepped the boundaries now, but Ruddock backed off.

'Just so long as I'm happy you are doing all that you can, er, Superintendent,' and he edged to the door. 'I will report to the Council . . .'

'It's nothing to do with the Council, Mr Ruddock . . .'

Clearly, the Council had used Ruddock, and as Mark watched him go, he didn't smile. The bastards . . . they never gave up trying . . . they were like woodworm gnawing at sound wood until it was rotten and was replaced by inferior timbers . . .

When he returned to the Incident Room, he called Inspector Larkin over.

'Paul,' he said. 'Put a team on to Councillor Hogbin, will you? Let's see what our Council Chairman's been up to recently. If he's making a fuss about us asking questions, we might be getting too close to him and his sexual peculiarities. Instruct the team to be very discreet, he must not know we're checking on him. Let's see if there's any truth in those rumours about him and those boy scouts. And we'll leave our Police Authority Chairman till later . . .'

There had been something of a rumpus around the council estates and tower blocks because of the increased number of police raids. But these were proving a success. As predicted by Moore, the petty villains began to reveal their sordid little secrets to prevent themselves getting too heavily implicated in the web-like murder investigation. Instead of lying or pretending they'd been elsewhere, they did admit to minor crimes. Where stolen property, drugs, indecent films or obscene literature were concerned, the divisional police, under Abbott's guidance, had arranged search-warrants and raids. The haul had been good. Twenty-one arrests had resulted.

They included a team of professional shop-lifters who specialized in taking women's clothing from chain stores, two housebreakers who raided country houses for antiques, and members of a ring of pornographic film producers were being questioned. Enthusiastic detectives had even visited the working places of some of these people, a practice not normally resorted to unless there were urgent and mitigating circumstances, and NUPE had objected. Mark knew that this had resulted, however indirectly, in the visit by Ruddock and the tirade from Hogbin, especially as many members of that union had been arrested. Three had been caught carrying joints of beef from the canteen of the local comprehensive school and NUPE had grumbled that the arrest was victimization of the working classes. The young detective in question had retorted that catching these thieves was a triumph for those who really worked. The NUPE man had responded by making a formal complaint to the Police Complaints Board because the detective had been abusive in suggesting the 'victims' were guilty by referring to them as thieves when they had not been declared so by a court of law.

But for Mark Pemberton, this was all evidence of the value of their spreading enquiry. Of particular interest, however, was the number of drug-arrests. In hindsight, it did seem odd that the wily and experienced Patrick Roe had been caught in such a simple way at Pennine Flats.

As Mark thought about this, he did wonder whether there was any link between Roe's dealings and Sheila Wynn – she had been on the sidelines of drug-dealing, albeit some years ago, so perhaps there was a connection? It would be interesting to see whether his teams could produce anything to support that idea. Because the drugs raid had been a divisional matter and a completely separate incident, it had not featured in the murder enquiries – indeed, from the beginning, such a link had not been necessary for reasons Mark knew only too well. But Sheila Wynn's death had changed things and he decided he must see whether Roe had known the deceased. He rang Detective Sergeant Paul Barnett, the divisional drugs officer.

'Paul, it's Pemberton from the Incident Room. I'm ringing about Roe. Has he made a statement of any kind?'

'Yes, sir, he's been very co-operative. I've got a signed admission out of him.'

'That's unusual, isn't it? I remember Roe from the past – he would never admit anything.'

'We caught him bang to rights, sir, he could hardly deny possession.'

'But even so, he's not one for co-operating with us, is he? Could this be a smoke-screen for a bigger job, you reckon?'

Pemberton was very aware that he had staged the drugs raid merely as a diversion, so had Roe been doing exactly the same?

80

Had he allowed himself to be caught in possession while a larger haul was being delivered or transported elsewhere?

The absence of the pushers could suggest that – as a scenario, it was not impossible. The sergeant considered the question and answered, 'He has been rather more co-operative than I would have expected, sir, but we've received no intelligence about a bigger job anywhere in the region.'

'Where's Roe now?'

'In the cells. I applied for a remand at court, and got him remanded in custody this morning, for eight days.'

'I'm coming to have a word with him, Paul. I'd like you to be there.'

'Very good sir.'

Pemberton and Roe had met in the past, Roe being a one-time bus-driver when Pemberton was walking the beat. Roe had then been a law-abiding citizen, a young man with a pretty wife and a mortgage, but when his wife left him for a Royal Air Force Flight Lieutenant, he'd gone to pieces. Now, he was rather overweight with a beer-belly and his skin was sallow with a lack of fresh air and exercise. Thinning black hair and a propensity for brightly coloured ties made him easily identifiable but made him appear older than his years.

'Now then, Patrick,' said Pemberton as he led the sergeant into the tiny cell.

'Hello, Mr Pemberton,' smiled Roe. 'This is a surprise. So how's the murder enquiries going? I do read the papers, you know, even in here.'

'We're doing fine,' said Mark. 'Things are running according to schedule, I think – but would you happen to know either of our deceased ladies?'

'Is that why you're here, then? To quiz me? And I thought it was a social visit.'

'I don't have time for social visits, Patrick, especially when I'm working on a murder, let alone two murders. So what about the Green Lane woman?'

'Sorry, I can't help there, I've never come across that lady, so far as I know. But I did know the other one, Sheila Downes, as I called her.'

'Did you now? And how did you know her?'

'Through the Black Lion. I went in for a drink now and again.

She was always cheerful, friendly, willing to spend a minute or two chatting.'

'And the drugs? You've been more than honest about your latest drama, so what about Sheila? Was she involved in drugs?'

'On the sidelines, Mark, very much on the sidelines. She would give our pushers the nod if new customers were likely; she never handled anything, but we did slip her a few quid if a good contact turned up. She's dead, so you can't prove that against her or me, can you? Otherwise, I wouldn't be telling you this.'

'And did she deal directly with you?'

'No, we used pushers as contacts. But you don't expect me to name them, do you? That would be asking too much. I am helping, am I not? I liked Sheila and I dislike murder, you see.'

'You are helping, and I appreciate it. So when did you last see her alive?'

'Weeks ago. When I read about it in the *Yorkshire Post* this morning I tried to remember when I saw her. It must have been weeks, Mark, literally weeks, in the Black Lion, one night when she was working. Don't ask me which. I can't remember.'

'Was she with anyone? Has she fallen out with anybody?'

'Only that big bully of a husband of hers, he used to knock her about a bit, they say. She was seeing that pal of Frank Mayhew's, Miller. Stan Miller. Traveller of some sort. Nothing serious mind, just somebody to go out with, have a bag of chips mebbe or a drink at another pub. That sort of thing.'

'OK, now, this confession of yours. You seem very ready to confess to us. I think that's unusual, Patrick, I think you're hiding something. A big drop, maybe? Or something more sinister? What about the IRA? Are they into the drugs racket here? I've had our Special Branch chaps sniffing around but they won't even tell me what's going on.'

'Look, that IRA phase of mine was when I was twenty, bloody years ago, Mark. It was a stupid period, I was a silly Irish lad, all idealistic with no common sense, and I had no idea what those bastards were really up to and I opted out.

'As I said, I hate killing. So there's nothing sinister in admitting that drugs cop.'

'I still think you're being devious, as always. You always were a good con-man, Patrick.'

'Look, Mark, you caught me on a day when everything went

wrong – punctures on the M1, flat spare tyre, my bloody watch was slow so I missed my meet and then when I did get home, your lot were waiting . . . you get days like that. I just threw up my hands and admitted it. What else could I do? I just hope the courts are lenient, that's all.'

'OK, well thanks for talking. And, sergeant, let me have a copy of Patrick's statement, will you? For my murder files.'

'Does that mean I'm going to get grilled again?' asked Roe.

'It means you are now part of my on-going enquiry, Patrick, and that I might want more talks with you.'

'Why, for God's sake? I'm not in that league, I'm no killer, Mark. You know that.'

'But you might lead us to the guilty party, eh?' said Mark Pemberton. 'In your nasty, evil dealings, you might have come across somebody who would want to kill Sheila. Think about that and if you remember anyone, get in touch with me.'

'If I talk, does that mean I get bail?'

'I never make promises of that kind,' said Pemberton, who added, 'Although in the event of an arrest, I might tell the court that you had been very helpful . . .'

'You know I wouldn't want that! I'd get marked down as a grass . . .'

'Just get thinking then,' suggested Mark, rising to leave. 'You know that our net is reaching wider and wider right now, and we'll be pulling in more and more local villains, including some of your friends.'

'I'll bear it in mind,' said Patrick Roe as the cell-door clanged behind him. As he left, Pemberton was not in a position to see Roe raise two fingers in the crude V sign.

10

The telephone rang in Wilf Draper's office and caught him just before he went down to the canteen for lunch.

'Ridley, Eighth Floor,' said the Scots voice at the other end. 'I'm ringing all forces in England and Wales, Wilf, we want an urgent meeting tomorrow morning at the Yard, say at eleven.

We need every force to be represented. Sorry for the short notice, but can you make it?'

He checked his diary. 'Yes, if it's important. I've a Welfare Committee meeting but I can tender my apologies. What's this all about? Why the urgency?'

'IRA,' said Detective Chief Inspector Ridley. 'We've received some intelligence which suggests they're planning a bombing blitz on mainland supermarkets before Christmas. We're keen to have your Force represented; isn't the PM going into your patch soon to look at some supermarket sites?'

'Yes, he's digging the first sod,' confirmed Wilf Draper. 'OK, I'll be there.' And as he replaced the phone, he remembered the Green Lane woman's fingerprints in his drawer. He could ask the Yard to check them while he was in the meeting, except that this check would involve an examination of the security files. He was sure that's where he'd come across the prints. He was fairly certain he'd been shown them during one of the security courses he'd attended.

So that he would not forget to take one set of the fingerprints with him, he placed the copies in his brief-case in advance, then asked his sergeant to up-date him on very recent IRA activity within his own force area. He had to be well briefed for tomorrow's meeting.

Detective Sergeant Sally Merston and Detective PC Alex Groves had wasted no time beginning their Miller action. They began in the Collator's Office where comprehensive files were maintained on local criminals, suspected criminals and those on the fringes of crime and its associated underworld activities.

From Mayhew's file, they gleaned a substantial amount of intelligence about Miller. Stanley George Miller, aged fifty-one, was a salesman for an animal-medicine producer, visiting pet shops, veterinary surgeons and animal charities, as well as stables, catteries, dogs' homes and even farms to dispense his wares. He ran a company car, a blue Vauxhall Cavalier whose registration number was recorded, and he seemed to be content with his work. He had been with this company for several years.

Married with two adult children who worked away from the area, his wife was a nurse in a psychiatric hospital and she worked odd hours including weekends and bank holidays, leaving him a good deal of spare time when he was not working. He spent a lot of time at the Black Lion where he was a member of the pub's darts and dominoes teams.

It seemed he often went there for a snack in the evenings, especially when his wife was at work. It was there he'd met Sheila Wynn and their friendship had blossomed.

Detectives, who also visited the Black Lion from time to time in the course of their duties, had noticed Miller simply because he was often in the company of Frank Mayhew. Had he not been in his company, Miller would not have come to the notice of the police. But Frank Mayhew was a regular at the same pub and, being unmarried, he also came to eat from time to time, and so the two men had become acquainted. They would drink together, play darts or dominoes or they'd simply chat. The endorsements to Mayhew's growing file showed that Miller and Mayhew did, from time to time, visit one another's homes for social reasons, perhaps to celebrate a birthday.

As Sally read the file, it became clear that Miller had never been suspected of crime. Other than a careless-driving conviction when he was twenty-six, he had no convictions and had not entered any of the areas of suspicion, even though he was a friend of Mayhew. The detectives who, over the months, had compiled this dossier, had specifically stated he was not suspected of receiving stolen money or goods from Mayhew, nor was he believed to be involved in any way, however small, with crime or drugs. It was accepted that professional criminals did have friends and acquaintances who were not involved in their crooked way of life.

But as she studied his record, Sally did wonder how Miller had come to be on the fringes of the Pennine Flats drugs raid – why had he gone there? He'd not been with Mayhew, for Mayhew had not been seen around that time – nor since, in fact. But Miller had been spotted and his presence had been registered; indeed, he had been searched for drugs but none had been found on him and so he had not been detained. There was nothing here about his affair with Sheila Wynn, but as the illicit boyfriend of the woman who was now in the mortuary, he must be a suspect or at least of some interest.

'Is he a firearms-certificate holder, Alex? Or a shotgun-certificate holder?'

'I'll check,' said Alex.

'When you've done that, see me back at the Incident Room,' she told him. 'I'll be there, I want to check through the statement index and see what HOLMES throws up.'

Sally's perusal of both the HOLMES data and the statement index did throw up several references to Stanley Miller – his visits to the Black Lion, his presence near the drugs raid, his links with Sheila Wynn, but nothing new emerged. During her search, Alex Groves returned and he was smiling.

'Miller is the holder of a shotgun certificate,' he said. 'He's had one since they were introduced by the 1968 Firearms Act. But he hasn't got a firearms certificate.'

'A shotgun killed Sheila Wynn,' Sally reminded him. 'We're not looking for a man who used a revolver or a rifle.'

'So it's time we interviewed him, eh?' suggested Alex.

'Then let's go,' and they left in the small, red but unmarked police car, a Ford Fiesta, which had been allocated to them. Miller lived in a pleasing semi-detached house at 18 Westfield Road and the Cavalier was in the drive. That was a good start.

'We'll need that car for forensic examination,' said Sally. 'To eliminate him if necessary.'

'Right, I'll see to that.'

Alex parked the Fiesta immediately behind it, so blocking off its escape if that likelihood ever occurred, and Sally rang the doorbell. There was a long delay, but eventually a rather dowdy and dishevelled man in a dull grey cardigan, old brown slacks and slippers answered the door. He looked older than his fifty-one years, his grey hair being very thin and his face haggard, worn and unshaven.

'Yes?' he looked them up and down, not recognizing them.

'Mr Miller? Stanley George Miller?' asked Sally.

'That's me, who are you?'

'Police,' each showed the necessary warrant cards and then Sally continued. 'We are investigating the death of Sheila Wynn, also known as Sheila Downes, Mr Miller. Maybe you knew she had died?'

It was a cold and brutal start to the interview, but it was one which could shock people into being very co-operative.

'I know,' he said. 'I didn't go to work, I heard on the radio this morning, I couldn't face my customers after that. You'd better come in, both of you.'

He led them into the kitchen where the table was littered with cups and milk bottles; a copy of a morning paper was open and its headlines shouted, MARSHLANDS MURDER VICTIM.

He made a cursory attempt to tidy up but it defeated him and he just waved to a chair. 'Sit down, anywhere . . .'

He sat in his own chair and faced them.

'You'll want to know about my relationship with her? It wasn't very secret, was it?'

'No,' said Sally. 'Far from it. So what about your wife? You are married, I believe? Did she know?'

'Yes, but she didn't care; she's got her work, she's totally absorbed by that. You can find her at the hospital – she wasn't jealous, if that's what you are inferring. Margaret wouldn't kill Sheila.'

'We'll have to interview her though,' Sally reminded him. 'Now, Mr Miller, tell us about your relationship with Sheila. Everything please.'

'Look, I was about to make a cup of tea . . . I need one . . . can I get you one?'

Sally looked at Alex and then nodded; one had to be so careful about accepting hospitality from a murder suspect, but it seemed ungracious not to accept. Miller was clearly in need of some sustenance and conversation.

He made a pot of tea, put a sugar-basin and spoons on the table and let them help themselves to milk directly from the bottle. Sally watched him in silence, knowing he was working out the best way to tell his story.

'So,' she said as she raised the mug to her lips. 'What can you tell us, Mr Miller?'

He went on at length about his wife's long and unsocial hours of work and how, after the children had left home, he had been lonely and bored. The Black Lion had been his local, near enough to walk even on the worst of nights, and he found the barmaid's chatter welcoming and amusing. Eventually, they'd become friends; she would come into the pub when she was not working to be with him. She seemed to enjoy his company as much as he enjoyed hers; her husband was a lorry-driver and at the time of their first meeting, he'd been on timber waggons which necessitated long and unsocial hours . . .

'We were two lost souls, I suppose,' he said. 'And after that, we met often, mostly at the pub but if our respective spouses

87

weren't around, we'd go off for the day, to the seaside mebbe, or shopping or, well, anything. It was a cosy set-up, really. Friendly. Pleasant.'

'And what about sex?' asked Sally, not afraid to ask the question. Sex was the motive for so many murders; when a murder occurred, the first task was often to investigate the sex lives of the victims and all the suspects. 'Did you and she have sex?'

'Not at first,' he blushed slightly, but gave her the required answers. 'But, yes, eventually, sometimes here, sometimes at her place, sometimes in the countryside. She liked it, she was experienced, I could tell.'

'You knew of her past?'

'I knew she'd been married once, but not to that lorry-driver, Harry. They just lived as man and wife.'

'I meant her life before she met Harry Downes,' Sally said, slowly.

He shook his head. 'No, I know she's not a local woman, but I didn't pry.'

Sally decided not to reveal Sheila Wynn's past, at least not yet. Now came the tricky part.

'Mr Miller, we must explore every possibility in trying to trace her killer, and that means examining the movements of every-one associated with her. Close movements, I mean. So I need to ask you to account for your movements, for elimination purposes I might add, after eleven o'clock the night before last.'

'The night before last?' he frowned, trying to recall his own movements at that time.

Sally jogged his memory. 'Sheila was working at the pub. She finished at eleven and after clearing up, left the premises just before midnight. She took a taxi home and got there a few minutes later. Her husband told us that and we have confirmed it with the taxi-driver.

'We know that much, Mr Miller. But there was a row of some kind and either she was thrown out or she left home. The time would be about half-past twelve. She was never seen alive again. Her body was found yesterday evening, around five-thirty, in the lower reaches of Blue Beck. We want to know where she was between those times, who she was with and what she was doing. Now, with you being a friend and a lover, surely she would have turned to you?'

He shook his head.

'No, I never saw her that night. I was working late.'

'Where?'

'In the Manchester area, I came back via the M62. I didn't get home until after half-past two in the morning. I'd been to a sales seminar in Stockport . . .'

'Can anyone vouch for your presence there?'

'Most of the delegates, I would think. I can give you the organizer's telephone number. He'll vouch for me. It was nearly midnight when I left the hotel to drive home, Jack Campbell will confirm that. I helped him to get his car started, his battery was flat and I let him use my jump-leads.'

'You've got his address or telephone number?'

'Yes, sure,' he delved into his brief-case which was standing on the floor beside the table and produced a black contact book containing his business connections. He scribbled the relevant names, addresses and telephone numbers on a business card and passed it to Sally.

'OK, so you left Stockport and drove home. What time did you reach home?'

'Half-past two or thereabouts, I can't be exactly sure.'

'Did you come straight home?'

'I stopped at a service station on the M62, for some petrol and a coffee and to go to the loo. That's all. I've got the receipt somewhere, for the petrol, so I can claim expenses. It'll show the time and date, so you can check.'

He rummaged around in his brief-case and found the receipt which he showed to them and Sally accepted it. 'And you went nowhere else?'

'No, look, am I supposed to have done something during that trip?'

'By the time you returned, Mr Miller, Sheila had left home and was somewhere in the town. Her husband says he searched everywhere, but didn't see her. Did she go to your home? Did you see her?'

'No, never. I never saw her that night at all, I've told you, I was away from home, but I don't think she'd come here, would she? She knew I was away on business.'

'You're lying, Mr Miller,' Alex came into the questioning now, playing the part of the hard inquisitor after the gentle probing by Sally.

'Lying?' Miller's face turned almost purple. 'How dare you say I am lying . . . why should I lie . . .'

'You were seen with Sheila Wynn shortly after two o'clock that morning, the early hours of the day she was found dead.'

'Who says that? It's a lie! I tell you it's a lie!'

'Our officers saw you,' said Alex slowly. 'So think again, Mr Miller, think back to what you have just told us . . .'

'I've told you the truth, God knows I have . . . why should I lie . . .'

'So you came straight home from Stockport, without stopping except on the motorway . . . Think again. I suggest you did stop, I suggest you saw Sheila wandering about the town, perhaps hanging about outside your house and you went for a drive or a walk . . .'

'No!' Miller rose from the table and thumped it with his fist. 'No, I did not see her . . . if I had, I would say so . . .'

'Calm down, Mr Miller,' said Sally, inviting him to be seated again. 'Look, you were seen with a woman after two o'clock that morning . . .'

'Me? Where, for God's sake?'

'Outside Pennine Flats . . .'

'Oh, that!' he laughed and it was a laugh of relief. 'Sorry, I forgot about that. When I was on my way home, I drove past the Flats. There was a lot of activity, blue lights, police cars, dogs, uniforms, that sort of thing. I thought there was trouble, a fire maybe, so I stopped for a look, to see if I could help mebbe . . .'

'Did you get out of your car?' asked Alex.

'Yes, I walked across the grass in front of the Flats and stood there, at a distance, just watching.'

'Alone?'

'Yes, of course. I was alone.'

Alex rapped the question. 'You were not alone, you had a woman with you, a blonde woman, a woman answering the description of Sheila Wynn . . .'

Miller frowned as he tried to recollect the events of those few moments and then he said, 'Oh, her. I don't know who she was, she lived in a house near where I was standing and came out to find out what was going on. I've no idea who she was, she watched with me for a few minutes and then went home. And I did the same . . . I was only there a few minutes . . . ah,

I know how you know about that! I was searched for drugs, I had to give my name . . . God, you have been spying, haven't you . . . I was clear, by the way. Anyway, after that, I came back to my own house and went to bed.'

'We could ask at the houses to check on that blonde woman,' snapped Alex.

'I wish you would, then you'd know I'm not lying.'

'And your wife, Mr Miller,' continued Alex. 'Where was she that night?'

'At home. She spent the night at home, I think, watching television. She was in bed when I got in, we sleep in separate rooms, by the way, but I looked in as I always do. She was fast asleep.'

'So she could not vouch for your time of return?'

'No, unless she was pretending to be asleep. You'll have to ask her.'

'We will, Mr Miller, we will. So you deny seeing Sheila Wynn on the night or early morning before her death?'

'I do.' Miller stared hard at the two detectives, defiantly almost.

'Then we will need to examine your car, now. Today. For evidence of her presence in it, dead or alive. Lack of evidence will clearly be in your favour . . .'

'I can't stop you, can I?'

'No, we shall take it away now, you can have it back later today. I will return it for you, here.'

'You make me feel guilty for just knowing Sheila . . .'

'There's more, Mr Miller. I will now ask if I can see your shotgun. You do have a certificate, our records say.'

'God, you have been doing your homework, haven't you? Have I no private life . . .'

'You could blame your friend, Frank Mayhew,' said Alex. 'It's him that really interests us, he's not been seen for a day or two . . . we know you and he are pals. Where is he, by the way?'

'How should I know? We're just acquaintances, two lonely fellers who have a chat and a pint together, that's all. How he spends his time is nowt to do with me. Anyway, what about my gun?'

'We want to see it,' said Alex.

'It's upstairs, locked in a wardrobe.'

'Then let's go and inspect it together,' said Alex. When

dealing with men who had guns, you never allowed them to gain any advantage over you . . .

They followed Miller up the well carpeted stairs and into the spare bedroom. There was an old oak wardrobe against one wall, and a single spare bed against another. Miller found the key in the chest of drawers and opened it.

'I keep it here . . . oh, bloody hell . . .'

'What?' asked Alex Grover.

'It's gone,' cried Miller.

11

While Stanley George Miller was undergoing his ordeal with Sally Merston and Alex Groves, the manageress of the Messenger Building Society in Keswick was suffering an even worse ordeal. A man wearing a curious old-fashioned brown trilby hat and carrying a large Tesco plastic bag, had entered the office and was brandishing a sawn-off shotgun at her. He demanded all the cash in the drawers before her, and she found herself thinking she knew this would happen. Hadn't she warned Head Office about the lack of security? Hadn't she submitted a report suggesting a security screen? That had been nearly two years ago and they'd done nothing, they'd not even acknowledged her submission . . . and now this had happened. It's funny, the things that went through your mind at times like this . . .

'Never mind the coins,' the man was rasping as he pointed the gun at her head. 'Just the notes, all of them, don't try anything silly, it's not worth it . . .'

Trying to remain calm, she collected all the fivers, tenners, twenties and even a few fifties and thrust them into his Tesco bag. It took a few seconds.

Quite suddenly, he was walking out as if he'd just made a perfectly normal withdrawal of funds. She heard the click of the gun as he dismantled it and saw him push the two sections deep into the plastic bag, then he was gone.

*

Once outside, Frank Mayhew slipped down a side alley. He removed the trilby hat and replaced it with the *Coca-Cola* cap which he'd had folded in a pocket, stuffing the trilby into a dustbin in the alley. Then he pulled a second plastic bag from his trouser pocket, this one bearing the Austin Reed logo, and he thrust the Tesco one and its contents inside. Then he returned to the street and walked calmly away.

Equally calmly, having rehearsed this move many times, Olive Fraser followed the Society's procedures. She had obtained a good description of the raider and now rang the police. Taking a deep breath and determined to remain calm, she waited for the 999 girl to transfer her call. When she was connected, she said, 'Hello? This is the Keswick Branch of the Messenger Building Society. I am the manageress, my name is Olive Fraser. We have just been robbed. No one has been hurt, but the raider was armed with a gun and has just left . . .'

'Just a moment, madam, I'll divert a car to the scene,' and the Control Room constable did exactly that.

He sent Papa Kilo Two-Two hurtling through the narrow streets towards the Building Society. Then he prepared to take a description of the wanted man.

'Can you describe him, Miss Fraser?'

'Yes, I got a good look at him. He is medium height, about five feet ten inches tall, I'd say, average build, white with dark hair. I could just see a bit of it under his hat.

'He wore an old-fashioned brown trilby pulled down over his eyes and face, and carried a Tesco plastic bag. He made me stuff the money into the bag. It's all in notes. Then he walked out. He had a gun, by the way, a shotgun, sawn-off. I know a sawn-off shotgun when I see one. No shots were fired.'

'And how much has he stolen?' asked the constable.

'I cannot be sure until I do a check, but I'd say around £3,000.'

'Did you know him? Recognize him? Has he been hanging around the office lately, inside or out? Had he a car? An accomplice?'

Olive answered all his questions and even as she put down the telephone, the police car arrived with blue light flashing and warning sirens filling the streets with the sound of an emergency. A young constable rushed in, red faced and eager to catch his first major villain, but he found Olive at the counter looking serene and relaxed. She described the robber all over again, albeit briefly, and the constable rushed off to search the town, saying a CID man would be calling to interview her. He would take a more detailed statement from her so perhaps by that time she could make an accurate assessment of the amount that had been stolen? Olive said she could – furthermore some of the notes were traceable through their serial numbers because they were brand new. She would endeavour to provide those numbers too. The constable thanked her and radioed the details to Control.

In the Cumbria Police Control Room, the inspector in charge heard the news and said, 'It looks like the Shotgun Raider to me, lads. OK, set up Exercise Highwayman.'

'Highwayman' meant that road-blocks were established on all roads leading out of the county; all vehicles would be stopped and checked, all suspected persons interviewed and all suspicious bags examined. All building societies and banks would be warned of the raid, all local radio stations alerted with the news so that motorists would be told of the fleeing vehicle or man, and so the county would have thousands of ears and eyes.

But Frank Mayhew did not flee from the town. Having disposed of the Tesco plastic bag in a car-park litter-bin some distance from the Building Society, he went into a hiking and climbing clothes emporium and bought two large white sweaters with some of the cash. He used the old notes. Outside, he slipped one of them over his overalls, and went for a cup of tea and a biscuit. As he paid for his refreshments at the counter, a police car roared past with sirens blaring and blue light flashing. He smiled, thanked the girl at the till and found himself a table.

That same afternoon, the *Evening News* was on sale and its banner headline said 'FEAR STALKS THE STREETS'. There followed an article about the two deaths, that of Sheila Wynn being described as the murder of a popular barmaid.

Councillor Hogbin's words were printed beside it in bold letters but surprisingly, the police were not criticized by the paper; they let the readers make their own judgement of Hogbin's vituperation. The paper seemed supportive and asked that, as citizens of the town, all its readers must co-operate with the police if the killer was to be caught. It mentioned suspicious neighbours being reported, or even friends and relatives who had been behaving oddly or those who were absent longer than normal. That would please the Chief Constable.

The snag with the lead article was that it implied that one killer was responsible for both deaths whereas the police had taken care never to make the suggestion. One valuable paragraph asked everyone to check with their neighbours to see if any ladies living alone were missing, to ring or call on their parents, aunts or other relatives, to check on those who were known to be in hospital, homes or care of any kind just to make sure they were still where they should be. Shotguns were mentioned too, the town's citizens being asked to check to see whether their own guns, if they had any, were still where they should be, or to report any that might have been discarded.

From the police point of view, it was on the whole, a useful article but it did highlight the terror felt by women. Some had been interviewed to add strength to the story – one said she'd been chased along a street while coming home from work at a supermarket when it opened late, another claimed she'd been grabbed by a man in back alley.

Several said they'd disturbed intruders on their property and so the aura of real fear was being perpetuated. Women said they would not go out alone . . . men said their women would not go out alone . . . schools said young girls must be accompanied and late-opening businesses like hotels, clubs and pubs said they would ensure their staff were taken home by taxi. The police, although aware of the fears that were circulating, could not investigate the paper's claims of assaults or intruders; if the victims chose to report the matters officially, then they would be examined, but so many people did use an opportunity of this kind for scare-mongering. And some women loved the publicity that went with a nicely told tale of near-rape or panting pursuit . . .

But the report did bring a rush of telephone calls. Many helpful citizens did call the Incident Room or visit the local police station with snippets of helpful information or to report suspicious things found in their gardens or hedgerows. One pensioner did find a gun, but it was an old discarded air-rifle. He was thanked; the gun was labelled as an exhibit because it might have been used in a past crime . . . empty purses and wallets galore were handed in, old shoes were found but none fitted Sheila Wynn, hats, coats, underwear and socks were discovered and examined . . .

But nothing was of any known value to the investigation, except for the fear of arrest that was now increasing among many lesser villains.

By four-thirty, 18 Westfield Road had been thoroughly searched for the missing shotgun. Miller described it as a single-barrel twelve-bore weapon, Stevens make, dating to 1928. It was not a British weapon, Stevens being an American manufacturer. Miller had never used it; it had been left him by his father and he simply kept it as a family heirloom. It was not in perfect condition, for the stock was cracked and the barrel was slightly pitted with use and age. It might even be dangerous to fire it.

But Miller himself, with the two detectives, failed to find it. They searched every likely place including the loft, the garage, the garden shed and the outside toilet.

They examined wardrobes, cupboards and the car itself. The search was as meticulous as only a thorough police search can be, and it embarrassed Miller for the house was dirty and untidy, showing deep signs of domestic neglect. Miller excused it by saying he was on the road most of the time while Margaret was always at work, her duties entailing very long and exhausting hours. She had no time for household chores, and most evenings she was too tired to get out the Hoover or the feather duster.

'Mr Miller,' said Sally after a second search. 'A shotgun cannot just disappear. I will have to bring in our Task Force and they'll take the floor-boards up and might even dig up the garden. You realize a shotgun killed your lover? It is vital that we trace yours.'

'I know, I want the sodding thing found!' he snapped, exhausted by the day's awful events. 'Look, I did not kill her, how could I?'

'We will have to check every minute of your alibi,' Sally warned him. 'It doesn't take long to shoot somebody. We must also speak to your wife, she has a motive for killing Sheila, has she not? Even if you believe she was not jealous, she might have worried about the strengthening relationship.'

'Margaret's a nurse, damn it! She cares for people, she doesn't want to kill anybody . . . God Almighty, this is terrible . . . how can I convince you people I'm not guilty? That my wife's not guilty . . .'

'You could tell us where to find that gun for a start,' snapped Alex Groves.

Leaving Miller with his worries, the detectives drove from Westfield Road, Alex taking Miller's car for its examination and Sally announcing she was heading for the hospital.

Mrs Miller had to be interviewed without delay. Sally asked at reception and was told Nurse Miller was with a patient, but if she could wait a while, Nurse Miller would be able to see her. Sally waited in a small ante-room which she had requested due to the private nature of the forthcoming interview. She waited for half an hour. Nurse Miller was a small, heavily built woman of about forty-five who waddled rather than walked. She had thick legs and ankles, but a round and cheerful face that beamed a welcome as she settled down beside Sally Merston. As she sat down, Alex returned, saying:

'I got a lift over. The car's being checked straight away, Sarge.'

'Thanks, Alex. Well, so you are Mrs Miller?'

'I am,' she responded cheerfully. 'And you are both detectives? That's what reception said. Let me guess – one of our patients has escaped?'

'No, Nurse Miller, it's worse than that. We have just come from your house, from interviewing your husband.'

'Our Stan? What about?' she shrieked.

'It is delicate, Nurse Miller, but are you aware of the murder in the town?'

'That woman in Green Lane? Yes, I heard about it. We had your chaps around here, checking to see if she was one of our patients. She wasn't, thank God.'

'There has been another death, you know. Sheila Wynn; you probably knew her as Sheila Downes . . .'

'Oh my God!' she gasped. 'I heard about it, but they hadn't identified the body then. Is it really Sheila? That's our Stan's fancy piece!'

'So you knew? About your husband's relationship?'

'Course I knew, he was making a fool of himself over that

97

cow, she was nothing better than a pro, a real tart . . . anyway, why talk to our Stan?'

'Because of his relationship with her. We need to establish his movements over the time she was shot. And because he is married to you, we need to establish your movements over the same period.'

'Me? Do you think I'm a jealous wife or something? The proverbial woman betrayed, no hell hath a fury like me, is that what you're hinting? That I shot her?'

'No, but we must ask everyone linked with her, however remotely, to account for their movements, for elimination purposes.'

'Well, I wasn't linked, not even remotely as you put it.'

'But you are linked, Nurse Miller,' stressed Sally Merston. 'Even if you don't want to be. You could have a motive . . .'

'Don't be daft!' she spat. 'Why should I want to kill an old slag just because my silly husband takes a shine to her? Let him have his fun, that's what I say, it'll wear off in time. He's had women before, he always gets fed up and settles down. He's bored, you know, he doesn't know what to do with himself when he's at home; he has no hobbies outside work and I'm never around to entertain him. I'm too busy here, what with night-school, keep fit . . . you name it, I go to it. I can give dates if that's what you want.'

'Yes, we would like that,' said Sally, and so Nurse Miller pulled a pocket diary from her handbag and began to reel off dates and times. It seemed that when she was not at work, she was attending something or other; even in the mornings when she was working a late shift, she attended a pottery class. Quite literally, she was hardly ever at home.

'So,' said Sally, listening carefully. 'That's a very impressive list of outings; we'll have to check with others in the classes, with the registers perhaps, to substantiate your story . . .'

'You leave nothing to chance, do you?'

'Nothing,' said Sally. 'Now, Stanley's shotgun. What have you done with it?'

The nurse's face darkened visibly and then she smiled again.

'Done with it? Why should I have done anything with it?'

'It's not at the house, your house. It's gone from its usual place in Stanley's wardrobe. Stanley was surprised, we believe, when we asked him to show it to us. The place where he kept it was empty; we have searched the house. We are sure he has not removed it and that he does not know where it is. That leaves you.'

She did not answer them for a moment, her dark eyes studying their faces.

'You really think I did her in, don't you? Look, I don't know how to use a gun, I've never handled that old one of Stanley's, I've never seen it for years. I have not moved it, I have no idea where it is. There, how's that?'

'So where were you the night before last, Nurse Miller?'

'God, you never give up, do you? I'll check,' and she referred once again to her diary. After studying it for a moment, she said,

'So there we are, a most unusual thing. I was at home. I finished my shift at eight o'clock, bought myself a take-away supper and had it at home, all by myself. And I went to bed early with a nice Catherine Cookson.'

'You never went out after that time?'

'Nope, not even to fill the coal-scuttle. I enjoyed the relaxation.'

'Did anyone call to see you? Anyone who could prove you were at home?'

'No, no one. Not a soul.'

'And where was your husband?'

'At a meeting out Manchester-way, he said. He came in late, very late. I heard him.'

'How late?' asked Sally.

'Half-past two, later even. We use separate rooms, but I heard the light switches and the loo being flushed.'

'And what about Sheila? Did you ever meet her? Go for a drink with Stanley when she was around?'

'No, never. We went our own ways, we're not lovers any more, although we are not divorced. We just share the house and that's all. I do what I want and so does he. Besides, I don't particularly like the crowd that gets into the Black Lion, I don't know what our Stan sees in them.'

'OK, Mrs Miller, well, thanks for sparing us the time,' Sally apologized. 'I do not like visiting witnesses at their places of work, but this was urgent.'

'You've a better chance of catching me here than at home,' Nurse Miller stood up, barely rising to five feet two inches.

'Sorry I can't help any more. But Stanley could never kill a woman, he hasn't the guts,' Nurse Miller opened the door for them. 'I wish he was a bit stronger, that he had a bit more go in him . . . other men would have been a sales director now, or a company director or even have their own business, but not our Stanley. He's still a bloody motorized salesman after all these years with one company or another . . . and you wonder why I spend all my time out of the house and out of his way?'

Sally smiled at her remarks and they left.

In the car on the way back to the Incident Room, Sally asked Alex, 'Well, what do you make of her?'

'I'd say she was just the sort of woman to bump off Sheila Wynn – she had access to a weapon, she has a motive and she had the opportunity. And she can't support her own alibi, can she? She says she was at home, but who can prove it?'

'So I'll recommend to Pemberton that she goes into the frame?'

'I think so,' agreed Alex Groves.

'Right, so the next step is to find that missing gun.'

'I think she knows where it went,' said Groves.

'And I think you're right, Alex, my instinct says she was hiding something. I wonder what?'

12

At 6.30 p.m. the two inquests were opened. That upon the body of Sheila Wynn was for purposes of identification only. The coroner's officer, a police constable in civilian clothes, identified the body he had witnessed being taken from Blue Beck and said it was the same one that had been the subject of a post-mortem which he had also witnessed. The post-mortem had been conducted by Doctor Dai Andrews. The constable then told the coroner that he had been present with the same body when it had been viewed by Mr Harry Downes who had identified it as the woman known locally as Mrs Sheila Downes, also known as Wynn, née Hadfield. The coroner, having formally recorded the identity of the body, adjourned the inquest pending the outcome of police enquiries into the circumstances of her death.

With regard to the body of an unknown woman found in Green Lane, the coroner heard that the police had received several possible names but none of the suggestions had proved positive. The woman's identity remained unknown and enquiries were continuing.

He therefore adjourned this inquest *sine die*.

One of those welcome flukes of coincidence which can make the difference between success or failure in any project happened to Detective Sergeant George Lloyd.

He was the driver of a car which was stationary at a set of traffic-lights in Dover Street when a large white van eased to a halt behind him. It was about the size of a small personnel carrier. Lloyd was *en route* to the Incident Room, having spent a fruitless day trying to trace Frank Mayhew. Even now, his partner, DPC Don Kent, was waiting outside Mayhew's old house, discreetly concealed in a plain car.

But as he glanced into his rear-view mirror, he saw that the man at the wheel of the van was none other than Frank Mayhew. The van's seat was higher than Lloyd's and he had a clear view of the van's elevated driving compartment. A black Labrador dog was sitting on the passenger seat, peering ahead as the van waited at the lights. Lloyd checked again; although it was dark, the light which reflected from the vehicles themselves and from the street lights was sufficient to identify the driver. The dog helped to clinch it. So where had Mayhew been and what was he doing in that van?

The lights changed and Lloyd eased away as the van tucked in behind him. Now he wanted to shadow Mayhew, but he did not want his target to be aware of his interest. Lloyd found himself in something of a dilemma; he knew of the building-society raid in Keswick because news had been flashed to all police forces. Operation 'Highwayman' had been stood down, having failed to catch the villain and Mayhew had not passed through any of the check-points.

A description of the raider and a note that £3,850 in notes had been taken had also been circulated and a specific call had been made to the local CID because Mayhew resided in their patch. They were asked to find him and check his movements. What Mayhew could not realize, and what the Press had not been told, was that the serial numbers of one batch of stolen notes were known. If Mayhew could be arrested with those notes in his possession, it would be conclusive proof of his guilt. A copy of those facts had been sent to the Incident Room and so Lloyd was made aware of his quarry's suspected behaviour. Cumbria Police had specifically stated that the raid had all the hallmarks of the Shotgun Raider. But Lloyd was alone and unarmed, and Mayhew was known to carry a gun.

Stopping him right here to conduct a search of the van and an interrogation was therefore out of the question. This villain needed careful handling, careful attention. Lloyd was now stalking his prey, using stealth and cunning and he knew that if he lifted the handset to call the Control Room for assistance, Mayhew might see what he was doing. If he did, he would recognize the move; if that happened, he would take evasive action and this wonderful opportunity to catch him in possession of the stolen cash would be lost. The only solution seemed to be to follow him in the hope that Mayhew would finish at a place where a detailed search and interrogation could be made.

Lloyd tried to anticipate Mayhew's direction of travel, for it seemed he was not heading for home, although he was in his home town. He had had ample time to return from Keswick after committing that robbery. Lloyd knew he needed assistance and that he must inform Control of Mayhew's whereabouts and bring other cars into the area to effect an arrest before Mayhew had time to get rid of the cash. First he must take up a position behind the white van. In the late evening traffic, therefore, he eased over to his offside at the next mini-roundabout by signalling his intention to turn right and this encouraged Mayhew to overtake him on the nearside. As he did so, he was able to obtain the van's registration number.

Lloyd made a complete circuit of the roundabout to take up a position behind the white van, albeit with three private cars between him and his target. It was an ideal position for shadowing and it was aided by the darkness. In Mayhew's mirror, he'd be merely a pair of anonymous headlights. Lloyd was now able to radio the Control room.

'Charlie Four-Six to Control,' he began and upon the response, he continued, 'Am shadowing Frank Mayhew, currently heading along Dover Street and wanted for interrogation about the Keswick armed raid today. He's driving a white Ford Transit 35cwt. van bearing the logo "Jacob's Self-Drive Hire".'

Lloyd provided the registration number and Jacob's address from the sides of the van, then asked if immediate enquiries could be made from the hire-company.

It was necessary to ascertain the name and address of the current hirer, and the date and time of hire. Control said this would be done immediately. Lloyd went on to request assistance. He asked that Detective Superintendent Pemberton be informed and that he be made aware of Lloyd's request for a team of armed CID officers to be available. In addition, teams of detectives from the Murder Room were required to shadow Mayhew, including DPC Kent who could be withdrawn from his current pointless observations of Mayhew's house.

'If the selected officers liaise with me over the air, I will continue to shadow the van and we can arrange a road-block or ambush,' he suggested.

'Ten-Four,' responded Control. 'Your location now, Charlie Four-Six?'

'Passing the Bay Horse Hotel, Dover Street, heading east,' he said.

'Ten-Four. Over and out,' and Control went about their arrangements as George Lloyd drove at a safe distance behind the Ford. Lloyd's radio message galvanized the Control Room and the Incident Room into instant action as they sought to accommodate his requests and to effect the arrest of this notorious villain. DPC Kent was told to withdraw from his current observations and to liaise with his sergeant as his quarry was now heading east, well away from his home address.

From among the officers engaged on the dual murder enquiry. DS Gavin Manners, an ex-SAS officer, was issued with a rifle and his colleague DPC Gordon Shaw with a revolver and they were told to liaise with Lloyd. Teams comprising six further officers were recruited from those currently visiting the Incident Room and they abandoned their immediate tasks to join the chase. Detective Superintendent Pemberton was delighted with this unexpected development. If his men could arrest and gather sufficient evidence to convict Mayhew of at least one armed raid, the whole of this exercise would be justified. He hurried to the Control Room to take charge of the drama and contacted Lloyd over the air to make his presence known. Then he asked for Lloyd's location.

'Charlie Four-Six. Now in Creighton Avenue, heading south towards the shopping precinct in Michaelmas Court. Please instruct all mobiles to keep their distance, we want no marked police cars in the area.'

'Understood, Charlie Four-Six. Control Out.'

Pemberton knew only too well that some keen young patrolling constables in their blue-lighted Ford Fiestas could converge on the operational area just to be part of the fun. They must be ordered to keep away . . . he relayed that instruction over the air. His only hope was that Mayhew was not listening to police frequencies. At the moment, the only car with Mayhew in its sights was Lloyd's unmarked CID car and it remained at a safe distance.

Mayhew probably considered himself secure. But the other CID cars were heading across town and speeding towards him. One was going ahead, a small dull red Viva with a man and a woman aboard – Pemberton wanted it to drive ahead of Mayhew and to keep him under surveillance in that way. From the town map in the Control Room, the Inspector, with Pemberton at his side, began to direct the operation. It was like a set of spiders moving in to take a fly that was in the centre of a web . . . but this fly was a dangerous and cunning one, more like a hornet . . .

As they worked, a call came from Cumbria Police. The operator asked for Pemberton who accepted it.

'Cumbria Control here, sir, at Penrith. Chief Inspector Watkins speaking. It's about Mayhew and the hire-van.'

'Fire away,' said Pemberton.

'A hire-van was left at Jacob's Keswick depot just before five this afternoon; it had earlier been hired the day before by a man calling himself Eric Barnes who gave a Middlesbrough address. He produced a valid driving licence in that name. He left the first van and hired another, the one bearing the number you gave us earlier.'

'That's the one we have under surveillance, Mr Watkins. The driver is Mayhew.'

'So he avoided our road-blocks?'

'He would never risk driving through them, he'd wait in town until the blocks were stood down, then drive home in a different van and by a cross-country route along minor roads. Did the hire-people give a description?'

They had. The description could have fitted Mayhew but it was not positive enough to carry any weight in a court of law. At the time, he'd not been wearing any form of headgear, for example, and the only clothing the hire clerk had noticed was his white sweater. She had described him as an ordinary sort of chap, about medium height, between thirty and forty-five years old, with dark hair. It could fit millions of men in Britain.

'It was Mayhew all right, but we'll never prove that. OK, Mr Watkins, leave it with us. We'll continue with our surveillance and I'll let you know the outcome.'

The target van had passed through Michaelmas Court with Charlie Four-Six on its tail. Delta Zero-Seven was now on Michaelmas Lane ahead of the target; Delta Zero-Four was parked out of sight in the grounds of Michaelmas Lane Primary School awaiting instructions. The armed officers, both in Hotel Sierra Eight-Eight, were mobile, but cruising through the streets two blocks away, awaiting any development.

'Charlie Four-Six,' said George Lloyd in due course. 'Target now turning left off Michaelmas Lane. He is moving into Newburgh Road. Am following. Over.'

This precipitated a rearrangement of the other cars, for Newburgh Road emerged onto the bypass at a roundabout.

Pemberton instructed cars to hurry to the bypass to begin patrols there; if they waited at the next convenient roundabout for orders, there would be sufficient vehicles to both precede and follow the target.

'Target now on bypass, heading east,' came the soft voice of George Lloyd.

'Ten-Four,' said Control. The assisting cars were given their orders.

One was now ahead of the target, travelling well ahead, far enough in front of it to be out of sight of the target. This car had entered the traffic at a roundabout ahead of Mayhew. Several more were behind the target, including Lloyd. The target van, well illuminated in the dark, was cruising at sixty-five miles an hour and held its speed for several miles before turning off the bypass and into a country lane. The signpost said 'Charlton 2'. Lloyd relayed this to Control but did not pursue the target down that lane. He had been behind the target long enough for

Mayhew to be aware of his presence and so he drove past the lane end, asking Control to send the next following car in pursuit. That was Delta Zero-Four who took up the pursuit.

Lloyd drove on to the next junction on his left, signposted 'Charlton 2½'. He knew Charlton. It was a small community of some 600 people, a pleasing village tucked away in the hills on the edge of town, close enough for commuting but far enough to be rural with no hint of urbanization.

Lloyd's first reaction was to wonder what on earth Mayhew was doing out here.

Delta Zero-Four took up the commentary. He had the target in view now. It was slowing as it entered Charlton and so the police car halted, allowing the target to proceed without a tail. Pemberton, from his map, saw that the road through Charlton had no junctions or crossroads until it reached Ewebury. The only road out, apart from the one used by the target, was another which led in from the bypass, and the target had passed that junction. It was along this road that George Lloyd now drove. A further car was positioned in Ewebury to report its arrival there, if and when it did so.

But it did not emerge from Charlton.

'Control to Charlie Four-Six. Over.'

'Receiving, go ahead,' acknowledged Lloyd.

'Target appears to have gone to ground. Suggest a foot search of the village. Over.'

'Received. Will all mobiles rendezvous at the village church? Maintain one at each exit road; they should look out for the target van, or something else driven by Mayhew. If the target van is located, do not approach, repeat do not approach or touch it. Just report direction. Over.'

Control asked all mobiles to acknowledge that instruction in turn, which they did, and George Lloyd drove to the church with its slender spire to await his teams. As they arrived they doused their lights.

It was Hotel Sierra Eight-Eight that found the van.

'It's on the pub forecourt,' said Detective Sergeant Manners. 'Deserted'.

'So it looks as if chummy's in the pub? I didn't know he used this place? It's a bit off the beaten track for him. Has he a meet here?' wondered Lloyd. 'Right, so we search the pub.'

With his teams around him, Lloyd despatched two to cover

the rear door, two to cover the van and two to enter the premises, the latter being himself and DPC Shaw. His revolver could be concealed from the regulars; Manners' rifle would be all too obvious and so he opted to watch the van. If chummy fled to the van, he wouldn't get very far.

Allowing time for all to reach their positions, Lloyd said, 'Right, me and Gordon Shaw will enter the bar. I know Mayhew by sight. If he's there, we will arrest him on suspicion of committing the Keswick raid and fetch him outside. If he's not there, we will search the pub – bedrooms, toilets, kitchens, the lot. If he's not in the pub, we'll have to start asking questions around the village or even consider searching every house. Now, he could be dangerous, but it's said he's never used his gun. But there's always a first time and this could be it. Right, Gordon?'

'Right, Sarge,' and Shaw fingered the pistol which was in a shoulder-holster beneath his left armpit. It was secure and out of sight, yet available for immediate use.

'Right, in we go.'

But Mayhew was nowhere in the pub. Lloyd, with the anxious landlord following everywhere, searched the entire premises as the bemused locals looked on in wonder. When they had convinced themselves that he was not hiding in the loft or the loos or anywhere else, Lloyd addressed the landlord. His name was Keith Collins.

'Sorry about that, Mr Collins, but we had a tip there was an armed raider in here.'

'Some nutter ringing you, I'll bet,' said Collins who had remained calm during the search; he recognized the merits of this intrusion because once the story had circulated, it would bring in some extra customers.

'Do you know a chap called Mayhew?' asked Lloyd. 'Frank Mayhew,' and he described him briefly.

'No, sorry,' he said and the regulars all shook their heads too.

'Has anyone like that just come in here? Within the last five or ten minutes?'

'No, nobody's come in for ages.'

'There's a white van on your forecourt, a self-drive and hire-van, Ford 35cwt. It's only been there a couple of minutes or less. Any idea whose it is?'

'It'll be that new chap at Rose Cottage,' chipped in one of the regulars. 'Only moved in yesterday, he did, in the early hours. He used one of them self-drive and hire-vans for his stuff.'

'And where's Rose Cottage?' asked Lloyd.

'Right across the green,' said the regular. 'Next door to the big white painted house. He left first thing this morning in his van, did the new chap. He looked like a van-driver. He's got a dog, a black Labrador.'

'Thanks,' said George Lloyd. 'You've been most kind.'

Leaving the members of the bar more than puzzled about their reasons for the search, Lloyd and Shaw left. Outside, Lloyd gathered his men together and they all moved across the green to Rose Cottage, with the exception of one man left to guard the van. It was a small detached cottage of mellow brick with a holly bush beside the front gate. There was no garage nor even a car-parking space, but the lights were on.

'I think that's where we'll find Frank Mayhew,' said Lloyd. Carefully, and without any noise, he encircled the cottage with his teams in much the same way as he'd covered the pub. This time, both the armed officers accompanied him, with Manners making no effort to conceal the rifle. They went to the rear door, for the kitchen light was burning, albeit behind closed blinds.

Lloyd knocked loudly.

22

A large dog barked and a man's voice said, 'Lie down, Ben,' then the door was opened by Frank Mayhew wearing a white sweater. 'Why, it's Detective Sergeant Lloyd! Hello, George,' he greeted his old adversary. 'I see you've brought your minder, armed as well, eh? Now, you know I'm not a dangerous man . . . so what can I do for you? Looking for an escaped convict, are we? A lady-killer perhaps? Doing house-to-house?'

'So what are you doing here, Frank?'

'I live here, this is my house.'

'Since when?'

'Since yesterday. I moved my few sticks in yesterday.'

'There's no bloody wonder we couldn't find you . . .'

'Let me guess . . . you've been watching my previous address! Wanting to talk to me about those murders, I'll bet? I'm in the firing-line for every crime that's committed between here and Land's End, eh? Good old Frank Mayhew, the chief suspect for everything . . . I'm not a killer, George, I wouldn't hurt a fly. I love all creatures great and small, just you ask Ben.'

The dog looked happy at the sound of its name and wagged its tail. It showed no animosity or fear of the detectives.

'I want to know where you've been today, Frank.'

'Sure, I'll always chat to my favourite detective. I've nothing to hide. Come in, and bring your minder with you.'

Mayhew stepped back to allow them entry.

'Coffee? Tea? Something stronger?' he asked as he led them inside.

'No, thanks, nothing,' and Lloyd, followed by Manners, found himself in a tiny kitchen with a cheap Formica table in the centre. Mayhew offered them chairs and they sat down.

'So, George, what is it this time? What am I supposed to have done now? Robbed another bank or something?'

'Today, Frank. Where have you been today?'

'Out and about,' he said, teasing them.

'The Lake District perhaps?'

'I can see there is no point denying it. Yes, I went for a day out in the Lake District, seeing the sights of Keswick and enjoying the charms of Derwentwater. I walked and strolled beside the lake and beneath the trees, watching the chip papers fluttering and dancing in the breeze . . .'

'And how did you travel?'

'I had hired a van to shift my bits of furniture and one of the depots which would take it back was at Keswick. So I thought to myself now there's a chance for a day out. So I went to Keswick and returned it there. Jacob's is the name.'

'And how did you propose returning if you'd left your transport there?'

'A chap I'd met a couple of days earlier said he'd meet me there and bring me back. He was fetching some Lakeland slate back here. It seemed a good chance for me to have a day out.'

'And who was this chap?'

'Feller by the name of Eric from Middlesbrough. I don't really know him, we met in a transport café over plates of greasy

chips, you know how it is. But he was as good as his word, well
nearly. In Keswick I met him in the George over some scampi
and a pint and he said his plans had been changed. He couldn't
fetch me home because something had cropped up, so he hired
a van for me. It was from the very place I'd left my first one.
Jacob's. Very handy. I drove the hire-van home. It's out there
now, on the pub forecourt. If he doesn't come for it, I've got to
return it to the depot here by six tomorrow night. So there,
that's my day out after being let down by a mate. Fascinating,
stuff, isn't it?'

'I don't believe a word of it, Frank, and you know it.'

Mayhew grinned. 'I have a feeling I've heard this conversation before. You're going to accuse me of robbing that
building society in Keswick, aren't you? I heard it on the news
as I drove back. Just because I was in Keswick . . . trouble
seems to follow me around . . .'

'I need to know where you were around three-thirty today.'

'In Keswick, George. Having a cup of tea in a café if you want
to know. Here, there's a chit,' and he delved into his trouser
pocket and pulled out a small plastic wallet. As he opened it to
find the till voucher, a second piece of paper fell to the floor.
Like lightning, George Lloyd put his foot on it, preventing
Mayhew from retrieving it.

Then Lloyd picked it up.

'Mine, I think,' said Mayhew, holding out his hand.

'Just a moment,' said Lloyd, not returning it immediately and
not troubling to open it. He knew what it was; he'd used just
such a piece of paper, bearing the same coloured printing, a
couple of days ago . . . and a whole new concept of this
criminal's behaviour came into Lloyd's mind. But first, he did
examine the till receipt and it provided the name of a Keswick
café, with details of the purchase, totalling eighty-five pence. A
cup of tea and cream bun were listed. And like so many modern
VAT receipts, it gave the date and time of payment. Fifteen
forty-six today.

'I'll keep this,' said Lloyd, pocketing the receipt. 'It might be
useful evidence . . .'

'I've admitted I was in Keswick,' said Mayhew.

'Yes, but if we take you before the court for robbing that
building society, you might deny you were ever there. Now, I
can prove you were. But this cock-and-bull story about meeting

110

this Eric chap, well, I don't believe that, not for one minute. What I believe is that you hired this van under a false name, as you've done on previous occasions, Frank. You would use a false driving licence, eh? You do not own a car, so you hire vehicles for your raids. We know that. So I think you drove a similar van to Keswick, raided the building society in your hat and with your Tesco bag, and then sat tight in town.

'You hid from the police over a cup of tea, waiting for a couple of hours or so until the fuss had died away. Then you came home in a different vehicle . . .'

'You ought to go in for writing television scripts, George. That would make a nice tale, bags of imagination and drama . . .'

Still clutching the piece of paper, George Lloyd ignored the sarcasm and said, 'Now, how about me and my lads searching your house and that van outside, eh?'

'Search? What for?'

'Evidence, Frank. Evidence of the crime you committed today, the crime you'll never admit. We might find a sawn-off shotgun perhaps, or money, plastic bags, some funny hats, indeed anything that will prove you raided the building society in Keswick this afternoon.'

'And if I refuse?'

'We will remain here until my colleagues obtain a search warrant for this house, and the other cottage in town. The warrant will authorize us to use such force as is necessary and that includes taking up floor-boards, digging up the kitchen and anything else we might feel necessary. Right?'

'Then help yourself, George. I can show you my guns, you know that. I never hide them, I am authorized, I do hold a current certificate and if I carry them with me, they're always in their gun-covers, as the law demands.'

'I'm interested in the cash, Frank, and a sawn-off shotgun!'

'Then search away, George. There's not many places to search here, it's a tiny house with precious little furniture. You don't need a warrant . . . you've got my permission because there's nowt here.'

Manners opened the door and called in three detectives. He obtained the van key from Mayhew and instructed one of them to search the van; if nothing was found, the van would be seized as evidence and meticulously searched at the police station. It might have to be examined by the Forensic Lab. The other two detectives were asked to search the cottage. And as they did so, George Lloyd sat and watched Mayhew. Mayhew, for the first time since George had known him, was showing signs of unease. He could not prevent himself looking at the piece of paper clutched in George's fist, although he was trying not to suggest that he was concerned about it. George now knew the reason for this concern . . . he was almost sure he would soon have enough evidence to nail Mayhew, at least for the Keswick raid . . .

The detective who had examined the van returned to say he'd found nothing incriminating, but the van was now formally in police hands, having been seized as evidence. The police would notify the hire-company. It took the other men half an hour to thoroughly search the cottage, (albeit without taking up floorboards and knocking out cupboards); they knew that as Mayhew had only just bought the cottage, he had not had the time to create secret hiding-places.

'The guns are all there, sarge, five of them. In a locked cabinet. There's another standing against the wall in the back entrance, in a gun-cover. It doesn't smell as if it's been used recently. No sawn-off guns. Nothing else, no money, no evidence of the raid,' they reported.

George Lloyd smiled.

'Good,' he said.

'Good for me!' beamed Mayhew. 'No evidence, eh? Nothing to link me with the raid, lads. I'm in the clear. So why's it good for you, George?'

'Because it reinforces my belief,' smiled George Lloyd, opening his hand to highlight the piece of paper.

'That's nothing,' said Mayhew.

'Isn't it? Then why is my possession of it worrying you, Frank? Just what have we here, eh?'

'I don't know, you tell me. What is it?'

'It fell out of your pocket, Frank, you saw it.'

'I admit nothing!' his attitude now changed. Gone was the friendliness. Now he was a criminal defending himself.

'I witnessed this fall from your pocket, and so did Detective Sergeant Manners. We can prove it was in your possession, can't we? It might even bear your handwriting and we could prove that as well, if need be. You know that, Frank.'

'It's not important . . .'

'It is very important, Frank, because it is a Certificate of Posting for a Royal Mail Special Delivery package. And I see that the date stamp shows that the package in question was mailed today, from Keswick post office.'

'So?'

'So the name and address shown here, the name and address of the recipient that is, will be visited by us. It's a Mrs Vincent, Edith Vincent. In Crowther Street here in town, number 16. So who is she, Frank? A friend, a former colleague, mistress, aunt or just a poor old lady you've conned into becoming an accommodation address to take in your mail? Well, we shall see. Because Frank, you posted something to her. Cash perhaps? Cash from a raid on a building society? There is no cash in the house or that van, no proceeds of the raid and that pleases me because it reinforces my theory. It compels me to ask – if Frank nicked that money, where is it? What have you done with more than three thousand in notes, eh? Popped it into a jiffy bag perhaps and posted it by Special Delivery to avoid police searches?'

'It's a sweater, George. I bought her a Lakeland sweater, a new one like mine, and posted that . . .'

'Really? Why mail a new sweater?'

Mayhew did not answer, merely shrugging his shoulders. 'A surprise present for her. She's old, she's known me since I was a kid.'

'So tell us, Frank, where were you yesterday morning in the early hours? Say between midnight and two o'clock?'

'Now what the hell are you getting at?'

'Murder, Frank. I take it you have read the papers or heard the news? About Sheila Wynn, or Downes as she is better known.'

'Yes, I have. Look, I had nowt to do with that, I'm no killer . . .'

'A shotgun was used, Frank. You've got half a dozen.'

'You've no proof that I was involved in that, George, and you know it. You can examine all my guns, not one's been fired for months, you can check that, I know; your forensic people can tell that sort of thing. Now, look, if you're trying to set me up for that one . . .'

'Set you up? I'm not trying to set you up for anything, but, for your own sake, we do wish to know your movements between midnight and two o'clock yesterday morning. And don't forget we need corroboration, witnesses, proof.'

'I was moving house,' Mayhew told them. 'I had hired that other van and started to load it about eleven. It took me till about two o'clock yesterday morning, you could ask the neighbours.'

'We already have,' Lloyd lied, albeit recalling that one of the pub regulars had mentioned this.

'Bastards! Then you'll know I worked alone, I always do and I drove to this place after two-thirty or so, I can't be sure of the exact timing. Then I unloaded.

'It took me most of the night. I like moving house at night, out of the view of snoopers . . .'

'OK, we'll check that as well, we'll take no chances with your alibis. Now, Sheila Wynn . . .'

'I knew her as Downes.'

'Right, what do you know of her? If you didn't kill her, Frank, who did? You know the villains of this place. And what about the Green Lane woman, eh? You might have found her . . .'

'If I hadn't moved house, I would have found her, me and Ben between us. And I'd have informed you lads.'

'So what's the whisper in town, Frank? You must have heard something? You, of all people, must know something? Gossip? Who'd shoot Sheila and ditch her like that? Who'd smother the other woman and why? So what's going on in this place all of a sudden? Why two deaths? Two women, eh?'

'George, you must be bloody thick. I'm not a killer, I don't know anything about those deaths, nothing at all. I was busy at the time, moving house, and I was away all day today, so I've not been in touch with anybody about them. I know nothing, absolutely sod all.'

'So where's your shotgun?'

'What shotgun?'

'The one you used for that raid.'

'George old son, you are not going to terrify me or bully me into admitting robberies with a shotgun just to get me off the hook for a murder.'

'I'm seizing all your guns, Frank, as evidence.'

'Examine them, George, feel free, but let me have them back. You go ahead and try and prove what you can.'

'Well, Frank, I reckon we can do that, at least for the robbery in Keswick. Now, I've news for you. You're under arrest on suspicion of committing that robbery in Keswick today. You are not obliged to say anything . . .' and Detective Sergeant Lloyd chanted the formal caution.

'You've got no proof . . .' shouted Mayhew.

'I will get proof after I've had words with the Post Office Investigation Division,' said Lloyd. 'Come on, Frank, you're coming with us.'

'What about the dog?'

'He can come as well, come on, Ben, you're nicked as well.'

'I want a solicitor,' said Mayhew as he was led away with Ben at his heels.

'Do you want one for the dog?' asked Lloyd.

Detective Superintendent Pemberton was delighted with the news and so was Mr Moore who had called the Incident Room to check on progress. He expressed his pleasure at recent developments and praised all the teams. He was pleased the exercise had produced some good results, if not quite the one he was seeking . . . but there was still some time for that . . .

In the basement of the police station, after having all his personal belongings removed, along with anything by which he might harm himself such as belt, shoe-laces and sharp objects, Mayhew was placed in the cells. It was not the first time this had happened but he knew enough about police procedures and the rules of evidence never to admit anything. From this moment, he would say nothing nor would he sign a statement or admission. He would deny everything he'd earlier said to the police, for no court these days would believe the word of the police. These days, most criminal juries now believed the accused rather than the police. Mayhew saw no problems ahead; he just hoped they looked after Ben.

But in fact he had made a rare and uncharacteristic mistake. Had he posted the money, then thrown away the certificate of posting, there would have been no evidence to link him with the Keswick raid. But, rather stupidly, he had retained the certificate just in case the package failed to arrive. And the police were now exploring that avenue. Detective Sergeant Lloyd felt the excitement of success in his veins. He rang the

North-West Region of the Post Office Investigation Division at Manchester and explained his request, adding,

'Mayhew posted a parcel at Keswick earlier today. I have the Certificate here, the registration number is K 482546, and the addressee is a Mrs Edith Vincent, of 16 Crowther Street here in town.'

'Thank you, Sergeant. And?'

'And, having just used the system myself, I know that your system records the precise time of acceptance of the package and a date stamp.'

'You want us to intercept the package?'

'No, I think for the court's purpose, it might be wise to let it proceed through the system. I'd like to have it delivered to Mrs Vincent – if we talk to her, I'm sure she will implicate Mayhew. I'm sure the parcel contains the stolen cash. He says it has a sweater inside. We did not find a new sweater at his cottage, other than the one he was wearing.'

'As you wish, and I agree, by the way. So you'd like me to check to see if the package has in fact been posted and is proceeding normally through our system?'

'Please, and can you call me back?'

'Sure, Sergeant.'

And Lloyd made sure that he detailed a detective to wait outside Mrs Vincent's tomorrow morning when the postman arrived.

Before knocking off for the evening, Pemberton re-examined the current progress. If Mayhew was in custody, and if his story about moving house could be verified, it seemed he was not in the frame for Sheila Wynn's death. And the lads seemed to think he was not linked to the other death; for that aspect, Pemberton was content that Mayhew had been arrested.

At last it seemed there had been a breakthrough so far as Mayhew was concerned; now there would be evidence to link him to the raids. But because the murder weapon had not been found and Mayhew was a known user of shotguns, he must remain in the frame until properly eliminated. The ballistics people would say whether any of his guns had been fired recently.

The top suspect therefore remained Wynn's common-law husband, Harry Downes. Miller seemed to be in the clear, having produced evidence of his whereabouts at the material time, but what about Miller's wife? Miller's shotgun had vanished and that was ominous. Had Margaret Miller shot her husband's mistress and disposed of the body? Mrs Miller, as a nurse, would be accustomed to handling bodies whether dead or alive, so could she have shot Sheila and dumped her from a car? There was more work to be done upon Mrs Miller. It seemed the Wynn death was gathering momentum but the Green Lane one was sliding down the scale of interest, so by concentrating his mens' minds upon the real murder, he could divert their attention from the Green Lane body. The exercise was now superfluous and he was pleased the Wynn death was uppermost in the mind of his teams. As he prepared to leave the Incident Room, he smiled as he saw Amanda waiting for him. But his plans were interrupted.

'Sir,' said a detective constable. 'I've a man on the line from Nottingham, says the Green Lane woman sounds like his sister. He is most insistent, he demands to see the body.'

And Mark Pemberton could not refuse.

14

Detective Chief Inspector Wilf Draper caught an early Intercity train to King's Cross. A taxi would deliver him to New Scotland Yard before the conference so he'd have time to make his visit to the fingerprint bureau. As the train carried him south, he pondered upon the mystery death. From his own long experience, there seemed distinct oddities about the circumstances. He was unable to elaborate upon those feelings, unable to express the intuitive concern that he experienced; if he'd been asked to present his worries in a report, they would not have appeared important but yet, instinctively, he felt there was something peculiar about that murder, something that did not add up, as he would say when trying to explain. No one had seen or heard anything; it was almost as if that woman had appeared from nowhere. He'd never known a murder enquiry which had resulted in so little feed-back from the public. So far, the appeals had produced absolutely nothing.

But, he tried to tell himself, it was not his problem. Mark Pemberton would have to sort it out and, so far, he seemed to be getting nowhere fast. According to canteen gossip, he was no closer to an identification than he had been at the outset; it was true that the second death had aggravated that process, but a good detective would have overcome that problem.

After today at the Yard, therefore, he might be able to suggest a name for the woman of Green Lane, but that depended upon the skills of the fingerprint-researchers in Room 8101.

Wilf tried to force to the back of his mind his fascination for the mysterious death as he settled down to study his intelligence reports on the local activities of the IRA and any security problems associated with the PM's visit.

At 8.30 a.m., the gentleman from Nottingham arrived at the hospital. The visit had been arranged over the telephone by Inspector Paul Larkin. Pemberton did not want to get involved in this one – he only hoped to God that this was *not* the fellow's long-lost sister. If it was, the ramifications would be horrendous . . . he must keep away, keep his distance. And if it did turn out to be the man's sister, what then? Would the man have to be told the truth? Or could there be some sinister reason for this character's presence? Had Moore told everything to Pemberton? There were times that Mark Pemberton felt there was more to this exercise than merely Moore's whim, so could Pemberton himself be operating blind?

'You look after him, Paul,' Pemberton had said.

Using another phone in a distant office, Mark then rang Doc. Andrews to warn him of this development. It was due to consultations with Doc. Andrews and this visitor that an early visiting time had been fixed.

The gentleman was Lieut.-Col. Roderick Abrahams, retired. Over the telephone, he had explained in his very clipped tones that his sister, Elspeth, had abandoned her family links more than forty years ago when she had married a man of whom his family disapproved. The man, called Stuart Bass, ran a chain of second-hand car dealerships and had a background of scrap-metal dealing and itinerant trading. Elspeth, on the other hand, had been privately educated.

Bass, so the family had constantly maintained, was hardly suitable as the husband of a woman whose breeding included a high proportion of aristocratic blood and a line reaching back to the Vollens of Stamper Castle. Owing to family disapproval, Elspeth had never again visited her parents or her brother, and no one knew what had become of her.

Years later, Lieut.-Col. Abrahams had written to her old address and had even hired a solicitor in an attempt to trace his sister.

He had never lost sight of the fact that she might have been divorced, or that she may have died without the family knowing, but his efforts produced no result. And now, with the reports of the woman's body lying in the very same town as that motor-trader, he felt this might be her. Certainly, the physical description reported in the Press could match her. Larkin, after his consultations with Pemberton, had agreed to escort the old soldier to the mortuary and in the meantime, he set a team upon the action of investigating the past record and present circumstances of Stuart Bass and the Cherryspink Motor Group. If the dead woman had links with that group, then the killer might be found among the family, staff or associates. And so the net continued to enlarge and spread.

When Larkin drove to the mortuary, he had no difficulty recognising Lieut.-Col. Abrahams. He looked like an old soldier of high rank. Tall and distinguished, the white-haired old man emerged from an ancient Rover 2000 which was immaculate in its warm brown livery. Dressed in tan cavalry twill trousers, a smart brownish-green tweed jacket and a matching Sherlock Holmes type of cap, he walked without a stick towards Larkin. He must be well into his late seventies, thought Larkin. His grey eyes were alert above a thick white moustache and Larkin wondered what stirring military actions this old man had witnessed in his career. Larkin identified himself and the old man did likewise. He said he'd driven up from Nottingham this morning and would be returning later today.

In the reception area, Larkin explained the daunting procedure involved in the identification of a dead body, but Lieut.-Col. Abrahams said,

'I've seen dozens of corpses, officer, on the battlefield and off. They hold no terrors for me, you know, I'll be one myself before long . . .'

119

'This one could be your missing sister, you mustn't forget, sir, it's not just any corpse.'

'Damn it all, man, I know that. That's why I'm here. But I've not seen Elspeth for years, I'm not emotional about it, you know, I just want to get the bloody matter cleared up after all this time. She doesn't deserve it, I know, but for the family record, I want to sort it out. God knows why she deserted her family to marry that rogue . . .'

'I'll call Doctor Andrews,' and Larkin asked the girl at the desk to call him.

Andrews shook the old man by the hand and himself explained what was to follow, whereupon the three men entered the depths of the hospital, following the labyrinth of clinical-scented corridors until they came to the mortuary. The old man seemed anxious to complete his task and warded off all attempts to mollycoddle him. When they entered the theatre, the corpse was already on the slab, having been withdrawn from the freezer drawer a few moments earlier.

It was covered by the large white shroud with the head, chest and feet making little tents along the fabric.

'Ready, sir?' asked Andrews.

Lieut.-Col. Abrahams nodded.

With mixed feelings of worry and anxiety, Andrews peeled back the shroud until the calm, white, waxen face was totally revealed and Lieut.-Col. Abrahams studied the woman for a long time. No one spoke. In the sepulchral atmosphere, they waited for the old man to decide and he sighed heavily.

'She's lost a lot of weight,' he said gently. 'Elspeth was much, well, heavier, more solid. But the face is like her . . . so like her . . . that nose, the line of the chin . . .'

'If you are not sure, Colonel Abrahams, we can pursue this further,' said Larkin. 'Once we get a lead from a possible name, we can examine the home of the deceased and find fingerprints there, on doors, mirrors, picture frames and so on. And then we can compare them with those of the deceased – that way, we can almost certainly prove identity. If you think this is your sister, but cannot be sure, then we would follow that course. A name and, of course, an address, gives us a valuable starting point and it also helps us to prove, if necessary, that it is not the person you think. Also, if we do get a name, we can check via dental records. If she'd had treatment, a dentist could check against his files.'

'She did marry that rogue who ran the Cherryspink Motor Group, you'd have to check his records . . . it was years ago . . . her marriage to him, I mean. There could be grandchildren now.'

'So, you cannot be certain this is Elspeth? Did she have any other identifying marks? Scars from childhood? Moles? Broken limbs whose repairs might still show on an X-ray?'

He shook his head. 'No, that's the trouble, she had nothing like that, not that I'm aware of.'

'So,' Larkin needed a firm yes or no at this stage. 'You cannot swear that this is your sister Elspeth?'

'Sorry, no, but she does look so like her . . . I mean, officer, it is more than forty years . . .'

'All right, I will take a statement from you, we'll do it back at the police station, and we will start enquiries from Cherryspink to see what happened to Bass and your sister's marriage and whether we can confirm or deny her identity. We will, of course, keep you informed.'

'Thank you, officer.'

And they all left the mortuary.

If the visit by Lieut.-Col. Abrahams had caused Pemberton and Andrews more than a little private concern, it did raise the hopes of the investigating teams. The possibility of an identification of the Green Lane woman created a wave of interest through the Incident Room and was good for morale.

As the old man was examining the body, the detectives were gathering for another morning conference. To assuage his concern, Pemberton sent a message to Moore via his secretary, asking him for a talk later this morning.

The Chief must be made aware of this development.

Already, a team had been allocated an action for Bass and the Cherryspink Motor Group with a brief to find out what, if anything, lay behind that link. But the old man himself was not free from investigation – another team would discreetly ferret into the background of Lieut.-Col. Abrahams. In spite of the Colonel's visit, the chief topic of conversation and morale-booster among the gathering detectives was the arrest of Frank

121

Mayhew, albeit not for murder. When Mark Pemberton rose to address his team, therefore, he began by thanking them for their efforts to date, following which he highlighted the circumstances of Mayhew's arrest.

'George Lloyd and Don Kent are awaiting the postman about now. The POID have been marvellous and it seems the cash is on its way to the address Mayhew's been using. If any of those numbered notes are in the package, Mayhew's going down for a long time. Now, back to the two deaths. In the frame, we still have Harry Downes. What's new on him? Where's Roger?'

Detective Sergeant Daniels rose and said,

'He's coming in stronger, sir. John and I have been visiting neighbours and acquaintances. It seems Downes can be violent when the mood takes him, one set of neighbours can confirm he has beaten up Sheila on several occasions, often before throwing her out. With regard to the bruises on the body, sir, Doc. Andrews was not prepared to say whether they were caused by rocks in the river or by other means but did say they could be the result of a beating or severe struggle. Could they have been done by Downes?'

'Are you implying he went too far the other night? That he beat her and she died . . .'

'I don't think the pathologist said she'd died from a beating, sir, he was quite specific she'd died from gunshot wounds. But if Downes had lost his rag with her, he might have thrashed her and then shot her.'

'Has he been quizzed about beating her up?'

'No, I want a bit of ammunition before I throw that one at him. But he's our favourite, sir. He's leading the field by a furlong or two.'

'OK, have words with him. If necessary, bring him in.'

Sally Merston reported next. She told the conference that her action on Miller had brought Mrs Margaret Miller into the frame while reducing the odds against her husband. Miller had an almost watertight alibi which was supported by a petrol receipt and a blonde woman who'd agreed she'd spoken to him while watching the drugs raid. She had not known his name, but confirmed she'd spent a few minutes watching the raid with a man of that description. The only problem with the Millers was his shotgun which had not yet been found; that Downes could somehow have gained access to that shotgun was a possibility.

Pemberton said he would again highlight the search for the murder weapon at the news conference which followed; Miller's gun might well be the one they were seeking.

The other detectives followed with their own snippets of information – the twitcher, Cedric Halliday, had been eliminated because, after close questioning, his account did bear scrutiny. He said he'd seen five hikers near Blue Beck Reservoir half-an-hour before his awful discovery, and the keeper of the reservoir had confirmed this sighting. He'd seen Cedric and he'd seen the group of hikers, but not together. Nonetheless, it did support Cedric's tale, and his other movements had been confirmed, especially during the critical moments of Sheila's final hours. The security men at the reservoir did add that Cedric was a regular visitor to the reservoir and was well known to the staff, but they'd reported nothing else that was considered suspicious.

Several courting couples, amongst whom had been the inevitable secretive liaisons, had been traced. There would have been more had this been summer, but a winter night spent in a car did stifle a lot of ardour. None of the lovers had seen anything suspicious around the Blue Beck area before departing at eleven or eleven thirty. If that enquiry was drawing a blank, then the overall outcome was better. As a direct result of the murder enquiries, a man suspected of indecent assaults on elderly women had been arrested and he had been charged, and a prostitution racket had been discovered. It was operating in good-class hotels and, as a consequence, observations would now be instituted with a view to gaining evidence for a prosecution.

Also surfacing among the muck which was being churned up by the questioning were vague but strengthening rumours of an active paedophile ring said to be operating in town. This came from Detective Constable Ted Wilson.

He explained, 'I got the gen from a customer of one of the pros; he'd seen young girls in one of the flats – schoolkids, ten or twelve, as young as that – and he'd come across reports of the same kids being in the Grand Hotel when a bash was being held. I've done a bit of digging, sir, and there does seem to be an active paedophile ring in operation. I think it's more than a rumour – some of the kids are being recruited from the poor families in Pennine Flats, they're getting paid for their services. Poor little deprived sods . . .'

'Right,' said Pemberton. 'I know this is a murder enquiry, but I think those evil bastards want sorting out. Stick with that enquiry, Ted, find out what you can. Get names and locations. If necessary, we'll fix a raid but remember we want cast-iron evidence against those filthy-minded villains if we're going to prosecute.'

'Sir,' said Ted Wilson.

The other team members reported their own successes or lack of success, all this being logged into HOLMES and the statement-file index, and Pemberton had to decide what would keep the enquiries alive in the media. The Press had to be kept interested and new developments were needed.

The continuing hunt for the murder weapon was one factor that must be kept alive in the papers and on local radio, but the overall impression was that the investigations were losing steam. All the right things had been done, all the right moves made, the right questions asked and the right procedures implemented, but nothing positive had resulted. There was no arrest for murder and no immediate prospect of one.

At this stage, Pemberton did not want to highlight the likely identification of the Green Lane woman – in his own mind, he felt she was not the Abraham woman. Moore would not have selected a body that might be identified, would he? But it was just possible something had slipped through the security net . . . he decided not to acquaint the Press with this development until something more positive had resulted. He knew that if Downes was arrested on suspicion, it would prevent any future speculative coverage in the Press. Upon an arrest or impending charge, the *sub judice* rule came into effect and halted all speculative publicity – the Press would and could only say that a man was helping with enquiries.

No further speculative reporting could be published or broadcast until the trial. He did not want that – he and Moore both wanted maximum coverage throughout the exercise and so it was prudent not to have an arrest at this stage. Besides, he needed maximum coverage to help solve the Blue Beck murder.

It was Amanda who produced some highly interesting new information.

Pemberton smiled at her, but she conducted herself with professional detachment.

'Sir,' she said when most of the others had completed their discussions. 'I'm on house-to-house in the Hemsworth area of town, working with DS Harvey. He's at court this morning, by the way, with a shop-lifter.'

'Yes, Amanda? You've got something for us?'

'Well, sir, it might be nothing. But when I was doing St Joseph's Street, that's where a lot of students live in rented houses, I came across a house full of young people who are not students. They don't appear to have any work. But it was what a neighbour told me that made me wonder. She said that the house was occupied by a Miss Garnett, a reclusive old lady, until recently. Number Ten it is. The neighbour does not know what happened to Miss Garnett, but she's not there now. I just did wonder if the Green Lane lady could be Miss Garnett.'

'Right, well, let's look into that possibility,' agreed Pemberton. 'What did the present occupants have to say about it?'

'I can't get any answer, sir. I've been back several times and they won't answer the door. Loud music is sometimes playing but I'm sure they know I'm there, ringing the bell. They just refuse to respond.'

'You've never driven up in a police car or given them cause to believe you're a policewoman?'

'No, I've always been dressed like I am now. I could be anything from a woman doing a door-to-door washing-powder survey to a DSS investigator, but they clearly don't like strangers. The nearby neighbours know nothing about them, and don't know who the house belongs to. They thought it belonged to Miss Garnett when she was there but it seems it was rented.'

Pemberton's mind did a rapid assessment; he remembered Draper's unusual visit to the Incident Room, Moore's insistence on a flood of house-to-house enquiries during this curious exercise, and continuing hints that there was an IRA cell based in town . . . had Amanda stumbled upon precisely what Moore wanted?

'Amanda, this is good, an astute piece of deduction on your part. Stay behind when the others leave, you and I will discuss this with a few more teams. And the rest of you, off to your duties. And good luck.'

15

Detective Constable Amanda Wallbridge was twenty-seven years old and had been in the force for six years. After her two-year stint on the beat, she had been selected for CID training and was now showing her mettle. Alert and intelligent, she was a small and slender woman with a bob of short light-brown hair and a hint of freckles on her rather plain square face. For reading, she wore steel-rimmed granny specs and her hobbies, when she had time, were rambling, going to the theatre and listening to operatic music. She did not look at all like a police officer, especially when in her casual clothes, consequently Pemberton thought it odd that the people in St Joseph's Street had refused to open the door. She could have been a neighbour bidding welcome or wanting to borrow some Gold Blend.

'Tell me about 10 St Joseph's Street,' they sat in his office, each with a coffee as the door stood open. Friends and lovers in private, they were now professional colleagues.

'It's a large Victorian terrace-house,' she began. 'It's one of lots in Hemsworth which are used by students. They rent the houses, usually with four or five sharing the costs. But there are some privately occupied houses. It's a decent area, sir, not run-down although I'd say the people there were not wealthy. They're ordinary folk like bus-drivers, shop workers, council staff, factory operatives and so on.'

'I get the picture. So tell me about your calls.'

'I made my first visit the day before yesterday, I was alone. DS Harvey was doing the other side of the street; we were asking the standard questions. I got to Number 10 by about five thirty in the evening. The lights were on and I could hear the television, the *Neighbours* music came on while I was waiting at the door. I couldn't see inside, the curtains were drawn.'

'Were you at the back door?'

'Yes, in the backyard. Those houses all have backyards which are enclosed. The door leads into the kitchen, the kitchen light was on, but no one was in there. Anyway, I knocked and waited, but no one came. So I went away. I came back about an hour later and could hear voices. DS Harvey came to help, he knocked again but we got no response; no one even came to the door or shouted "Who's there?" or anything like that. So we tried the front door, it had a bell which did ring, we could hear it ringing inside, but no one came.'

'They might not have heard you, Amanda. It might be as simple as that. With noisy TV, people talking, it's easy to miss a knock on the door or a ringing doorbell.'

'We went back, several times. I *know* they were in. Anyway, because we got no response, I tried again yesterday. I'd completed my allocation of streets but went back during the daylight hours. I went back every hour between eleven and four yesterday – six times, and not once did they respond.'

'So then what did you do?'

'DS Harvey and I did a mini-house-to-house in the St Joseph's area; we learned they are not students. The local people don't often see them, although one said he's seen them leaving the house early in the mornings sometimes, as a group. Four men and a girl, they think. I couldn't get a description of the men except they're all youngish, under thirty. They don't dress like townspeople or even hikers, just jeans and trainers, sweaters or anoraks. There's one girl who does a bit of shopping. She is described as being white with very dark hair worn loose down to her shoulders, about twenty-five years old who dresses in jeans and bright sweaters, pillar-box red being one of her regulars. They don't go out to work and I did make local enquiries from the DSS, Job Centre and so on, but they don't appear to be on the register for the dole or other state handouts. They don't owe money – they pay cash for their groceries, and the poll tax for the quarter has been paid in cash. They asked to pay quarterly, by instalments. I checked with the Council. It seems they came here in June or July and poll-tax records show the house occupier as Eammon O'Brien.'

'And I suppose the girl speaks with an Irish accent?' he smiled.

'No, not according to the grocer. She has a Midlands accent, he felt.'

'So is it an IRA active-service unit, or people pretending to be IRA? What about a vehicle? Have they got transport?'

'We did a PNC check on all the cars parked in the back streets near the house, there are no garages to any of these houses. We could account for all of them, although they could be renting a garage in another part of town. But none of the locals has noticed a strange car in the street. I did ask at two local garages to see if they've been in for petrol but they couldn't help.'

'You have been busy!'

'You'd think, with five people living in a house for several months, somebody would know something about them. They are not complete hermits but they do seem to favour solitude and don't welcome visitors.'

'So are you suggesting these five are deliberately avoiding their neighbours, the police and other Nosy Parkers?'

'I started by being worried about Miss Garnett's disappearance, but it seems there could be something else, couldn't there? Like an IRA cell? I have heard the rumours.'

'Well done. It might be an active-service unit, looking for somewhere to plant a bomb or two this Christmas. That's a matter for the Special Branch, Amanda, so I'll inform Draper's office. If you have uncovered a possible IRA cell, then we all owe you a debt of gratitude. In the meantime, let's get back to our own enquiry. You mentioned a Miss Garnett?'

'Yes, she's gone. I did wonder if she is the Green Lane lady.'

'Right, that needs checking. If these peopole came and took over the house, they might have ousted the poor old thing. To be honest, I doubt it; they seem to be doing their best to avoid any kind of law-breaking or trouble, they do not want any sort of unwelcome attention so I don't think they'd do her in. But we must be certain. Check with the registrar of births and deaths to see if Miss Garnet has died recently or ask at the welfare services to see if she's in an old-folks' home. Find out who owns that house – try the income tax people or the Council, someone should know. Then we need to find out discreetly who the present occupants are. And do it now, Amanda, quick as you can but I'll get SB to do their bit as well. Don't return to the house. We don't want them to become wary of us – find out as much as you can about it from a distance. OK? And keep me informed of your progress. Right?'

'Yes, sir,' breathed Amanda Wallbridge and, having addressed him formally following his orders, she left to continue her exciting enquiries. Pemberton watched her walk across the Incident Room. She was an interesting woman and he wondered if her dedication had uncovered something important – lots of other detectives would not have bothered to return to that house time and time again. But Amanda was different from the others. He recalled Moore's words now – Moore had wanted concentrated house-to-house enquiries, so had he known this might occur? Were these people known to the security forces? Mark felt Moore had not told him everything.

Outside Number 16 Crowther Street, Detective Sergeant George Lloyd and DPC Don Kent waited for the postman. The small red van arrived and parked at the end of the street and they watched the postman's progress towards the front door, which he knocked.

An elderly lady opened it.

'Mrs Vincent?' asked the postman as he clutched a large Jiffy envelope.

'That's me,' she smiled as she signed the postman's register. The postman thanked her and slipped the register back in his bag. When he'd gone, Lloyd and Kent approached the house and knocked. Mrs Vincent came to the door once again, expecting to find that the postman had forgotten another package.

'We're police officers,' Lloyd introduced himself and Kent, each showing their warrant cards. 'We are interested in the parcel that has just arrived. Can we come in and inspect it?'

'Police?' a look of horror came upon her wrinkled face.

'There's no need to be alarmed, Mrs Vincent, it is just that parcel that interests us . . .'

'It's from Frank, my friend's boy, he often sends them here . . .'

'I know and I'm afraid we will have to confiscate it. We will give you a receipt . . . Now, if we can have the parcel . . .'

'Well, I don't know what Frank would say . . .'

'Neither do we, Mrs Vincent, but he does know we are picking it up, I can assure you. We have told him.'

'Oh, well, in that case I suppose it will be all right,' and she went into the house and returned with the huge Jiffy bag. They accepted it, gave her a receipt and left the old lady, intending to open it in the Incident Room.

*

With Pemberton looking on, Lloyd carefully loosened the flap and peered inside. There was a white plastic shopping bag without any logo and it contained a thick white woollen sweater. The disappointment showed on Lloyd's face, but Pemberton said, 'Try deeper inside. Don't touch the plastic, though, it might have his prints on it.'

And as Lloyd delved deep within the package, tucking his hands into the warm folds of the sweater, he found the money.

'It's packed with notes,' he said, beaming.

'Leave them, let SOCO open it, we need photographs of it and the contents, and a scientific analysis . . . I'll tell you what, George, we ought to have words with the POID about other raids, eh? They'll keep detailed records of these packages?'

'They're all listed, they're not supposed to be used for cash like registered letters, but folks use them to guarantee a delivery next day.'

'Which means the Post Office looks after them. So, when you've explained things to SOCO, have another word with your contact in POID, see if they have records of Special Delivery packets to this address on the dates of his other raids.'

'It's a hell of a risk, sending cash through the post!'

'It's better than risking prison if he's caught in possession, George. So this is great, well done. Ask the Post Office to check if similar parcels have been sent to other addresses too, from towns where raids have occurred. We might prove system here . . .'

'I've already asked them to do that, sir,' smiled Lloyd.

'Good man, well, look, you stick with Mayhew and the Shotgun Raider jobs. If he knows we've got him fair and square for this raid, he might tell us about the others.'

'He won't,' said Lloyd. 'He'll tell us nothing.'

'We can always try,' said Pemberton. 'Well, I must get cracking, it's news-conference time.'

Twenty minutes after the news conference had concluded, the constable on the reception desk buzzed Pemberton on the intercom.

'Sir,' he said, 'I've a Mr Fisher in reception, he wants to speak to you. It's urgent, he said, something to do with the murder enquiry.'

'OK, send him up.'

Fisher was heavily built and wearing a dark grey suit; bald with but wisps of greyish hair about his ears, he carried a brief-case and looked like a commercial traveller. Pemberton welcomed him and took him into his office, asking if he wanted a coffee. Fisher accepted.

'So, Mr Fisher, you've something to tell us?'

'Yes, I've found a gun, a shotgun, a sawn-off one, Superintendent.'

'My God, where?'

'In a barn, well out of town. It's on land owned by a Mr Reuben Close at Manor Farm, Rickaby. That's about six miles to the north-east.'

'A farmer, is he?'

'Yes, but the gun's not his, I asked him. He was there when I found it, so I said I'd report it. I read about you wanting to know about guns, in the paper it was.'

'Great, this is just what we want. So, how did you find it?'

'Mr Close is putting the old barn up for sale, he reckons it will convert into a house or a bungalow. I'm with Stapleton and Kitchen, the estate agents, you see, and was examining the barn with a view to handling the sale. It's full of junk actually, old ploughs, a tractor, bales of hay and so on, and on one of the high ledges, I noticed the gun. I pointed it out to Mr Close, I thought it was one of his that had been abandoned, so he took it down. He said it was a sawn-off shotgun and it wasn't his. We put it back. So here I am.'

'This is just what we've been looking for. Now, hang on, I'll see if I can raise Detective Sergeant Lloyd, he's out in his car somewhere. He's dealing with that aspect. Can you wait ten minutes?'

'Of course, I'll be pleased. So this is what an Incident Room looks like?'

'I'll show you around,' said Pemberton as a token of gratitude, 'although I know you'll realize there are some things we can't let the public see . . . Inspector, a moment, please,' and he beckoned to Larkin.

He asked Paul Larkin to raise George Lloyd over the air and order him back to the Incident Room. It looked as if Miller's gun might have been found, albeit doctored to produce the sawn-off barrel, although it might also be Mayhew's – had

Mayhew a local, secure hiding-place for the weapons he used on his raids? Did he pick it up before the event and return it afterwards? He was never found in possession of a sawn-off shotgun; his were always legitimate.

Lloyd would have to sort it out, bearing in mind it might be the murder weapon. By the time Pemberton had given Mr Fisher a cursory tour of the Incident Room, Detective Sergeant Lloyd had arrived. Pemberton asked him to accompany Mr Fisher back to the barn, to examine the scene and to seize the gun as evidence while ensuring it was preserved for finger-prints. If it was Miller's, it would probably have been cleansed of any identifying marks, and if it was Mayhew's, it would certainly have been cleaned.

'So,' said Pemberton, 'let Forensic have a look at it; they might tell us if it's been fired recently. I realize Miller's not your action, but Sally's busy with Miller right now and don't forget this gun could have been planted by Mayhew. He has never fired his gun, has he, during a raid?'

'Not that we know of, sir.'

'So if it has been fired recently, we are even more interested.'

'Yes, sir,' smiled Lloyd. Now, things were moving fast and moving in the right direction. 'Come along, Mr Fisher,' he invited. 'Show us what you've found.'

Detective Sergeant Sally Merston and DPC Alex Groves had revisited the Millers' home. Stanley George was out on his rounds, having made a determined effort to return to a normal way of life. Margaret, however, was at home this morning, for she had a late shift to work, beginning at three this afternoon. She let the two detectives into the scruffy kitchen, sweeping aside some dirty breakfast dishes and coffee-mugs.

'Coffee?' she asked.

'No thanks,' Sally did not relish the idea of using mugs from that table.

'Stanley's at work,' she said. 'He won't be back till late, he's in Northumberland today.'

'It's not Stanley we want, Mrs Miller,' Sally had not yet seated herself at the table. 'It's you. We need to discuss your where-abouts on the night Sheila Wynn disappeared.'

'I've already made a statement about that,' the stout little woman's eyes flashed with anger. 'I've told you all this. I was at home, here, all that evening. I never went out.'

'But we need proof, Mrs Miller, we are double-checking everyone's statements now, going into infinite detail. At what time did you come home?'

'My God, you lot never accept anybody's word for anything, do you? There's no wonder the police have a bad name . . . pry, pry pry . . .'

'Just answer the questions, please,' said Sally with her customary patience.

'I had been at work all day, a day shift, a long one. Like I told you, I got myself a take-away and came home.'

'Times, Mrs Miller, times please,' said Sally.

She sighed with a huge heave of her massive bosom. 'Eight. I finished at eight. I'd be at the take-away by, what, twenty-past or so. I got a Chinese, chow mein if you must know, and I ate it here with a glass of wine.'

'Do they know you at the take-away?'

'I should think so, I'm a fairly regular customer.'

'We'll check.'

'You do.'

'So you got home, what time?'

'Half-eight.'

'Alone, were you?'

'Yes, I've no feller, I don't bring lovers in when my husband's away. Besides, I'm not much of a glamour girl, am I?'

'So you ate your supper, then what?'

'Watched a bit of telly. After the news on the Beeb and a play, I went to bed. I didn't see the end of the play, *Winter Of Love* or something it was called, because I was shattered. So I turned in and read my book, I went upstairs just after ten. Read a few pages of my Catherine Cookson and crashed out. I did hear Stanley come in, but really I can't be specific about the time, except it was late, two or after.'

'Any callers?' Alex Groves put this question.

Margaret Miller hesitated just a fraction, but it was sufficient for Groves to realize she had to consider the question with care.

'We have been doing house-to-house enquiries around the town,' interrupted Groves in what sounded almost like a challenging tone. Mrs Miller recognized the power of those words; she lowered her head.

'I lied,' she said. 'Last time you saw me. I lied.'

'So who was the visitor?' Groves was tempted to thump the table-top as he shouted the question, for he had no idea there had even been a visitor. But his tiny ploy had worked – it would not have worked with a professional villain.

'Look, I know what you're going to think, but I assure you I had nothing to do with what happened afterwards . . .'

'Mrs Miller,' Groves' voice was softer now. 'Your visitor, who was it?'

'It was Sheila.'

'My God, she's dead and you told lies to us about her . . . Look, this is bloody serious, Mrs Miller. How could you lie about a thing like this?' Sally's exhortation filled the kitchen as she stamped around and around, her contempt for this fat woman overriding her usual calmness. 'Do you realize we have wasted hours trying to find out her last movements and now you tell us this . . . What time? What happened?'

'It was late,' Miller sat down and whispered . . . 'My God, I wish I hadn't . . . look, she came to the house. I was in bed, like I said, reading. It would be half-twelve or so, not any later, well, not much. A minute or two maybe. I heard the doorbell. At first, I thought Stanley had forgotten his key so I ignored it. He could sleep in the car, I thought, coming home that time of night. He needs teaching a lesson sometimes.'

'Were there lights on?' asked Groves.

'Lights? Yes. Downstairs, we leave them on until the last one's in bed. And my bedside light was on. Anyway, it rang again and so I looked out of my window. I saw her, standing there, under the light at the front door . . . She was crying.'

'Did you speak?'

'Before I could say anything, she saw me looking down, I'd moved the curtains, you see. She shouted up at me to let her in, she said she'd been thrown out and could she stay here . . .'

'And what did you do?'

'I told her to sod off,' said Margaret Miller. 'I told her she must sort out her own problems, and no cow like her was going to make a mug out of me . . .'

'And?'

'I went back to bed.'

'What did she do?'

'She rang the bell again, two or three times, then I heard her

walk away down the garden path. I never heard her again . . .
God, I wish I'd let her in, I really do, nobody deserves what
happened to her, nobody . . .'

'Did you tell your husband?'

Again, she hesitated. 'Yes,' she said. 'When he came in, I
went downstairs and told him Sheila had called, I said she
sounded distressed and was looking for shelter.'

'So what did he do?'

'He went out to look for her,' she spoke softly.

Sally Merston and Alex Groves looked at each other and it
was Sally who asked the obvious question.

'Did he take his gun?'

Margaret Miller's shock was evident in her eyes now.

'Gun? No, of course he didn't! He went to find her, to bring
her here, I said she could stay overnight, on the settee . . . he
just went out looking. I heard him return, oh, very late. Half-
past four or something, later even. I could tell he hadn't found
her, only one person came in. Him.'

'Why didn't he tell us he'd been looking for her?'

'I think he was frightened what you would think . . . we both
were . . . I mean, our Stanley would never harm her, never . . .'

'So,' said Alex Groves. 'Both of you have lied; if that had
been in court, it would have been perjury. As it is, it could
amount to an offence of wasting police time, so I need a full
statement from you, Mrs Miller, with everything, but before I
take it down in writing, I need to know one more thing, one
more piece of truth.'

'Yes?'

'Which of you shot Sheila Wynn?'

16

'We didn't shoot her, God, we wouldn't do that. I lied, I know
I shouldn't, I knew at the time but I couldn't help it . . .'

'Then where is the gun?' Sally put the question very softly.
'If we cannot account for the whereabouts of that shotgun, Mrs
Miller, you and your husband could find yourselves under
arrest on suspicion of murder. Already, the circumstantial

evidence against you is fairly strong, you especially in view of your possible motive . . . and you were the last person to see her alive, the last in our records, at any rate. Now, if we can trace the gun, and if we learn that it has not been fired recently, it could prove your innocence. It's vital that we know where it is. Do you understand?'

'I gave it away,' she said.

'Mrs Miller, it's lie after lie . . . Now, you say you gave away a gun? Who to, for God's sake?'

'A scrap-metal dealer, he came to the door asking if we'd got any old scrap metal so I gave him the gun.'

'To keep?'

'Yes, I wanted rid of it, I wanted it out of the house. I hate the things.'

'And you didn't tell your husband what you'd done, am I right?' interrupted Alex Groves.

She nodded. 'No, it had belonged to his father and, well, Stanley just wanted to keep it. He went about it the right way, got a certificate when his dad died, and so on. But he never had ammunition for it, he never used it. It was a keepsake really.'

'So why did you get rid of it? It wasn't yours to do that with, was it?'

'No, that's why I never told Stanley. I daren't, I knew he'd be upset, hurt, angry. I just took it out of the wardrobe one day and let the chap have it. Stanley never missed it.'

'How long ago was all this?' Grove continued.

'A long time, months. Eight or nine months maybe. I'd forgotten about it myself, I kept thinking I'd tell Stanley but, well, time slips away and I just never got round to it. You know how it is . . .'

'Why did you do this?'

'My brother. He comes to stay from time to time, He's, well, sick, mentally I mean. Suicidal at times. He knew the gun was in the house and on one occasion I found him playing with it, toying with it . . . well, I didn't want him buying any cartridges and injuring himself, or us. It was the sort of thing I thought he was capable of, so I got rid of the gun . . . Samuel, my brother that is, often stays.'

'OK, now, back to your husband. He came home from his conference in Lancashire after two o'clock, and went seeking Sheila?' Alex continued his questions. 'Did he take his car?'

'Yes, he did.'

'That means he would cover a lot of ground in and around the town. So what time is he due back from his rounds today?'

'I don't know, it's usually around six or six-thirty unless he tells me different.'

'Then we will call back. Now, I need a written statement from you detailing everything you have just told me.'

'Yes, all right. Look, I'm sorry I was not truthful before . . .'

'Then let's be sure you include everything in the statement, Mrs Miller. The lot, everything that you know about Sheila Wynn, your husband's relationship with her and what happened on the night in question, what you did with the gun, who the scrappie was that you gave it to so we can find him . . . For, as they say, the truth will out, you know.'

'I know,' she said with a certain resignation.

By lunch-time on that third day, the effects of the continuing enquiries were increasing the clear-up rate of crimes and offences around the town. A total of twenty-one defendants had appeared before the magistrates that morning on various charges as a direct result of the aftermath of the drugs raid on Pennine Flats.

The big fish, Patrick Roe, however, was not among them for he was already on remand on more serious charges relating to controlled drugs.

The police wanted him to be tried at Crown Court and so the Crown Prosecution Service was compiling the necessary file of evidence.

Two more burglars, a pair of brothers, had been arrested; they had found themselves under suspicion of murder because of their unexplained absence from home on the night that Sheila Wynn disappeared. Their mother thought they'd been to a party and told the police that; the police had checked the story to learn there'd never been a party and so the lads had found themselves sweating before two determined detectives. Rather than face a grilling about the murder, they had admitted burgling two old-folks' bungalows to steal a mere £15. And they also asked for fifteen similar offences to be taken into consideration, all at old-folks' private houses. It was a good result for the detectives, and it would also make an impact on the monthly crime-detection figures, apart from reassuring the public that the police did get results.

But the surprise catch was Councillor Raymond Hogbin, the Chairman of the Council.

'So what have you got on him?' Mark Pemberton asked Detective Constable Ted Wilson.

'It followed from the raid on the brothel in the hotel, sir,' he said. 'We traced those schoolgirls, Hogbin was visiting one of them, photographing her in scanty underwear, naked in the bath and having sex with her. He's been at it with boy scouts too . . . for years, it seems.

'He's been giving money to kids from the council flats, from Pennine Flats among them, no wonder he was sweating at our interest in the place.'

'Is the evidence sound? Kids can be a problem.'

'I think it will stand up in court, sir, but we've a lot of work ahead. But we've nailed him and I thank God for that. We've got a confession out of him, by the way, he's in the nick now.'

'Does the Press know?'

'No, sir.'

'Then I might just arrange a leak at an opportune moment,' smiled Pemberton. 'Great stuff – is this child-porn ring very widespread?'

'We've got a mailing list from Hogbin's flat, sir, there's over a hundred local folks getting filth through the post, it turns out he's the distributor. So much for caring councillors helping the downtrodden of our society . . . and he was even nicking official envelopes to mail the stuff! We found a pack of 500 buff ones with the Council logo on, in his flat. If nothing else, we can get him for theft of those. He lived there alone, by the way, a bit of a weirdo by all accounts. His mother died eight or nine years ago.'

'Great. That's the sort of villain an enquiry like this brings in, and so it should. Right, make sure the case is watertight, we don't want him wriggling out of this one. I think I'll tell Councillor Ruddock about this, it will give me great pleasure to break the news to him. It'll let the Chairman of the Police Authority know we *are* doing some good and productive police work!'

Pleased at this development, Pemberton went into his office and called in Inspector Larkin. Paul updated him on the current

138

developments, including the interview with Mrs Miller and he said:

'Right, Paul, we need a time-chart, eh? Showing Sheila's movements. Can we do that? Make good use of HOLMES. We know she was alive at 12.30 a.m. three days ago, that's Monday morning. Downes said he searched the town between 1 a.m. and 6 a.m., and now we know Miller went looking for her between 2.30 a.m. and 4 a.m. or so, according to his wife. He used his car, and he'll have to be seen. Where did they search? Did Miller and Downes meet each other during that search? When did Sheila die? Where did she die? How was her body transported? She wasn't found until 5.30 p.m., so was she lying in that beck all day?

'Now, Miller. We have him sighted at Pennine Flats around 2 a.m., at home about 2.30 a.m. and back in the town until after 4 a.m. Downes's search isn't confirmed at all, he just says he went out looking at 1 a.m. and kept searching till 6 a.m., making himself late for work. He doesn't know where he went – then he found the other body.'

'I'll do a time-chart for her, too, sir, but we've nothing much there. Courting couples were in the lane till 11 p.m., they saw nothing until Downes found her. No one on a passing train saw anything . . . this one's drawn a blank.'

'OK, so make a chart for her as well,' agreed Pemberton, who had almost forgotten about that corpse. 'Dredge HOLMES for additional links between the two, other than Downes. Where's he today?'

'On a milk run, sir, Daniels and Watson are going to have him in when he gets back, to talk about the bruises on Sheila's body.'

'Make sure they ask him if he saw Miller in town that night. Get him to say exactly where he was during the search, you'd think they'd have met, eh?'

'Yes, sir, they must have checked the same places, you'd think. Now, there is another thing. Lieutenant Colonel Abrahams. I rang Nottingham to check him out. He's a con-man, sir, he's well known to them.'

'Oh, bloody hell.'

'He's had us up the proverbial creek! Every time he reads about an unidentified middle-aged or elderly woman lying dead, he goes to see the body, claiming it might be his long-lost sister, Elspeth. It never is; it seems he did have such a sister who died years ago. He never got to the funeral, and never accepted she'd died; he was in Burma at the time. He was a corporal, by the way, he's never been a commissioned officer but did well in business after the War. Hotels, I think. He still believes Elspeth may be alive and is always looking for her and so a prosecution for wasting police time would hardly seem apt.'

'The silly old buffer! But what about the car firm he complained about?'

'Cherryspink? They're real enough, sir, and so is Stuart Bass, but he doesn't know the old man and never married his sister.'

'Then why did he pick on them?'

'I asked Nottingham Police about that aspect – he always seems to pick on a company local to the deceased person, sir. They think he gleans information about the bosses from the financial pages and claims that any successful man is a villain who had his evil way with his sister years ago. A lot of forces have fallen for his tales, if that's any consolation.'

'He should be locked up,' said Pemberton.

'I think Bass became very worried, sir,' grinned Larkin. 'When our lads got there this morning at half-eleven, he did a cover-up job, it seems he's knocking off his secretary and had to do a rapid check in his diary to prove his whereabouts over the last few days . . . But he'd never heard of Elspeth and his family have no known links with Abrahams or any of his sisters or relations. We've no reason to link him in any way with our murders. He seems a normal businessman but he might be worthy of a closer look, and the old codger, well, he's a nutter who likes looking at dead women.'

'So where's the old man now?'

'Driving back to Nottingham in his lovely old car.'

'So, he'll be awaiting another dead old lady, eh? It's been a trip out for him and who knows, we might get something from Cherryspink Motor Group after all. It's amazing the muck we turn up in a murder enquiry. We should consider charging him with wasting police time. I'll think about that. So who have we still got as a possible name for the Green Lane woman?'

'Just Miss Garnett, sir. Amanda's chasing that one. We keep getting possible names, but can rule a lot out by their physical characteristics. We had one name a couple of hours ago, a man looking for his wife who'd cleared off and left him fifteen years ago. But she had only three toes on one foot.'

'Great. So the homing pigeons are slowly returning to roost, aren't they, Paul.'

'We do seem to be making some modest progress, sir.'

'Indeed we are. At first, it seems to be all questions, questions and questions, but now we're getting some answers. Not always the right ones, mind, but they are coming in. And when every question's got an answer, we can chuck it all in, eh? And we need more answers from Harry Downes, don't we? Is he still Number One?'

'Yes, he's leading the field, Miller's dropped in the frame.'

'And Mrs Miller?'

'Well down the list but still in the running. After all, she does have a motive. And Mayhew's still there, but he's well down the list, although he was seen moving his furniture.'

'Anything on that found gun yet?'

'SOCO have it in for fingerprinting, sir.'

'Any sign of it having been fired recently?'

'Apparently not, sir, the barrel looked as if it has never been used for ages. There was dust inside, years of it by all accounts, but not necessarily from that barn. I reckon some other villain dumped it there. Not Mayhew.'

'Has Mayhew been questioned about that gun? Or his possible involvement in the murders?'

'Not yet, sir, not until we get the fingerprint results in. If we're to interview him, we need sound facts to go on.'

'That makes sense. Now, what about Mayhew's own guns?'

'Negative, sir, none's been fired for years. They're mainly antiques, good-value guns, not nicked either, a nice collection. I don't think we can lay murder on his doorstep.'

'OK, well done. So we are making progress. Right, well, I'm off for a sandwich and a pint. See you after lunch.'

At the Yard, a fingerprint officer from the Eighth Floor was waiting for Wilf Draper's meeting to break for lunch.

'Mr Draper, those prints you left us. It's going to be a long job, I'm afraid, longer than we thought. There's nothing in our current files so it means a search in the basement, through old records. It'll take a day or two.'

'That's fine, I can wait.'

'Am I right in thinking the subject has been murdered?'

'Yes, she was found dead on our patch the day before yesterday, strangled or smothered, naked as the day she was born. Dumped from a vehicle, we think. The local lads haven't an identity for her, but don't think she's from the area.'

'Our Chief asked me to confirm that. OK, we'll be in touch, probably in a day or two.'

'Thanks', and Wilf Draper went off to have a pint in Scotland Yard's bar, the so-called Goldfish Bowl, with his colleagues. He was pleased the Eighth Floor hadn't quickly dismissed his request and it was interesting to know that they were taking the trouble to delve into their old records. They went back years.

17

Amanda Wallbridge had little trouble locating Miss Garnett. Enquiries to the Social Services Department quickly produced the old lady's name and the fact that she was alive and well and currently residing in an old-folks' council home. She had been admitted because, having reached the age of eighty-four, she was incapable of caring for herself. Her grandnephew had not objected.

This was good news for Amanda because it meant that the Green Lane victim was not Miss Garnett; nonetheless Amanda went along to the Andrew Nicholls Home for the Elderly. The matron was understanding and said Miss Garnett was in the lounge, but said that it was not very easy to communicate with her due to her senility. Amanda therefore explained her request to the matron.

She replied, 'Her rent was paid through her bank, Miss Wallbridge. Miss Garnett is a lady of means, as they say, although she never owned her home. It was paid to Ellis's, they're the estate agents in Grosvenor Street, and they operate on behalf of the owner. I understand her grandnephew has taken over the tenancy, at least temporarily, while he seeks work. His name is O'Brien, Eammon O'Brien, he does visit her.'

'He sounds like an Irishman?' Amanda commented.

'I don't think he is,' returned the matron. 'I believe he's from the Midlands, the Birmingham area, although I confess I do not know much about him.'

'Can I speak to Miss Garnett?'

'Of course.'

The matron led Amanda into the lounge which bore the unmistakeable scent of old folks and introduced her to a very stooped lady seated in a high chair. Amanda shook the proffered, frail hand and sat opposite Miss Garnett. Miss Garnett had a pinched face which was surprisingly pink and smooth, with bright blue eyes and an engaging smile. She was very deaf and Amanda found it difficult asking questions, but she did learn that Eammon was her sister's grandson. Her sister was Mrs Edith O'Brien, her son was Joseph and Eammon was his eldest boy. A nice lad, very kind to her. No, they were not Irish, they lived in Birmingham . . . no, she had no idea who Eammon's friends were . . . Eammon used to work in a hotel on the catering side . . . yes, it was in Birmingham she thought . . . no, he had no job now . . . he and his friends wanted to work here, so they'd taken over the house, and the furniture . . . she had let them have it all, she had no use for it now and no other relations . . .

Miss Garnett was helpful and Amanda gained the impression that she had no idea she was talking to a detective, even though Amanda had taken care to stress that.

The outcome was that Amanda had confirmed an important name which she could pursue through her own channels. She returned to the Incident Room, gave details to Inspector Larkin for inclusion in the growing mass of data stored in HOLMES, and asked the computer to check that name against other entries. There was no other O'Brien in the system.

'Ring Birmingham,' Larkin told her. 'Ask for CID, see if they know the name.'

Detective Sergeant Bidwell in Birmingham said he'd check and ring back in about an hour. In the meantime, Amanda wrote up her own information in the form of a statement so that it could be logged in the file, indexed and double-checked with HOLMES. Pemberton came to see how she had progressed and after hearing her story, said,

'It looks as though we'll have to mount covert observations

on that house, I think. Things don't seem normal there, Amanda, we need to know more about the occupants. Maybe you and I should volunteer to do the job?' he smiled at the suggestion and implications. She did not respond! 'I'm sure they're not linked to our murders, but they do appear to be worth investigating. As soon as you get a reply from Birmingham, let me know the result. If it means Special Branch involvement, we'll have to turn the enquiry over to Draper, although he's away today. We can wait till he returns.'

Bidwell rang from Birmingham within the hour and told Amanda that she had scored a bull's-eye.

Intelligence from various parts of the West Midlands Police area and further afield, had shown that O'Brien and a cell of four others were suspected of a long series of acts of sabotage.

'They're extreme left-wingers,' he said. 'Fanatics, obsessed by a drive against capitalism. We've not once secured a conviction against them – they're a small, highly effective outfit comprising a rat-bag of disaffected socialists from the Workers' Revolutionary Party and their ilk. They attack public utilities which have just been privatized or which are on line for privatization. They're not IRA in spite of O'Brien's name, but like people to think they are. It's almost certain that some of their sabotage has been blamed on the IRA, if only in public opinion. They were suspected of damaging rural telephone exchanges while British Telecom was being privatized; a gas mains went up with a hell of a bang near Shrewsbury and they were in the vicinity of an explosion at Manchester Airport just after British Airways was de-nationalized. And now, with water and electricity being recently privatized, and other public services in line, they're operating again. They laid low for a while and we lost track of them. They've money, God knows where from, and they move around the country to strike their targets. They're known to use violence but no convictions have been secured against them. So, Miss Wallbridge, it seems to me that you could have a problem on your patch unless your lads do something to stop them.'

'I'll inform my Super,' said Amanda.

'Isn't the PM visiting your patch soon?'

'He is, the day after tomorrow in fact.'

'Then your men will have to be alert, they're not in your town for the good of their health, nor to enjoy the countryside. They mean business, nasty business.'

'Thanks for that. Do you have all their names?'

'Sure, got a pencil?'

'Yes, I'm ready.'

'OK. The leader is the one you mentioned, Eammon O'Brien born 12.3.1962, 6 feet 4 inches, dark brown hair, brown eyes. He is an ex-IRA operator who got sickened off when the IRA started killing innocent civilians and babies. He turned to having a go at the Government in this way.'

'Right.'

'Next, Darren Smith born 5.4.63, 5 feet 8 inches, light brown hair, brown eyes, an ex-British soldier, he's their explosives man. Then Terence Baker, a one-time bouncer in a night-club, born 23.11.63, 5 feet 8 inches, dark hair, blue eyes, and Roderick Taylor, born 14.8.64, 5 feet 9 inches, fair hair, blue eyes. He's never had a job that we know about, he was recruited from the dole queue. They're the Mr Fixits, going out on recce parties, obtaining things like vehicles, ladders, or whatever they need for their raids. The *femme fatale* of the group is Tracy Shields, born 16.7.63, 5 feet 3 inches, blonde hair worn long, blue eyes, who once worked for ICI as a secretary.

'She met O'Brien through an event they both attended – he's the brains behind the outfit. They call themselves CLAP – Citizens' League Against Privatization – but their wider recruiting attempts have not been the success they wanted. They're still a small outfit. That's how we know of them – they tried to recruit an undercover detective, an SB man who was watching them! And he's still around to tell the tale.'

'How do they operate?' asked Amanda.

'They always go for government property which is recently privatized or about to become so. They used the anti-poll-tax feeling to vent their anger on some council properties which were being sold off to private enterprise. And they've one major fault – they try to let the public think it's the work of the IRA, which doesn't please our friends across the Irish Sea. They do not court publicity for their actions, they operate very secretly and so far as we are aware, they do not know that we have any information about them and their antics. O'Brien is a clever tactician, he's no fool, he learnt a lot while working with the

IRA. Now, Miss Wallbridge, that is briefly what we have on your new friends.'

Amanda had managed to make a note of all these factors and told the detective she would pass the information immediately to her boss. She was wise enough to realize that intelligence of this kind was not for young officers to cope with and so, after thanking Bidwell, went to seek Pemberton.

Mark listened intently, muttered something like 'Oh, God, what next?' and in view of the security problems thus presented, said he'd have to have words with Goddard about his two suspects. In the circumstances, he repeated his instruction that Amanda keep away from 10 St Joseph's Street and suggested she spend some time in the Incident Room. She could sift through the gathered mass of information to see if those five suspects had cropped up elsewhere during the current murder enquiries. That way, he could watch her at work. The notion pleased him. Now he must update the Chief.

Pemberton buzzed the Chief Constable's secretary on the intercom and asked for an urgent meeting with him. Moore, just back from a late lunch, agreed and told him to come immediately.

'Well, Superintendent, what is your news?' he asked as Mark entered his office. Today, Moore wore a smart lovat-green suit with a white shirt and dark green tie, and his black hair was as immaculately groomed as ever.

Mark explained and Moore listened without a word and then beamed. 'Mark, this justifies everything! This is precisely what I wanted. It absolves us from any criticism should the exercise go wrong . . . it is tremendous news. It means we can clear the scene before Mr Major arrives. This really is tremendous stuff, so leave this with me. I must contact the security services before we make any further moves. I'll be in touch.'

'Should we be keeping tabs on them, sir? I mean, if they are active, they could be planning something or putting one of their schemes into operation right now.'

'Exactly, Mark, and this is a job for the SAS or the security forces, not the police. Leave it with me, I'll be in touch. Now, is anyone pestering them now? Trying to reach them?'

'No, sir, I've called off my teams.'

'Good, then keep them away; they mustn't even get a hint that we're interested in them.'

'Understood, sir,' and Mark took his leave to return to his Incident Room.

At about the same time, Detective Chief Inspector Wilf Draper was leaving Scotland Yard for his long journey home by train, albeit without any results from his fingerprint request. He made a mental note to attend the CID conference at the Incident Room in the morning.

Also at the same time, Detective Sergeant Sally Merston and Detective Constable Alex Groves had a small success. Following Margaret Miller's claim that she had given the shotgun to a scrap-merchant, the two detectives began visiting those who operated in the town, commencing with those who travelled from house to house. Several did this.

The scrap-merchants toured a given district to drop leaflets through letter boxes asking that scrap metal be ready for collection two or three days later. On only their third visit, Sally and Alex produced a result. The place of trading was called Montgomery's Yard and the boss was Nathan Montgomery. When he saw the detectives arrive in their small car, he thought he was to be subjected to a quarterly inspection of his records at the least or a search for stolen scrap at the worst.

'Hello, Nathan,' greeted Sally.

'Hello, Miss Merston, when I saw you coming, I thought this was another raid.'

'Now, why should we raid an honest and upright citizen like you, Nathan? No, it's not a raid, it's just an enquiry.'

'Ah, so you want information? I'm not a grass, you know.'

'It's a murder enquiry, Nathan, therefore serious. Now, we're looking for a shotgun and a Mrs Miller who lives in Westfield Road, number 18, tells us she gave you one. It was when you called for scrap. Eight or nine months ago, it would be.'

Nathan had no idea whether he was suspected of being a killer or whether the gun had been used to kill somebody before he'd acquired it, and so he was not sure how to respond. Being a devious character, he always scented trouble even when it did not exist and rarely admitted anything. Sally recognized his hesitation and reassured him.

'Nathan,' she said. 'I'm not suggesting you have killed anybody, so don't look so worried. It's that Wynn murder, the woman found dead at Blue Beck the other day. We just want to eliminate Miller's gun, that's all.'

'So it wasn't hers that was used then?'

'No, we don't think so. It couldn't be, if you've got it, could it? We want to be sure, you see. We want to know if Mrs Miller's telling the truth about its whereabouts.'

Nathan understood now.

'Oh,' he said. 'Right, yes. I remember it, it's not often I get guns handed to me.'

'Tell me what happened, Nathan,' invited Sally as Alex watched. Alex wondered if a male detective would have been so successful in getting Nathan to co-operate.

'Well, it's not hard to remember. I was doing my rounds, like I always does, I'd left leaflets earlier and followed 'em up with the waggon, collecting. This woman asked if I'd take a gun away so I had a look at it, it wasn't much of one, Miss Merston, not a Purdy or owt like that if you know what a Purdy is, but I took it off her hands. For nowt. She just wanted shot . . . shot, eh? Funny that, eh? A joke! Anyroad, she wanted shot of it and so I took it. There was no ammo, nowt like that. So I put it in the cab.'

'And what did you do with it?'

'Do with it? I kept it. I've got a certificate, you know, for shotguns. Your uniform lads will know that, they check it now and then. I need a shotgun here, for rats and vermin.'

'We'd like to take it for forensic examination, Nathan, to eliminate it. We'll give you a receipt and let you have it back when we've done – now, have you fired it recently?'

'As a matter of fact I haven't, not yet, not at all. OK, pleased to help, it's in the office.'

He led them into his dirty and untidy office and from a steel cabinet, which he unlocked, he produced the gun. Groves accepted it, checked that it was not loaded and thanked him. He issued a small receipt which he handed to Nathan.

On the return journey to the Incident Room, Sally said to Alex Groves,

'So this means Mrs Miller was telling the truth, Alex,' she mused. 'And that suggests she did not kill Sheila Wynn because she'd got rid of the weapon a long time before the murder. And therefore it is equally unlikely that Stanley Miller killed her because he didn't have his gun either.'

'So that puts old Harry Downes even higher in the frame, doesn't it?' said Alex.

'I wonder how Roger and John are getting on?' smiled Sally. 'The last time I saw them, they were trying to trace Sheila Wynn's movements after visiting Margaret Miller, but weren't having much success.'

Detective Sergeant Roger Daniels and Detective Constable John Watson had had very little success. The news of Sheila Wynn's visit to the Miller home around 12.30a.m. on the night of her disappearance had added to their list of sightings, but no one seemed to have seen her after that. Dennis Lewis, the landlord of the Black Lion, couldn't help. The detectives felt sure that the pub would have been one of the first places she'd have sought shelter or help, but according to Dennis she had not called there. He did say, however, that shortly after 12.30a.m., someone had hammered for a long time on the back door, but everyone was in bed and no one had replied. He'd never looked out and the knocking had soon stopped. People did tend to hammer on pub doorways at nights, drunks especially. They came, trying to get in by asking for extra drinks and so such nuisance visitations were generally ignored.

From a long list of acquaintances and friends the detectives had visited, none acknowledged that Sheila had sought their help that night. And then came the stroke of fortune. Roger Daniels was chatting to a taxi-driver called Gerry Wake outside the railway station, explaining the extent of their enquiries and the driver said, 'Sure, pal, I saw a woman that night. Chatting to a bloke in a car, she was. She had a red sweater on, or a red coat or something, blonde. I thought she was a kerb-crawler, that she was after picking up a client.'

'Young?' asked Roger.

'No, knocking on a bit. Brassy, mutton dressed as lamb I'd say.'

'Where was this?'

'Not far from the Black Lion, in the same street, outside the cleaners. The cleaners' window lights were on, that's how I saw her.'

'Time?' asked Roger.

'Late, after half-twelve. Twenty to or a quarter to one mebbe. I was due to knock off at one, and was on my way back to base to do a last call. A short run. I remember because I thought how daft for a woman to be alone like that in the street at that time of night, it looked as if she was cadging a lift. I never saw what happened after that because I passed on.'

Roger knew that it took three minutes brisk walking time from the Millers' house to the Black Lion, and only a minute or so from there to the dry-cleaners. The timing was about right.

'This is great, Gerry. I can't be sure it was Sheila but the time and description does fit. So the chap? What was he like? Or his car?'

'He was in the driving-seat, sergeant, so I didn't get a good look. I was heading towards him, mind, and I'd say he was in his late thirties mebbe, with dark hair, a bit thin on top. He looked tall, his head was near the roof, if you understand.

'The car was modern, clean and in good nick by the look of it. In the artificial light, it was hard to say what colour it was, a light one, tan mebbe, or off white, yellow even or light green, that kind of range. I'd say it was a Vauxhall Nova or something similar. It had lights on, headlights burning. He had a light top on, a pale blue I think, sweater mebbe, or light jacket of some kind. She was on the pavement, the door was open on that side, the passenger side, and she was bent down talking. I mean, Sergeant, I didn't take particular notice . . .'

'You've done well, Gerry. This could be the last sighting of her alive. So all we've got to do is find that man. Do you think he was local, Gerry?'

'Well, I have seen that car around at night, sergeant, quite often. It's one of those you often see but don't take much notice of, if you know what I mean. But I don't know who it belongs to. If I see him around again, I'll jot his number down, shall I? Then give you a bell?'

'That would be perfect,' smiled Roger Daniels.

18

When Harry Downes returned home after finishing his run, the CID were waiting.

'Can't you buggers leave me alone?' he unlocked his back door and they followed him in. 'It's bad enough losing her, but having you sods on my backs all the time . . . you might at least give me time to get in and get the kettle on . . .'

'Harry, I know you want us to catch Sheila's killer and we can't do it without your co-operation,' Roger Daniels said. 'So, the sooner we get this over, the sooner we can get off your back. Now, first things first. Your car. Forensic have done their stuff and I thought you'd like to know it's clean, no blood, no evidence of it being used to transport a body. From your point of view, that's good news.'

'That's what I told you all along! So what about that other body, am I clear of doing her an' all?'

'We have never suspected you of harming that woman . . .'

'God! I hate to think what you'd have done if you had suspected me. Who is she, then? Haven't you got her named yet?'

'No, not yet, nor have we traced her killer. So, back to Sheila. You've been away? We've been looking for you.'

'Away? I haven't, just doing my job, that's all.'

'Right, now, we've been making enquiries around the place, about you and your life with Sheila. A bit stormy, wasn't it?'

'No more than other married folks,' he grunted. 'You know that anyway, I've admitted I clouted her sometimes.'

'So we want you to tell us once again about the night she left home.'

'Again?' Harry sat down at the kitchen table, 'I've told you God knows how many times.'

'But we want you to go over it again, Harry, minute by minute from the time she came through that door.'

Patiently, Harry repeated his story, struggling at times to recall precisely what he'd said on the earlier occasions, but the two silent detectives let him ramble on without any prompting.

He concluded by saying, 'I told her what I thought of her and she went, like I said.'

'What was she wearing, Harry?'

'That red coat, the short one . . . I can't remember what colour shoes or skirt, dark I think. A white blouse.'

'It was a fine night, then?'

'Aye, surprisingly mild for the time of year. No frost. No rain . . . not Christmassy at all.'

'Weren't you worried about her being alone, at night, without any real warm clothing in December?'

'Course I was. I went looking, all bloody night!' he shouted.

'So how did she leave? Was she crying? Did she run away? Did you chase her out, Harry? Bully her out of the door, thumping her perhaps as she tried to prevent you . . .?'

'Beating her up? Are you bastards saying I beat her up? Are you saying I killed her by bashing her up?'

'We found bruises all over the upper part of her body, Harry. Lots of them, on her upper arms, torso, stomach. Big bruises, the sort you'd get from fists, from a pummelling . . .'

'I never laid hands on her, not that night, anyroad.'

'The neighbours said you did beat her, she's complained at times, but she didn't leave you, did she? She must have loved you, Harry . . . now, listen, we have forensic scientists available who have carried out a very careful examination of Sheila and they say she had been soundly beaten before she died . . . before she was shot.'

'I had to force her out,' he said weakly.

'Force her out?' queried Daniels.

'She wouldn't go, I was mad at her . . . I chucked her out.'

'How do you mean, Harry? Chucked her out?'

'I . . . well, I mean, er . . . I ordered her out, she wouldn't go, we shouted and swore, she was hitting me, lashing out all the time, flying at me for saying she'd been with that other chap . . . so I opened the door and tried to push her out . . . she refused. I clouted her, *yes I bloody clouted her*, so there! She deserved it, she deserved more, the cow . . .'

'How did you clout her, Harry? With anything you'd picked up? Fists? How many times did you hit her?'

'Fists,' he whispered. 'I just bundled her out, lashing out at her while she had a go at me . . . don't know how many times I hit her . . . she fought like a bloody tiger, trying to stay in the house but, well, I'm a big chap and I got her out, bundled her out, she was crying then but I slammed the door and locked it. I never looked out again.'

'So you lied to us, Harry?' the chill in Daniels' voice was all the more threatening as Harry began to sob. The huge man buried his head in his folded arms on the table and began to weep.

'But I never killed her, I loved her . . .'

They waited as he regained some of his composure and then Daniels resumed.

'What time was all this, Harry?'

'After midnight, just before half-twelve, I told you that.'

'But you've lied once, Harry, you might have told more lies. You lied about finding the other body, didn't you? You said Sheila would confirm your story about being late for work, but she was already dead, wasn't she? You knew that, you tried to pretend she was still alive, didn't you? By trying to trick us . . .'

'I didn't know that, did I? How could I know she was dead then? God, I'd searched everywhere, I thought she was shacking up with a fancy man or something, gone back to the pub mebbe.'

'But you lied, Harry. You were covering up and if we told that to a court of law, to a jury, what would they think? They'd think you had killed her, that you had chased her out of the house while attacking her and that your attack might have got out of hand, that you had a gun somewhere and used that, then spent the night getting rid of the body, Harry . . .'

'What do I have to do to convince you blokes I didn't do her in . . .'

'Just tell the truth, Harry, that's all. Right from the start. So, shall we begin again? The truth in every word, Harry.'

Detective Constable John Watson brewed a cup of tea in Harry's kitchen and gave a steaming mugful to the tanker-driver with some for himself and Daniels. Harry was now more composed as he sat opposite Daniels who now had a statement form on the table. Harry had decided to tell the truth about his violent attacks upon Sheila, attacks that he could not control when his anger grew black and deep, and so he told them about his earlier attacks upon her, always when he was dog-tired, always when he thought she'd been unfaithful . . .

It was a moving confession of his domestic violence towards

Sheila and it culminated in that terrible row on the night she disappeared.

Having admitted his assault upon her he stoutly denied killing her and he stoutly denied using a gun.

'Now, Harry,' Daniels' voice was softer at this stage. 'You went out looking for her? Tell us about that? What time did you begin?'

'One o'clock or thereabouts. I waited for her to come back, waited for her knocking to come in, but she didn't. I'd cooled down by then, you see, and knew I'd been too hard on her, she'd only been working late . . . so I got the car out and went into town. I drove round for ages, walked a lot, asking at all-night cafés, checking at the bus station and railway-station buffet, the Black Lion but they were all in bed and the lights were out, I went to Miller's house but got no reply . . .'

'What time were you there?'

'Late, after two I think, there was a downstairs light on, but I got no reply. People often leave lights on at night, and then I thought if she was there, they wouldn't have answered my knocking anyway.'

'But you weren't sure she was there, were you, because you continued searching all night, so you told us before.'

'Well, I thought if she had gone there, and got no reply like I did, because they were out, she might have gone somewhere else. I didn't know many of her haunts, I thought she might be wandering round so I thought I'd check the streets until I found her . . .'

'Did you talk to anybody?'

'Yes, a few. A policeman in fact, standing on the corner of Blenheim Place. I asked him if he'd seen her, he said no. I asked at that all-night garage in Crossfield Road, the attendant hadn't seen her, then a customer from the Black Lion pulled in, Paddy he's called. I'd seen him there sometimes, chatting her up but he hadn't seen her. I asked a few taxi-drivers, but they said she'd not taken one to go anywhere.'

'What about Miller? Did you bump into him that night, in town?'

'Miller? No. Why?'

'He went out looking as well.'

'He did? How did he know she was locked out?'

'She called at Miller's house, not much later than half-twelve.

154

Miller wasn't home, he'd had a late conference in Manchester, but Mrs Miller saw Sheila.'

'Saw her?'

'Mrs Miller was in bed, she looked out of the window and saw Sheila at the door, but told her to clear off. Sheila went, and then Mrs Miller regretted it, she thought Sheila was in need of help. So when Miller returned, about half-past two, his wife told him of Sheila's call, and said she could stay on the settee if Stan could find her. He went looking as well, so he says, until about half-past four. In his car.'

'It's a big town,' said Harry. 'I never saw him.'

'OK, so this all-night garage, Harry, would the attendant remember you calling?'

'I would think so.'

'What time would that be?'

'Quarter to two I'd say, summat like that.'

'We'll have to check.'

'I hope you do, then you'll know I'm not lying.'

By closely questioning Harry about his movements that night, the two detectives did eventually glean a lot of information; Harry had been able to recall several of the places he'd visited, and they would now be checked. The people who worked nights there might be able to prove Harry's innocence.

'So, when you'd finished searching, then what?'

'I came home, parked the car and had a quick wash and shave, and something to eat, then went to the tanker to start work. I was late by then, like I said, and, well, I took that short cut and found that other woman . . . it was unbelievable . . .'

'It must have been a shock,' said Daniels.

'You can imagine what I thought when I first set eyes on her, in the headlights . . . I thought it was Sheila . . . I honestly did . . . so when I stopped and found it wasn't, God, was I relieved . . .'

'And we have grilled you about that too, haven't we?'

'I never knew I'd be going through all this, honest, it's bloody terrible . . . I've not slept a wink since . . .'

'OK Harry, we'll leave you now. Now look, if you think of anything else you've forgotten, folks you met that night and haven't told us about, people calling on Sheila, ringing her up, that sort of thing, enemies she might have . . . give up a call. It is in your own interest, you know, unlike lying all the time . . .'

155

'Aye, right,' said Harry Downes, who was too exhausted physically and mentally to see them off his premises.

'What do you think?' asked Daniels of his partner as they drove away.

'I don't think he did her in, Sarge,' admitted John Watson. 'He lied, but a lot of fellers would in his circumstances. Would you admit thrashing your missus if she'd been found dead a few hours later? I think he's just been caught in a bloody awful web.'

'But he's still Number 1 in the frame, according to the lads. And he is one link between the two bodies.'

'Even so, in my view, he's done neither of them in, and that means we've no real suspect in the frame,' said John Watson. 'I don't think Harry did either of them in, I don't think Miller did, or Mrs Miller or Mayhew, so who else is there?'

'Search me. Come along, let's see if we can find that petrol-pump attendant before we knock off.'

Having spent time interrogating HOLMES and reading through the statement file in the Incident Room while enjoying a coffee with Pemberton, Amanda Wallbridge decided to have a chat with Cedric Halliday, the twitcher who had found Sheila Wynn's body. She called at his modest home in Victoria Terrace for it lay within her house-to-house visiting area, and she found him with his mother, having tea. They liked the look of this slender girl detective and invited her to join them. She smiled and accepted, seating herself at the table as Mrs Halliday organized things.

Amanda explained how she'd been checking his statement and said she was interested in the five young people he'd seen near the reservoir. Could he describe them in a little more detail? she asked.

Being a skilled ornithologist, Cedric had keen powers of observation and he admitted secretly watching them for a few minutes through his binoculars.

'Why did you watch them?' smiled Amanda charmingly.

'They didn't seem right somehow,' he said. 'They looked out of place up there, they weren't dressed for the countryside they were in, it's bleak moorland up there, rough and cold, especially at this time of year. They had jeans and trainers on, the sort of dress you'd see in a city-centre bar in summer rather than the open moors in December.'

'So what did you think?'

'Well, at first I thought they were students on a project of some kind. They seemed to be examining the reservoir closely, but not watching the wildlife like I was. Mind, it was nearly dark as well. It gets dark very early this time of year, and that surprised me, them being up there with darkness falling.'

'Had they transport?'

'Now it's funny you should mention that because I did wonder how they'd got up there. There is a road up, you know, from the west and they might have had a car parked somewhere down there. But I couldn't see it, it might have been behind the hill.'

'And what time did you see them?'

'It's about a forty-minute walk from there to where I found that woman, so it would be about half-past four, I'd say. I'd watched them for a few minutes, so, yes, about half-past four.'

'Now, Cedric, can you describe them?'

'Not in any real detail, it was too dark.'

'Generally though?'

'Like I said, they were young, like students, with jeans and white trainers. One was a girl, I could see that, a blonde. One was a lot taller than the others and seemed to be telling the others what to do. One of the men, not the tall one, had a white jacket or sweater on, he stood out in the dark.'

'And did they carry anything?'

'Not that I could see.'

'Do you think the man in charge of the reservoir would have been able to see them?'

'Yes, they made no attempts to hide themselves. But it was dark and the security man was in his office, it's on top of a tower at one end of the dam, and the lights were on. With lights on inside, he'd never be able to see what was going on outside.'

'And is that area open to the public?'

'Oh yes, there's a public footpath which runs parallel with the water, but fenced off at several points to stop people actually getting to the water's edge. There's no boating up there, nothing for that sort of visitor, except fishing from specific places and bird-watching. But these weren't fishing or watching birds, and they certainly weren't hikers.'

'In your statement, you said the security man saw you there?'

'Yes, I'd been there a while, watching some wild geese which had just come in from Scandinavia, and he came for a chat, he knows me well. We discussed the birds and I told him about the black woodpecker I was looking for, in the woods on the lower slopes of the moor.'

Amanda found that Cedric could not help any further and thanked him for his contribution to her enquiry.

He asked if anyone had been arrested for the murder of the woman he'd found and she had to say 'no' although she did qualify it by adding 'Not yet'.

She returned to the Incident Room to report this conversation to Dectective Superintendent Pemberton.

19

Pemberton told Amanda to go straight up to the reservoir to interview the security officials and he briefed her carefully. Full of enthusiasm, she drove there immediately, using a circuitous route which carried her through the early-evening traffic and well away from the Blue Beck marshes. She parked on a gravelled area before the high stone tower. Like a squat light-house perched on the end of the dam, the windows around the top were illuminated, and to reach it she climbed the stone stairs with their iron handrail and rang the bell.

A middle-aged man opened it and stared at her.

'Who are you?' he asked.

'Police,' she replied and showed her warrant-card.

'Come in then,' he growled, closing the door to keep out the cold. 'Fancy summat to drink? I've a coffee-pot on? It's nice to have a bit of company up here.'

'Thanks,' she smiled at him. He was a stout man in his middle forties and was wearing stained overalls over a grubby white shirt. He said his name was Alf Porritt, and in his small office with its dials and lights he made the coffee and placed a packet of digestive biscuits before her on his tiny table.

'Help yourself. So what's this then? Summat going wrong? You're a detective, aren't you? Summat to do with them murders, is it?'

'Not really,' Amanda said, and she then mentioned the five young people and Cedric and asked if he had seen any of them recently.

'Cedric's often up here,' he said. 'Me and the other security blokes know him well, he's no bother.'

'And the five youngsters. Have you seen a group here lately?'

'Aye, we have, me and my mates. It'll be in the log, hang on, I'll get it for you.'

From the drawer of a tattered oak desk, he produced a large handwritten ledger in which the daily occurences were recorded in chronological order. She learned that the group of five had been seen around the reservoir at varying times during the last few days. There were always five of them; no vehicle had been noted and their descriptions were brief enough to suggest it was the same five that she had discovered – one very tall one, and one girl being among them.

'What about night time?' she said. 'You can't see anyone out there from this tower, can you?'

'We do patrols,' he said. 'But if anybody's up to no good, they'll see us leaving this spot and they'll hide in the dark . . . we've not seen that lot at night.'

'What action are you supposed to take about them?'

'Record their visits, like we've done, and ring our security office. That's at our Division Head Office in Leeds. I don't know what they do about it. We just tell 'em.'

'So what have this group been doing here? Any idea?'

'Nowt, so the book says. Just hanging around, wandering about, looking at things. But they're not bird-watchers, they've no binoculars or telescopes like Cedric, and they're not hikers because they're not equipped. I thought they were mebbe holiday-makers or students.'

'Then why record them in your book? You don't record every visitor, do you? This is a public road past here, lots of people come up here don't they? Especially on Sundays.'

'No, we don't note every single one, but we were told to look out for those five. Our security people told us to record what we saw, so that's why I noted them. I thought you must know that, coming here like you did.'

She did not respond to his remark, but she had not been told that wider observations were being mounted on the St Joseph's Street five. Had Mark been told? It was odd he had not mentioned it. 'But surely you had to do more than just record their visits?'

'If we saw them doing anything suspicious, then we had to ring Security, I mean, if we saw 'em messing about with the sluice-gates or pulling down the boundary fences, that sort of thing, then we'd do summat. Like the other night. I had to chase a bloke away in the early hours, half-one-ish. He'd got this blonde with him, then he'd climbed on to the dam and, well, excuse me lassie but I reckon he had a jimmy riddle right off the top.

'Well, he set the security lights off and when they flooded the spot, he ran like hell. I chased after him, but he got into his car and drove into town, like a bat out of hell. We needn't record that sort of thing. We'd record it if folks were seriously misbehaving; take car numbers, descriptions and the like. But those kids, and that bloke courting, well, they've done nowt wrong, not in my view.'

'But at night, in the darkness, you'd not see if they did anything, would you?'

'Oh aye, we would, if it was summat serious. There's several vulnerable places, like the pumping-house, the sluice and so on, the motors and electrics . . . if any unauthorized people tamper with them, indoors or out, hooters would sound and lights come on, like they did with that chap having a pee. They work an' all, so we'd know if folks were doing wrong. We'd do summat about that.'

Without voicing her thoughts, she realized that if any determined wreckers wanted to sabotage the reservoir, they could create a diversion so that the guard emerged from his tower; then they'd immobilize him and go ahead with their plans. Any lights and noise would not be heard due to the isolated nature of this place.

Before leaving, Amanda did ask about any sightings of Sheila Wynn or the other woman, but the man said he was too far away up here to see faces and identify folks. At night especially, you couldn't recognize people, and so she returned to the Incident Room to report to Superintendent Pemberton.

While Amanda was at the reservoir, Roger Daniel and John Watson were enquiring at the sales kiosk at Crossfield Garage in Crossfield Road. The night-duty attendant had not yet come on – he started at 10 p.m. and worked through till 8 a.m. It was his turn for a week of nights and so, having secured his name and address, they went to his home. He was Sid Hunt and he lived in Fortune Street. His wife let the detectives in to the small sitting-room where Hunt was watching television.

He did not stand up but he did switch off the set as he faced his visitors. After learning of their quest, he said, 'Yes, I remember that chap. A big chap? In overalls? He was on telly next day, he found that woman, didn't he? That wasn't his missus, was it?'

'No, it was another dead woman,' said Daniels. 'His wife was younger, blonde.'

'That's it! I remember. He said he was looking for his missus, she was in a red coat. She'd cleared off after a row and he was worried.'

'That's him. So what time did he call?' asked Daniels.

'Oh, blimey, that's hard to say. Late, it was, well after half-one.'

Daniels tried to jog the fellow's memory. 'He told us that when he called there was another chap there at the same time, Paddy he called him, a customer at the Black Lion, he said he pulled in. Would he be getting petrol?'

'Oh, that chap! He was in a rush . . . I remember now, yeah, it would be knocking on for two. You could check with the till records, he had a Vauxhall, a pale greenish one I'd say but it's hard to tell colours in them garage lights. Strip lights they are, they distort some colours. Anyway, he got a tenner's worth and paid in cash. The till receipts will show the time he called, and his car number. We take car numbers down at night, for security and in case the car's been nicked. The police are always popping in to ask us to check overnight sales against their list of nicked cars and waggons.'

'What did he look like? The car-driver?'

'He never got out, he paid cash through his window . . .

middle-aged, I'd say. Not young, not old, a bit under forty mebbe. Heavyish. Dark hair. I could see he had a beer-belly mind, when he fished for his money. Otherwise, nowt special about him really.'

'Is he a regular at your garage?' Daniels felt a tremor of excitement as he listened to the description of this man and his car.

'He's been before, I'm sure of that,' Hunt said. 'Not exactly a regular 'cos he never came every day or even every week, but, well, he does come in from time to time.'

'Local chap, is he?'

'I'd say so, but I don't know his name. He always pays cash.'

'OK, thanks,' Daniels was growing increasingly excited about this development. It matched the taxi-drivers account of the man seen with the blonde, and it also indicated that Harry Downes was telling the truth. 'Now, those till records, can we get access to them?'

Hunt checked his watch. 'It's ten to nine,' he said. 'If you get straight round, you'll catch the second-shift manager before he knocks off. He'll let you see them.'

They did arrive before the manager closed the office and when he learned they were engaged upon the murder enquiry, he was very helpful. He allowed them to peruse the night-sales records and eventually they found one at 1.41 a.m. showing a £10 cash sale. It bore a registration number, as did all the vouchers. Daniels noted down the details and included those of two other £10 cash sales. He thanked the manager and they left.

'The owner of this car's got some questions to answer,' said Daniels as he and Watson drove back to the Incident Room.

When they returned, the Incident Room was full of detectives gathering to book off duty. On a normal day during a murder inquiry, they finished at 9 p.m. but many lingered awhile to discuss the day's events, to have a coffee and then to visit a pub for a drink or two to continue their discussions. Among them, Pemberton was expressing his delight with Amanda's enquiries at the reservoir and she stood close to him with her plastic mug full of coffee. Daniels waited until his boss had finished his conversation with her. He ended by saying, 'Thanks, Amanda, you get away now and I'll see you later. I'll convey this to the Special Branch – I reckon that information's for them.'

As the young detective went to his house to await him he felt pleased with her work. She was a natural detective, resilient and persistent. Then Daniels reported his success.

'Does this mean Harry is sliding down the frame?' Pemberton asked.

'Well, it does suggest he's telling the truth about his wife, sir, and to be honest, neither John or I think he's guilty. But it's the driver of that car that's interesting us now.'

'Do a PNC check straight away. It'll only take seconds.'

Before anyone else came to badger Pemberton, Daniels went over to the PNC and keyed in the registered number of the Vauxhall. Pemberton watched with some interest for it took fourteen seconds for the computer to produce the registered keeper. The model was shown as a Nova and the computer said it was green.

'Well, I'll be damned!' he cried.

'Whose is it?' Pemberton leaned forward to read the name on the screen.

'Patrick Roe, 316 Pennine Flats . . .' said Daniels.

'That's the drug-dealer that Division nicked at the Flats,' commented Pemberton. 'You'd better have words with him, Roger, see if he remembers seeing Harry Downes or Sheila Wynn. I'm not sure whether he knows Harry or not, but he did know Sheila.

'She was involved on the fringes of his drugs ring, putting the word out if she found a new customer.

'When I had words with him, he reckoned he'd not seen her for weeks. He never said anything about seeing Harry that night so he might not know him; have a word with him about it. Does he know Harry by name? Does he know that he's Sheila's real bloke? He might just be the witness we need.'

'Is he still inside?' asked Daniels.

'Yes, Division objected to bail, he's on remand in the cells. See him tomorrow, he can't go far! It's time we all knocked off now.'

As the night-duty skeleton staff took over the Incident Room, the teams gradually filtered away. Mark Pemberton, tired after the hectic three days of the so-called exercise, was ready for his supper. He declined to join the others in the pub, saying he wanted an early night. He would walk the mile or so, to enjoy the crisp December evening.

But as he reached the door on the ground floor, Detective Sergeant Goddard hailed him. He had a white plastic carrier bag in his hand.

'Ah, sir, I'm pleased I caught you,' he said. 'You left these in the Q-van, I thought you'd better have them back before they get lost.'

'Did I? What have you got in there?'

'Two pairs of old shoes. I assume they're yours, according to the log, you were the last to use the van before I took it out on obs.'

Pemberton realized he'd made a mistake after dumping the body . . . He'd intended incinerating these. He and Doc. Andrew had left prints at the Green Lane scene and he'd seen plaster casts of these very soles in SOCO's files . . . but clearly, Goddard had not seen those marks.

Pemberton took the bag from him.

'You're not engaged on the murder enquiry, then, sarge?' Pemberton commented. 'So how did you escape my net?'

'Discreet observation duties, sir. I'm looking out for some suspicious lefties thought to be holed up here. We've had a tip from the Midlands, they might be aiming to sabotage our water supplies. We have names – which could be false – but we've not located them yet. I am checking your lists, by the way, but nothing's turned up there so far.'

'We did turn up five likely customers,' Pemberton told him. 'You know about them?'

'Yes, thanks, but they're not the ones I'm interested in.'

'All alone are they?'

'According to my sources, there's just the two of them, sir, and tonight I've got some gen about a pair of likely lads who are renting a flat in Sherman Terrace. I'm keeping obs. there tonight. Your teams haven't got to that part of town yet, eh? On their house-to-house?'

'Not yet, so I know nothing about those two. Keep me informed, I might be interested. Well, thanks for my old shoes. They're ideal for gardening.'

And Goddard returned to the battered old white Q-van which was parked outside, thinking it was just like the immaculate Pemberton to use a pair of old shoes while examining a murder

164

scene. Mind, the lads said he could walk across a ploughed field in pouring rain and emerge at the other side with clean shoes.

Mark Pemberton watched Goddard drive away. He knew that if any of the murder teams had seen these shoes, they might have recognized the patterns of the soles as those left at the scene and that could have given rise to some awkward questions. But on the way home, he passed the rear of a hotel with its array of dustbins and, on impulse, cast the bag of shoes into one of them. They would be collected in the morning and destroyed.

As he enjoyed the walk home, he reflected upon the events of the last half-hour. Roe's name had suddenly cropped up. Until now, Roe had never appeared in the frame, had he? Although Pemberton himself had interviewed him about Sheila, he'd not emerged as a suspect. But should he be in the frame? Division had dealt with the drugs raid and so its parameters were not an integral part of the murder investigations, although some of the facts had been logged in HOLMES; after all, the raid had merely been set up as a diversion.

But was it coincidence that Roe's name had suddenly cropped up? He remembered Bud Abbott's theories about coincidences and wondered if the presence of Roe as a witness, albeit a minor one in the murder investigation, was worthy of deeper examination? And, without thinking very deeply, he knew it was. Roe's movements *before* his arrest had not been checked simply because he had never come into the frame. Now he would be placed in the frame which meant he would receive the full treatment even though he was in custody for another offence.

And another puzzling fact was Goddard's observation for those two men. Did this link in any way with the five that Amanda had discovered? It was odd that both sets of men should be here at the same time, both from the Midlands. . . he would have to talk to her about it, maybe he'd give her a call.

He turned around and hurried back to the Incident Room.

He had some enquiries to make and work to do. Amanda would be asleep by the time he arrived home.

20

The small staff of night-duty officers were surprised by Pemberton's unexpected return that suggested something important had developed. It would relieve the monotony of their mundane role as glorified filing clerks.

'Sarge,' Pemberton addressed Detective Sergeant Matthews and let the others overhear him. 'It's amazing how a walk in the fresh air fortifies the brain! I'd like you to search HOLMES for me please. I'm interested in several matters relating to both murders – the first is all the references to blonde women. The next is every reference to a Vauxhall car, any Vauxhall car, with colours if possible, and finally, any references to Blue Beck Reservoir. That should be no problem, should it?'

'No, sir,' said Matthews, 'so long as your day shifts have programmed in all the data!'

'I'm sure they have. Now, while you are doing that, I'll be scanning Sheila Wynn's time-chart.'

Larkin had compiled a simple chart on lined paper and it was stuck to the office wall with Sellotape. It outlined the critical hours so far as sightings of Sheila Wynn were concerned. Ticks in bright pink flourescent markings indicated the positive sightings and known timings.

From the chart, he could see that around midnight on the day of her death, she had been seen at home by both Harry Downes and the taxi-driver who took her home. Each confirmed the other. That was a positive sighting. She had remained at home until about 12.30 a.m. when she'd been thrown out, bruised and crying. Harry was there. That timing, with an allowance for a few minutes either way, had been confirmed. Harry had admitted being violent, perhaps causing the bruises but not the shotgun wound.

She had been seen just after 12.30 a.m., and this was ticked as confirmed; the sighting had been by Mrs Miller at her home, and a few minutes later someone had knocked on the door of the Black Lion, then gone away. It could have been Sheila. An officer had timed the walk from the Miller's home to the pub and it was only four minutes; that route also passed close to Mayhew's former home, so had she called there? He'd not been asked that. And if she had been running, then the time could have been even less.

The next sighting, in the town, had not been confirmed but it did match Sheila's description. A blonde woman of her age and wearing a red coat or jumper had been seen by a taxi-driver outside the cleaner's, a short distance from the pub. She'd been talking to a man in a Vauxhall, probably a Nova, light coloured; he was described as being under forty with dark thinning hair. Roe? The time had been around 12.40 to 12.45a.m. The next positive sighting had been in the river at 5.30p.m., when she was dead. Where had she been during the interim time?

'Sir,' said a detective constable who came towards him with a file of papers in his hands. 'There is a reference to a blonde in this statement, it's not been programmed into HOLMES yet, that's one of tonight's jobs.'

'Where?'

'At the reservoir, sir, about half-past one that same morning, she was with a chap in a Vauxhall. They were seen by the night-duty attendant, it's on Amanda Wallbridge's statement file.'

'Let me see that,' and Pemberton studied Amanda's words, but the sighting had been insufficient to clarify whether or not it had been Sheila with a man. But the car was a Vauxhall.

'Great. Now, any more sightings of this blonde?'

There were none which matched Sheila's description until the discovery of her body at 5.30 p.m. Several other blondes who had become subjects of enquiry had been eliminated from the murder, but he found the reservoir sighting very interesting. At this early stage, the murder teams had paid scant attention to the reservoir due to its distance from town.

When he searched HOLMES for references to Vauxhall cars, there were lots. The computer highlighted Miller's car, for example, but after rejecting many of the others as inconsequential due to their timings or locations, Pemberton was left with the one seen at Crossfield Road Garage and the one seen by the taxi-driver. There was almost an hour between them; the woman in red had been seen talking to the driver of a Vauxhall outside the cleaners at about 12.40 or 12.45 a.m., he reminded himself.

Another interesting Vauxhall of similar size and colour had been spotted at Crossfield Road all-night garage at 1.41 a.m. The drivers of each were similar, too. And Patrick Roe was the owner of the latter. So had Roe seen Sheila in the early hours of that morning? Pemberton checked the timings again, comparing the Sheila sightings with the Vauxhall ones. Roe had claimed he had not seen Sheila for some considerable time and so Pemberton, with a pencil and paper, worked out a new scenario.

He based it on the fact that Sheila and Roe knew one another. They were both involved in drugs – that admission had come from Roe himself. In the early hours of the morning of Sheila's disappearance, Roe claimed he'd been to pick up the drugs without stating where, but he had said he'd suffered a puncture on the motorway with delays compounded by a flat spare tyre and a fault in his watch. He had been at Pennine Flats at 2 a.m., probably arriving just before then, when he'd been arrested with his drugs. And that had been odd – even to catch Roe in possession was considered most unlikely. But no one else had been caught in possession, another oddity.

Mark then examined the timings on the various sheets of paper around him. He envisaged Sheila being thrown out at 12.30 a.m. or thereabouts; she had fled the short distance to see Miller who was out. Miller's wife had given her short shrift so she'd continued to the Black Lion, presumably on foot. Her knocking on its doors had been misconstrued as a drunk messing about and so she had then sought further help . . .

Suppose she had then decided to walk to Roe's home in Pennine Flats? She knew him through her drug-dealings and from his visits to the Black Lion. Pemberton examined the street map of the town which was pinned to the wall and saw that her route from the pub to Pennine Flats would conveniently take her past the cleaners . . . so it was highly feasible and the timing of that sighting, around 12.40 or 12.45 a.m., was about right. So it could have been her talking to that man in the Vauxhall. Was that man Roe? Had she been talking to Patrick Roe outside the cleaners? If she had, then Roe had lied.

The next sighting of a suspect Vauxhall was at the reservoir about 1.30 a.m., with a blonde . . . and a man who had been scared off the dam itself . . . Had that blonde been alive then? If she had been dead, he might have intended throwing her in the water, so was the weapon already in the lake? Had Roe walked on top of the dam to examine it before lugging the corpse there, taking the opportunity to get rid of the shotgun? Had he not realized the place was staffed at night?

Pemberton grew excited at these possibilities. Then, if Roe had failed to get rid of the corpse at that stage, he might have driven to a convenient point at Blue Beck, near the marshlands, and dumped her there . . . Then had he gone back into town, filled the car with petrol at 1.41 a.m. to establish some sort of alibi which he could claim was linked to his drug-dealings? Having been caught in possession, Roe would guess the police would never check back in time. There was no need.

And no one, it seems, had examined Roe's car. Where was it? Hadn't tyre-marks been found near the dumping place of Sheila's body? Had a match been found for those? It must be found and its tyre treads must be compared with the plaster casts from Blue Beck marshes. But Roe's arrest at 2 a.m. in possession of drugs had taken him right out of the frame. Till now. Had that been planned? Had Roe actually engineered his arrest? If so, it meant someone within police circles had tipped him off about the raid . . . Mark groaned. That would explain why all the pushers had avoided capture. A mole . . . that was something he could well do without.

When Mark checked HOLMES for further references to the reservoir, he found them in Cedric's statement and in Amanda's enquiries into the mystery of those five members of CLAP. As he checked this data, he realized that Detective Sergeant Goddard's observations for the two suspected water saboteurs were not recorded here; after all, his was a separate SB enquiry and there was no reason to link those two men, or the five CLAP members, with the murder investigation. But now there was a link – that link was the reservoir.

He said to the detective constable who was working at his side on the large table, 'Get me D/I Abbott, will you? He won't be in bed yet, it's only just gone eleven.'

Abbott was not at home, for he was still at the divisional police station; two more drug-users had just been brought in, the aftermath of the raid.

'Sir,' he answered the phone.

'Can you come round to the Incident Room, Bud? I need to speak with you. It's important.'

'Sure,' and he left immediately.

When Abbott arrived five minutes later, one of the staff organized coffee and everyone sat round to listen to Pemberton's theory. Abbott nodded as each point was made and when Pemberton concluded, he asked, 'Well, Bud, what do you think?'

'After listening to this, I think Roe could be our killer, sir.'

'Do you reckon he got himself arrested to create what he thought would be an untouchable alibi?'

'It's a possibility, although I reckon it could be chance on our part. But it does raise another problem, sir. If he did await our arrival, he must have known, in advance, that the raid was to take place. I know we had only hours' notice ourselves, but somebody must have warned them . . . the pushers and users got away . . . instead, we caught Roe. That would not have happened normally, so I reckon questions must be asked.'

Mark was pleased to hear this man echoing his own worries. It was unscheduled support for the notion of a mole. Mark went on, 'And I agree with you, so there's the possibility of a mole within our own people? That'll mean we must set a trap . . . but first – Roe. What about his tale of getting a puncture and all that?'

'It was never checked out, sir, it was not relevant at the time. He wasn't a murder suspect. He was never part of the murder investigation. We got him in possession of drugs, and that's all that mattered at that time. He would know that.'

'Right, so his story needs checking now. And his car? Where is his car?'

'We did not check that either, sir, again because it was not relevant. There are no garages with those council flats, he probably rents one or leaves his car out all night.'

'We need to find it and examine it for blood stains or fibres from Sheila's red coat, and tyre-tread patterns . . . he had not time to clean it or dispose of it. If we can prove she was in that car, dead or alive, he's our man.'

Pemberton also referred to the various Vauxhall car references, asking Abbott to check those carefully too.

'We have the keys to his flat with us, sir, and to his car,' said Abbott. 'I'll get cracking on that one. What about interviewing him about the murders?'

'Test him about his car first. Watch his reaction. I'd like to

170

know the outcome of our search of the reservoir before we interview him formally about the deaths. But get him worried – it'll do him good to wonder how much we know. I want as much evidence against him as possible. Tell him we want his car for elimination; he might tell us where it is.'

'I agree,' smiled Abbott. 'We'll need absolutely positive proof to make any charge against him watertight.'

'Exactly, and so I'd like to know what clothing he was wearing when he was arrested, if you could find that out for me. Fibres from Sheila's clothes, or blood might show up.'

'Right, sir, well, I'll get cracking. His clothing will be no problem, he's still wearing it! Will you be here till late?'

'Yes, all night by the look of it. Now I'm going for a chat with the night-watchman at the reservoir,' said Pemberton, remembering he'd have to ring Amanda to explain his delay. But as he walked out of the room, Amanda was coming in. She said she'd remembered something about the reservoir, the blonde in the car.

'You'd better come with me,' said Pemberton.

The security tower was all in darkness and it took some persuasion on Mark's part before Alf Porritt would open his door. But he agreed when he learned the purpose of Pemberton's late-night mission. He opened it to find the detective and the girl who'd called earlier.

'I had that lass o' yours here earlier,' he grumbled to Pemberton. 'I told her it all.'

'One or two things have arisen since,' Mark exuded charm and patience. 'So we've had to come to check them out, DC Wallbridge has told me everything you told her. The thing that interests me is the man who was walking on the dam, Mr Porritt.'

'I never really got a good look at him.'

'Is it easy to climb on to the top of the dam from the shore?'

'Oh, aye. You just climb over a wooden gate and then a metal fence, it's not all that difficult. Fishermen used to do it regularly till we were privatized, then the new regime said it was private premises and we had to keep folks off.'

'But there are notices up? "Keep Out" signs, that sort of thing?'

'Since privatization, yes. I mean, the walk across the top is marvellous; it's as broad as a country lane with rails along both sides and, except for the pumps and things, there's no reason why folks shouldn't use it, it's just like a bridge.'

'And the man with the blonde. He was on that stretch?'

'Aye, he was, but at night, you see, we have these security lights and they come on if anybody walks over there. I can control them from here if I want, turn 'em on to manual.'

'Show me,' and at the press of a button, the entire length of the dam, some 300 yards in length, was illuminated.

'So where was this man when you spotted him?'

'See them rails, starting at this end? Well, count the posts . . . one, two, three . . .'

He halted at post number eight. 'He was about there, I reckon. That's what? Fifteen or twenty yards on to the dam.'

'And the time?'

'Half-one, or thereabouts.'

'Did you record this in the log?'

'No, not that. Not courting couples.'

'What about the timing? Could it have been a few minutes earlier? Or later?'

'Not later, 'cos I listens to the news on the half-hour and I heard it after he's cleared off. Might have been a bit earlier, aye, it must have been. A minute or two, no more.'

'And what was he doing?'

'Well, I thought mucky bugger because I thought he was pissing into the water . . . excuse my language miss, but I didn't really see what he was doing, but he turned back and ran like hell when the lights were on him. He jumped the fences, got into his car and went away like a bat out of hell.'

'Could he have thrown something into the water? It'll be deep at that point, won't it?'

'Oh, aye, that's the deepest part, being up against the dam wall. Aye, well, I suppose he could have chucked summat in, but I never saw him do that.'

'Now, you told Detective Constable Wallbridge he had a blonde in the car. Can you describe her?' Pemberton was airing the suspicions that Amanda had raised, suspicions strong enough to compel her to return to the Incident Room to check them out.

'Well,' said Alf Porritt. 'She never got out so I never got a good look. She was in the front, in the passenger side, and she had her head down, trying to keep her face away from the light, I reckon.'

'You mean your security light?'

'Aye, it shines on to the car-park, see?'

Mark looked out of the other side of the tower and, by shading his hands against the inside light, could view the car-park which the public used. His own car was there and the lights did shine inside, but not enough to identify from this point the features of a person sitting inside.

But the area around the park was well lit by this bright light.

'How do you mean, had her head down?' he asked.

'Well, when I looked at the car, when he was running for it, I saw her head. She had the seat-belt on, mind, it was sort of holding her up but her head was against the door post, slumped down as if she was asleep, I thought. And when he set off, she never moved. I thought she was hiding her face from me. They do, you know, all sorts of folks come up here for a bit of nookie and if they spot us looking, they try to hide . . .'

'OK, she had blonde hair. What about her clothing?'

'Red. A red jacket or coat or summat. I saw that, but nowt else. I couldn't say how old she was or owt like that. I never thought it'd be linked to a murder; you don't, do you?'

Amanda blushed and said, 'I'm sorry, sir, I should have asked all these questions when I was here . . .'

'Put it down to experience, Amanda,' cautioned Mark. 'You raised a question in my mind, and I think you were right. Now, Mr Porritt, when you scared the man, he jumped into his car and drove off, is that it?'

'Aye, like a bat out of hell. He never even put his lights on till he'd got well down the road, so I couldn't get his number.'

'What sort of car was it? I'd like you to be sure of this.'

'A Vauxhall, a small 'un. I'm sure it was, my lad has one just the same. Nova, a light green one. Clean it was.'

'And the man? What about him? Can you describe him?'

'Heavyish chap, I'd say. Quite tall, well made, somewhere between thirty-five and forty at a guess. Dark hair, heavy about the gut. He had a blue sweater on, pale blue or mebbe a very light grey, and jeans.'

'Mr Porritt, this is a tremendous help. Now, I must get it all down in writing, and then I'll leave you in peace . . .'

'There's no need to rush off on my account, Mr Pemberton and young lady, it's nice having a bit o' company at night especially on double shifts like tonight. My mate's gone sick, but the overtime'll be worth it.'

'Thanks, but I've a lot to do. Now, before I go, I must get permission from your bosses to search the reservoir, I want to bring our frogmen in at first light.'

'You'll have to ring Leeds, the night manager will be on. Use the private line, that green phone.'

When Pemberton explained his purpose to the Leeds supervisor, permission was readily given.

When they left the reservoir, they paid a quick visit to the scene of the dumping of Sheila's body, then drove to the all-night garage in Crossfield Road.

That combined journey, allowing time for a big man to lug a large woman from his car and cast her into the lower reaches of the river, took less than eleven minutes. If the reservoir man had seen Roe at twenty-past one or even twenty-five past, it was very possible. If his timing of half-past was precise, then it would have been a difficult journey to conclude within that time, but not impossible bearing in mind the desperate need of the driver. The security man did say the car had left a minute or two before half-past. It meant that Roe could have picked up Sheila outside the cleaner's at 12.45 a.m., killed her and then driven up here and left before 1.30 a.m., finally dumping her in Blue Beck before going to the garage. He got there in time to be filled up and given a receipt timed at 1.41 a.m. Just possible.

'So, Amanda, why would Roe kill the woman who was providing him with new customers?' he asked.

'Maybe she was cheating him, sir?'

'Maybe she was, or maybe she was blackmailing him, or maybe she just knew too much. Let's hope Abbott bears that in mind. Come on, it's back to work for me. You go home and get your head down, I want you back at the reservoir by 7.30!'

Mark Pemberton drove back to the Incident Room with a feeling of elation. On the way, he asked Amanda if she'd been told about Goddard's suspects or whether they had any links with the five youngsters she had discovered. She shook her head; although she'd heard of other obs. jobs, these two were unknown to her. Pemberton halted the car, kissed her briefly after checking they were unobserved, and dropped Amanda in the car-park where her little 2CV awaited. He waved her farewell.

Later this morning, a search of the reservoir might just confirm all his suspicions. Then he could close that enquiry and chalk up the Green Lane death as the exercise it really was.

As he walked into the Incident Room alone, he wondered whether Abbott would find Roe's car and if so, what evidence it would reveal.

21

When Detective Chief Inspector Bud Abbott interviewed Roe in the very early hours of Thursday morning, Roe refused to answer any questions about his car.

'You can't question me about that,' he said. 'I've been charged, you cannot question me any further about my offence.'

'It is not about that offence,' said Abbott at length. 'It is about another offence. Murder. I am allowed to question you about another offence, by consent of the Custody Officer. And he has agreed. This interview is being recorded.'

Roe said nothing. The expression on his face told Abbott everything.

'I want to know the whereabouts of your car, Patrick, for elimination purposes.'

Roe said nothing.

Abbott continued, 'We know that you are the owner of a Vauxhall Nova car, and we have the registration number,' and Abbott quoted it for the record. 'We know you called for petrol at a certain garage at 1.41 a.m. on the morning that Sheila Wynn alias Downes disappeared; we suspect you visited Blue Beck reservoir the same morning and we are aware of your claim to have had punctures prior to your arrest at 2 a.m. that day. We have witnesses who can state you had a woman in your car and that the woman answers the description of Sheila Wynn.'

Roe said nothing.

'We have plaster casts of tyre-marks taken from the scene of the dumping of Sheila Wynn's body. If we have access to your car, therefore, we may be able to eliminate it from our enquiries and so eliminate you.'

'Bollocks!' snapped Roe, who steadfastly refused to say anything more.

Amanda left the Police Station car-park at 1 a.m. to drive home. She had assured Pemberton she'd be back at work at 7.30 and he suggested she drove straight to the reservoir. He'd arranged for the search to begin at first light and she could help in those arrangements. Besides, Pemberton wanted her to share in his success, for he was sure the results would be positive.

As she drove through the Sherman Road area of the town, her headlights caught sight of a man, a tall man, a man rising to more than six feet in height. Eammon O'Brien. One of the St Joseph's Street five. In a green sweater, he was walking quickly towards her, head down and hands in the pockets of his jeans to keep warm. He was instantly recognizable from his photo. She was caught in indecision; she was not in a police car so she could not radio for advice or help. So where was he going? She could not let this moment pass. She turned down a side street, parked, switched off her lights and got out of her car.

It was bitterly cold, so she donned her white woolly hat, her thick red-and-yellow woollen jacket and gloves, the clothes she wore when rambling on the moors. Then she hurried back along Sherman Road in the rising breeze of that night.

He had vanished, but he must be only a mere twenty or thirty seconds ahead of her. She continued, listening to see if she could hear his footsteps and then she heard a yard door bang. It was down the street on her left. She turned down that street. It was called Sherman Terrace. She hurried along and saw a light in the downstairs front room of Number 27. It was the only one with a light downstairs. She halted outside, listening. There was no sound of a television operating or a party being held and so she ventured closer, tip-toeing up the short path into the yard. Beneath the bay window was a tiny rough lawn, unkempt and about the size of a kitchen table-top with high walls around it. She stepped on to that, hoping to peer through a gap in the curtains to see if O'Brien was there.

Gingerly, and with immense care, she moved closer and she could hear voices inside . . . she stooped to look through the tiny gap and he was there. Eammon O'Brien . . . so who were the two men he was with? Then she remembered Mark's questions about two more men, Goddards suspects, called Harris and Fife. What was their involvement? And then a hand came from behind to clasp itself around her mouth to stifle any cry and a powerful arm seized her waist.

'So who have we here, then?' demanded a man's voice.

Further news came into the Incident Room that night. The Millers' gun, now owned by Nathan Montgomery, had been examined and had not been fired for years. Thus it was ruled out of the murder enquiry. Nathan would be told and his gun returned, although there was a note from the examiner who said it was in very poor condition and likely to be dangerous if fired.

There were more minor arrests too, all a direct result of the investigation. An outstanding rape enquiry was finalized when the villain admitted a series of sex attacks, two of which provided alibis against his involvement in the murders; a stolen-car racket was broken too, the men being identified by those who had parked in a quiet place for a bit of courting . . .

As Pemberton looked at the mock-up racecourse runners' frame which hung from the wall of the Incident Room, he saw that in the hunt for Sheila Wynn's killer, Harry Downes was still leading, with Roe's name now a close second. Mr and Mrs Miller were well down the list and so was Mayhew, still to be interviewed. He could wait; he was safely in custody!

So far as the Green Lane mystery was concerned, several more names had been suggested for the victim and these were being examined, and Harry Downes' name was in the frame for that killing, but no others. Poor old Harry. Pemberton realized that it was Harry who had unwittingly led them to Roe; his visit to the all-night garage and his sighting of the man called Paddy who was filling his car had provided that lead.

If necessary, an identification parade with Harry as the witness should confirm that the man called Paddy was Patrick Roe and, as such, was a customer at the Black Lion and a person who knew Sheila. Would Alf Porritt be able to identify him?

As Pemberton pondered his next move, Abbott returned with news of his abortive interview with Roe. Pemberton listened

177

and said, 'He's done it, Bud. He's our man, he killed Sheila Wynn. So let's prove it. Tomorrow, the Task Force must examine every lock-up garage in town. His car must be here, somewhere in town. If you look at the time-sheet, he didn't have an opportunity to get rid of it, did he? There's no burnt-out cars reported, is there? If he'd set fire to it just before our raid, we'd have known. So it's waiting for us to find, Bud. You've got the keys?'

'Yes, the ignition keys and a Yale lock, probably from the garage he uses, were in his pockets when we arrested him.'

'I'll leave that one with you, Bud. You know what to look for?'

'Yes, sir.'

'Great, then I'm going home for a few hours of shut-eye – if I find the gun in the reservoir and you find the car, I reckon we can prove our killer is Patrick Roe.'

'I hope so, sir.'

When Mark entered his bedroom, Amanda was not there and the bed had not been slept in.

She must have gone to her own flat, perhaps for a change of clothes for tomorrow, although it was odd she hadn't left him a note or rung him. He knew she was a little worried about their relationship, wanting to keep it from her colleagues due to the wide differences in rank.

June hadn't been dead a year either, and sometimes Amanda had discussed the ethics of living together so soon after he had lost her. There had been no children of the marriage, which had been a happy one, so that was not the problem, although he was forty. But this was no crush of a middle-aged man's for a young girl; he did love her and he did need her.

He thought about her as he climbed into the cold bed and tried to snatch a few hours' sleep.

At seven o'clock that morning, the Underwater Search Unit's large vehicle, a converted ambulance, arrived in the reservoir's car-park where Pemberton was already waiting. The officer in charge was the appropriately named Sergeant Ronald Duck who had lived down his parents' awful choice of name to make a career in underwater diving and searching. His task was outlined by Mark Pemberton who took him along the walkway above the water to outline the extent of the required search. Sergeant Duck was in possession of a map of the bottom of the reservoir which showed the varying depths of the water, the Underwater Search Unit having a library of such maps for every stretch of inland water within the Force area.

By the time the plans were outlined, the men had assembled their diving gear and the inflatable boat had been tested; everyone had been briefed, and by the time they'd brewed a coffee each it was daylight. The moment it was light enough, the search began.

It started with a preliminary dive as Pemberton looked around for Amanda. There was now a total of around twenty officers here this morning, a dozen of whom were UWSU members in diving gear, the others comprising photographers and members of the murder team. It was now 7.45 a.m. and it was unlike her to be late. But it was a cold morning with a sharp frost and there was just a chance that her car had failed to start. He would allow a few minutes before asking for a check to be made. Perhaps she'd dropped into the Incident Room?

By now, the rubber craft was on the water with three men aboard and Pemberton shivered at the thought of them diving on this chilly morning. But the cold did not seem to worry them as they tested their apparatus yet again. They were going to carry out a meticulous, well planned search of the bed of the reservoir and had plotted the area on the plastic cover of the map.

'Ready?' the voice of Sergeant Duck carried across the still, morning water.

One of the divers raised his hand in acknowledgement, and then toppled backwards into the water to begin his difficult task. A second man followed.

Pemberton stood on top of the dam, resting his hands on the chill metal rails as he saw his men at work below. But he could not resist watching the car-park for Amanda's 2CV. When she had not arrived by eight o'clock, he returned to his own official car and radioed the Incident Room.

Inspector Watkins said she was not there and they'd had no word from her; he would ring her flat to see if she had left. Pemberton waited.

Watkins tried several times, then said, 'No reply, sir. I'll send a car round.'

'Do that,' said Pemberton with just a twinge of concern. 'I'll wait in my car.'

He was not doing this just because it was Amanda. It was routine action when any police officer failed to parade without notifying their supervisory officers of the reason. It took ten minutes for a beat car to be diverted to Amanda's flat and he reported that she was not there. A bottle of milk was outside and the newspapers were still in the letter-box; he had knocked and shouted, but the neighbours said she was not there. Her car was out, it was pointed out. The beat man relayed that information to Watkins.

'She's either not been in all night, sir, or she's gone out very early,' said Watkins to Pemberton.

'Exactly, Paul, that's why I'm concerned. She's not turned up – look, this is not like her at all. You'll have her car number recorded?

'Put an alert out for it, get all beat cars to search and let me know if they find it. And keep checking at the flat. I'll call you at intervals, I won't be within ear-shot of the radio all the time.'

Watkins could not fully understand Pemberton's concern for the slip of a lass who seemed to enjoy his company – the lads had noticed their closeness, but so far, nothing more than that had been noted. But you never knew – such liaisons did occur and inevitably, due to the differences in rank, they were secretive. So where was the silly lass? She'd probably just overslept. And as Watkins set the enquiry in motion, Pemberton returned to his vantage point.

The frogmen were sweeping along a swathe of about three yards directly beneath the outward-sloping wall of the dam, and from time to time he could see their black frog-like movements in the clear water. Occasionally, they touched the bottom and stirred up clouds of yellow muddy water which hampered their search, but they persisted with patience and skill. By nine o'clock they had found nothing and surfaced for another break. The reservoir security man had boiled his kettle and was producing cups of hot coffee which were welcomed by all. Pemberton returned to his car to radio Watkins.

'Her car has been found, sir, a traffic warden's put a ticket on it, it's on double yellow lines in Churchill Street. We've checked, it was there at five this morning, a milkman noticed it and thought it odd.'

'Churchill Street?' puzzled Pemberton.

'Off Sherman Road, sir.'

'Sherman Road? What the hell is she doing down there?'

'We don't know, sir . . . I don't follow?'

'Sherman Road, Paul . . . think man, Sherman bloody Terrace leads off it. That's where Goddard's suspect reservoir bombers are dossing down . . . he's watching out for them . . . or supposed to be . . . he was there last night, wasn't he? So get Goddard out of bed. I want to talk to him. I'll be there in a few minutes – make sure Goddard turns up, tell him it's urgent.'

'Yes, sir,' and so Pemberton, having left instructions with Sergeant Duck about treatment of any gun that might be found, raced back towards the town.

As he descended the twisting lane from the reservoir, he saw five young people walking up the hill towards it. One was the tall man called Eammon O'Brien; the photograph was a good one, and there was the girl, the man in the white sweater and two other young men.

He passed them by, and radioed ahead to the Incident Room to report their presence.

'That news is for Special Branch's information,' he said, pressing the accelerator. He had driven almost a mile before he realized why they were walking here.

22

By nine-thirty, the Underwater Search Unit had found a shotgun. It had clearly not been long in the water and it was retrieved with the practised skill and care of the police officers. The speed of their find was due to their knowledge of the reservoir aided by information given by the night attendant. The discovery corresponded with the position where he'd seen the man supposedly peeing into the water.

Sergeant Duck radioed the information to Control and asked that Pemberton be informed.

*

At around the same time, a pair of Task Force constables found a lock-up garage rented from the council by Patrick Roe. The key on his car key-ring opened it and inside was a Vauxhall Nova, a pale green one about six years old. A check with the Police National Computer confirmed that it was Roe's vehicle and it was therefore secured for evidence.

Later that morning, it was removed by a police Range Rover and low trailer, and taken to the Forensic Laboratory for a detailed examination. A quick visual inspection did indicate that the tyre treads were similar to the marks found at Blue Beck marshes at the point where the body had been thrown in, and there were patches of blood in the vicinity of the front passenger seat, and red fibres clinging to the seat-belt.

Control was asked to pass this information to Detective Superintendent Pemberton.

Pemberton was in Churchill Street, looking at Amanda's locked car. At his side stood Detective Sergeant Goddard, looking upset and tired. The fact that he'd been dragged out of bed hadn't helped, but he was deeply concerned about the implications of his predicament. It appeared he had not done his duty . . . Pemberton was standing before him, angry.

'So you never saw this car arrive, Sergeant? I thought you were supposed to be engaged on observations on this house?'

'I was, sir, but I was parked in Sherman Road. I couldn't see her approach or where she parked. I just saw them walking towards the house and then enter by the backyard-door.'

'So you never saw D/PC Wallbridge?'

'That woman I mentioned might have been her, sir. I had no way of knowing. My information was that two men were staying here and they might be Harris and Fife. I had to try and ascertain that, one way or the other. We had also received new intelligence that they might be contacted by one or more of five others who were living at 10 St Joseph's Street.

'SB was trying to establish their intentions. At 01.11 hours, I logged a man; I knew him as Eammon O'Brien. He entered the suspect houses. I radioed that to Control for onward transmission to SB Control. At 01.12 hours, a woman followed him inside.

'She was wearing a white woolly hat, a thick woollen sweater-cum-jacket in red and yellow; she was about five feet three inches tall, slim build; that's all I could see in the dark. I logged her entry as before.'

'You did not recognize her?'

'No, sir, I couldn't see her face.'

'Go on, Sergeant,' Pemberton spoke quietly. 'What next?'

'Another man came, sir, in darker clothing. Medium build, with a cagoule, pale green colour. The hood was pulled up over his head, I couldn't identify him. He went in to the house seconds after the woman. They all went in through the rear yard-door, they've always used that door. I lost sight of them as they entered the yard. I then logged another woman and two more men. Six in all. None came out. I came off duty at six this morning and my shift was taken over by DPC Soulsby, acting as a window-cleaner. But he did not watch this house – he had other premises to check.'

'What about the front of the house? Has it been covered?'

'No, sir, there's no suitable observation post there and besides, they've never used that door.'

'There's always a first time, Sergeant. Now, I can tell you that one of the women you saw enter was probably DPC Wallbridge, she had a red-and-yellow woollie and a white hat.'

'She was not expected, sir.'

'No, but she is a police officer. So either she's still in there, or she's left unobserved. Were observations maintained during daylight hours?'

'Not in this case, sir, we felt that would attract attention. It isn't as if we are wanting an arrest – it's just a watching brief.'

'Fair enough. So, I wonder why she went in? I reckon she must have seen something that prompted her to act as she did, like a good police officer . . .'

'We were under orders not to go in, sir, and not to let Harris and Fife see us. I did not see anyone come out.'

'But some of them *have* come out, sergeant, possibly after you went off duty. O'Brien has certainly left. He was at the reservoir this morning with his mates while we were searching it. I saw him. And I saw five people, not seven. So where are the other two? Your two, Sergeant? In here? With our DPC? Is she a hostage perhaps? I'm inclined to think these are beginning to look like real villains, clever, cunning and dangerous, especially if they'll detain a police officer. Now, I think they've set up a diversion for some other job. I think they want us to watch them up there, at the reservoir, I think they've led us on, the bastards . . . so the important question is – where are Harris and Fife at this moment and, more important from my point of view, where is Detective Constable Amanda Wallbridge?'

'I'm sorry I can't help more, sir.'

'We'll have to go in, in spite of orders. I can't risk anything happening to one of my officers. She must still be in there, with Fife and Harris.'

Six Task Force constables were in a personnel carrier awaiting orders from Pemberton. None was armed; it was not thought necessary.

'I'm going to upset SB's plans, Sergeant,' said Pemberton who had deliberately not informed Draper of this incident. 'The safety of a police officer takes precedence over your obs.' He turned and beckoned to the sergeant in charge of the Task Force unit and they emerged from the van to stand before him. These were experts at entering and searching houses and when Pemberton explained the situation, they took up their positions to the front and rear of Number 27. In keeping with all the accepted procedures, Pemberton stood back to wait and watch. As the officer in charge, he must not lead them into danger in case he was eliminated; someone must remain in command which meant the senior officer present had to stand back to direct operations. Some men, untrained in the sophistications of higher command, would interpret such actions as those of a coward . . .

In the time it took for half the search squad to assemble in the backyard, Pemberton found himself wanting to rush in and sort out Amanda's captors, but he steeled himself to wait in the street as the remainder hurried to the front of the premises. With radio contact, they would effect a simultaneous entry. There was no sound from the house. Some of the other residents had gathered to watch, but there was an air of calm about the terrace. Then he heard shouts.

Those would be the preliminary requests from his officers, seeking lawful admittance; they were repeated several times, and then came the sound of shattering glass. Then silence. Then nothing. Absolute stillness.

Several minutes elapsed without anything happening. There

was no action, no noise, nothing . . . Mark began to find he couldn't bear this, he had to know what had happened to Amanda, where she was, how she was, why she had come into this house. And to hell with orders, to hell with instructions from people in offices and to hell with the niceties of higher command . . . what in the name of God were the men doing? Everything seemed to have stopped. No one said anything, no one was doing anything . . . he couldn't wait any more . . . he went forward, wondering if he was walking into an ambush, wondering whether his men were crouching behind dustbins and cars for shelter but not caring, even if the occupants were armed.

He'd heard no shouts of warning . . . his heart was pounding now, the adrenalin was flowing, his spine was tingling with anticipation as perspiration began to dampen his back, making his shirt cling to his body. In meeting this danger, he consoled himself with the thought that he had not let his love for Amanda panic him into taking extreme measures, even if he was not working by the book . . .

Then he saw Sergeant Willis. The sergeant was in the backyard, behind the security of an outside toilet, listening.

'Not gone in yet, Sergeant?' the words emerged as a critical question as he felt his anger intensified.

'No, sir, we're giving them time to come out. We've called, we've smashed a back window to allow us entry, PC Royce reports the front door is open, it seems they might have gone, but if they are here they'll have heard our calls and should make a response soon . . .'

'Gone? They might have gone? This is bloody ridiculous!' in those tense seconds, Pemberton's patience ended. With no thought for his own safety or for Force procedures, he ran forward to the broken window. 'Why wait all this time?' he bellowed at no one in particular, pushing it wide open. 'Why hang about, for God's sake . . . come on, we're going in . . .'

'Sir,' cried the sergeant with some trepidation. 'Sir, no, wait . . . you need support . . .'

But Mark did not hear him.

He was climbing through the window now, then racing into the house through the kitchen and striding over abandoned bags of rubbish as he called for Amanda. It was dreadfully untidy inside, cheaply furnished with second-hand bits and pieces and it looked deserted. The birds, as they say, had indeed flown. The front door was standing open, allowing in a draught of cold air as a constable waited outside, ready to deal with any massed exit. As the anxious sergeant hurried in after him, Mark dashed into every deserted room calling her name.

'Sir, I don't think it's safe . . .'

Pemberton ignored the calls and took no heed of the worries of the support teams as he now galloped upstairs, taking them three at a time until he was on the landing. One door was closed. This had to be the one. He shouted her name. No reply. He kicked out at the latch.

· The fragile door swung open . . . he waited for a shot, for some reaction, but none came. He stepped inside.

And he found Amanda.

She was lying on the bed, trussed like a chicken with the deadly signature of a bullet-hole in her forehead.

'*The bastards*,' he shouted as the tears cascaded down his face. '*Bastards, bastards, bastards . . .*'

Two minutes later, Pemberton got the message about Roe's car and the found gun; the news was conveyed by radio from Bud Abbott who said he had confronted Roe with this new evidence, but Roe still denied responsibility for Sheila's Wynn's death.

Abbott added that Roe claimed the police had set him up; he would say in court that they had doctored his car with blood and treated the gun to make him appear guilty . . . he would point out that they had had every chance to do that while he was in custody . . . and who would believe the police these days? No jury would convict him if he persisted in his innocence and gave rise to doubts of police credibility.

'Deal with this death,' Pemberton snapped at the sergeant. 'It's murder. Full call-out. Tell Control. Tell the Chief. Seal the premises, call a doctor to certify death. Set things in motion. Use the existing Incident Room. Now, I'm going to visit Patrick bloody Roe!'

Pemberton swept into Roe's cell and the moment Roe saw him, he rose and smiled at the anticipation of another verbal contest; his was the smile of success and confidence, but Mark removed it from his face with one powerful punch to the flabby belly as he shouted, 'You bastard, Roe, you utter bastard . . .

She's been killed, you realize that? My girl. The best prospect I've got . . . all because you killed Sheila Wynn . . .'

'Mark, I never . . . not me . . .'

'You're an utter bastard, Roe, you really are . . .'

And Mark Pemberton, skilled in the martial arts, felled Roe to the stone floor of the cell and in a split second had the man's arm twisted behind his back and a hand at his throat, choking the life out of him . . .

'Help, God help me . . .' Roe, the one-time school bully who was frightened of any violence against himself, spluttered but no one could hear. They were alone and he was on the floor, gasping for life as Pemberton's savage temper had burst yet again.

'I'll kill you, I'll make you suffer . . .' all Pemberton's control had gone, he was a rough, tough kid from the back streets now, a kid who had been trained as an adult to deal with violence and one who could now kill with his bare hands without leaving a trace . . . and Patrick Roe knew this.

'Police corruption, Patrick? We fixed the evidence, did we? You'll tell the court that? That we made you appear guilty by fixing the evidence against you . . . they all say that nowadays. I know you killed her, Patrick. I know you did . . . so if you don't cough this one, you'll die now, or God help me . . . with one more pull of this arm, I can cut off your air supply . . . You'll die young and you'll die a guilty man . . .'

Roe, the coward and weakling struggled and coughed, sig-nalling with his hands that he wanted to speak. Mark released his pressure. Roe, whimpering with fear, crouched on the floor as he nursed his neck, and he did not attempt to rise.

'It was an accident, Mark, honest. I forgot about the gun . . . it was in the car, loaded. Protection against anybody who might waylay me.'

'Protection? For God's sake who from?'

'Druggies, users, addicts. Those who knew when I carried drugs; they're worth a lot, people get desperate . . .'

'And without a certificate? No wonder we didn't link you with guns . . . and it was loaded! You're a bloody fool!'

'So it was illegal and I was stupid. But I needed it . . . I needed some protection . . . that night, I picked Sheila up, she was crying, walking the town, so I parked and we talked a bit, then she offered me sex, relief, her thank you to me or

187

something . . . I forget about the sodding gun; I'd put it between the front seats . . . when we moved, we knocked it and it went off . . . it missed me, thank God, but she caught the whole bloody blast. Mark, it was awful, it was terrible . . . I panicked. What would you have done, eh? I ask you? Just what would you have done . . . well, I wanted rid of her body, so God help me, and I tried to cover my tracks by being caught in that drugs raid . . . What a God-send, I thought, what a perfect false alibi!'

'Who tipped you off – about our raid?' Mark was standing over his victim now, calmer, rational again, but still a threat. Roe simpered on the floor, almost in tears.

'Councillor Hogbin, through one of your Control Room's civilian staff; a man called French. He rang Hogbin, he's on Hogbin's mailing list, they're paedophiles, Mark, both of them, that's why I'm grassing, those sort are the real bastards . . . look, I'll admit to manslaughter of Sheila, but not her murder, Mark, and I didn't do the Green Lane woman in either.'

'I know you didn't, so let's get this confession to Sheila's death out of the way, Patrick, and we'll drop that murder charge and discount you for the Green Lane job.'

'I'll go along with that,' agreed Patrick Roe.

'Sorry about the attack,' Mark, quite unexpectedly and rather movingly, touched Roe on the shoulder, then helped him to his feet. He was still quivering with shock and panting heavily. 'I lost control,' Mark whispered. 'Sorry. I lost my girl today . . .'

'I heard and so I accept your apology, Mark. You and I have known each other a long time,' Roe added. 'I'll not lodge a complaint. I deserved it . . . my life's a mess, isn't it? You did warn me, years ago . . .'

'We were friends then . . .' and Mark Pemberton, with tears in his eyes, walked out of the cell and remembered a certain child-molester. Roe was right, such monsters were evil.

By eleven o'clock, he was standing in front of the Chief Constable who was already dressed in his best uniform in readiness for the PM's visit. Mark had explained Roe's confession and the awful outcome of the rest of the morning's work.

188

'I'm sorry, Mark, I'm dreadfully sorry. I know you thought a lot about that girl.'

'I did, sir,' and there were tears in Pemberton's eyes. 'She was the best.'

'She probably saved the PM's life, you realize that?' Moore said gently. 'Because of Amanda Wallbridge, we know those men have at least one firearm and we know they intend to use it.'

'She alerted us to them, Mark, she did everything expected of a competent officer; the sole purpose of my exercise was to locate and neutralize these men. Our intelligence was not complete, you see, we needed to learn more, we had to have an excuse for interviewing the whole town . . . so we're proud of her. I'll ensure she receives a posthumous commendation. I'm not saying she was expendable, but her death has been of great importance. All that remains is for us to get Harris and Fife, and we know where they will be heading very shortly.'

'I'll order the murder teams to remain on duty, sir, and for the Incident Room to continue to operate for Amanda.'

'Do that, Mark, and I have arranged for saturation cover of the visit site. The SAS will be there, under cover, as will the security services, acting as back-ups to our own men.'

'So the reservoir five were a diversion, sir?'

'Yes. Their objective was to mislead us into thinking they were going to blow holes in our reservoirs and pipes. While we were concentrating on them, the other two would be planning to execute the new Prime Minister. They thought we would be too engrossed in the security of the reservoirs to pay very close attention to Mr Major. But we anticipated some kind of distraction – hence the need to find out – and hence the need for our exercise. The five are now in our cells, by the way, under interrogation. And you can prove homicide by Roe as well?

'Good work, I accept your reasoning for a manslaughter charge rather than murder. And we've caught our mole; Hogbin is being interviewed about that now. We've broken a few false alibis, haven't we? So, in all, I think our exercise has been very fruitful, don't you, Superintendent?'

'It depends how you look at it, sir.'

'I've decided it will continue, Mark,' the chief went on. 'We'll record the supposed murder of the Green Lane woman as an undetected crime, so wherever we wish to have a purge on the town, we can do so with equanimity. The "unsolved murder" will be ours to resurrect whenever we please – or whenever it's needed.'

'Yes, sir,' said Mark without enthusiasm.

'Look, Mark, I know you've taken this hard . . .'

'It's cost a bloody good girl her life, sir . . .'

'It will raise the question as to whether police officers' lives are expendable in the national interest, Mark, and that is a question no one can answer. Now, back to your duty, there's important work to be done. I need you during the operation to stop these idiots shooting John Major. We've set up the scene so that there is only one site from which they can get a good aim – and we've fed another mole, one who works for the Council, with that information to ensure it reached Fife and Harris. That mole tipped them off about the visit well in advance; we've turned the tables by setting our own trap.

'We don't know where they are at this precise moment, but we do know they'll turn up at the pre-arranged sniper location. To get the necessary evidence, we will arrest them in possession of the firearm and will charge them with conspiracy to murder – as well as the murder of Detective Constable Amanda Wallbridge. I'm sure a ballistics examination will prove their guilt in her case.'

'I wish I'd been told of all this, sir.'

'I did say the exercise was on a need-to-know basis, Mark, and so it was. So, come with me and we'll make sure our own marksmen are fully briefed.'

Mark followed the Chief Constable out of his office and into his official car. The smooth machinery of a new murder investigation was set in motion to deal with the death of DPC Amanda Wallbridge as the legal machinery was set in motion to charge Patrick Roe with manslaughter and the unlawful possession of drugs. As they drove away, Mark shed a tear for Amanda and thought about poor old Harry Downes and the part he had unwittingly played. He felt sorry for the Millers, too, but experienced muted joy at the capture of Mayhew. Somehow, he seemed small fry now.

They had not yet found Mayhew's sawn-off shotgun, but did have enough evidence to get him a jail sentence for those robberies. It had been a good exercise, he supposed . . . Moore had been right; it had produced a mass of crime-beating information and it would help the crime-detection statistics.

But at what cost? Tonight, his house would be lonely, his bed would be empty and he would cry himself to sleep.

The visit of the Prime Minister went off without a hitch. The public never knew that two armed men were arrested in one of the derelict buildings overlooking the sod-cutting ceremony.

Four days later, Detective Chief Inspector Wilf Draper received a call from the fingerprint bureau at Scotland Yard, and sought an interview with the Chief Constable.

'Well, Chief Inspector,' smiled Moore as the Special Branch officer entered his office. 'What brings you here?'

'I thought I'd better come direct to the top with this, sir,' he began. 'I've had the fingerprints of the Green Lane woman examined by the Yard; I did it through their old records, security section, not criminal records.'

'Clever thinking, Chief Inspector.'

'Well, sir, they've come up with something pretty explosive. That woman, the one found dead in Green Lane, well, she's Olga Trubetchino, born 13 May 1928 at Tovarkovski in the USSR. She is a defector, sir, she came to this country in 1964 and sought political asylum, having worked for Russian Intelligence for thirteen years before that. The UK gave her a new identity . . .'

'Yes, I know, Chief Inspector,' smiled Charles Moore.